A BLACK DOG BOOK

LIE DOWN WITH
DOGS

Book 3

HAILEY EDWARDS

Copyright Information

Edited by Sasha Knight
Cover by Damonza

Interior format by The Killion Group
http://thekilliongroupinc.com

THE BLACK DOG SERIES

CHAPTER ONE

"Three wishes my ass," I muttered while crawling on my hands and knees behind a crate full of women's underthings. I snatched a pair of beige granny panties off the pile and used a plastic clothes hanger to wave them like a control-top flag. "Truce," I yelled at the djinn. "Put down your weapon."

"Hey, there you are. Come on out, dollface. The party's over here." His deep tone cracked when he laughed, shooting his voice two octaves higher. "Besides, it ain't a weapon if you're born with it."

If I rolled my eyes any harder, I'd be examining my frontal lobe.

His chuckles tapered into a slow exhale. "I just wanted to have some fun."

I bet. The exposed skin from my left elbow down to my wrist was shiny pink and still smarting from the scalding blast of super-heated vapor he had fired at me when I attempted to apprehend him. Who knew tarnished lamps made such versatile weapons?

"I won't hurt you," he promised.

Uh-huh, right. Djinns were liars and manipulators, much like my estranged pseudo husband. Not that I was hauling around emotional baggage with the Prince Regent's name on the tags or anything.

"Lower your weapon and put your hands behind your head," I called. "Kick the lamp to me."

"Play with me. It'll be our little secret." His voice dipped. "No. Make that our *big* secret."

Great. Not only was Herbert a teenage djinn on a crime spree, he had compensation issues too.

A lesser known fact about djinns was if you attempted to gain control of a magic lamp and failed, not only did your wishes go unfulfilled, but you accrued a debt equal to theirs. The tables turned, and the victorious djinn could then compel you to grant them three favors. I was just spitballing here, but I got the feeling Herb's wish list involved me, the risqué contents from one of the crates scattered throughout the warehouse, and the sexual education he had acquired via the Internet. *Thanks, Tumblr.*

The crate in front of me shimmied while faint pink mist smelling of roses spilled over its sides. Well, that explained a few things. Being his age was hard enough without having floral-scented mojo.

"You still want to rub my lamp, right, baby?"

Yeah, Rook, the aforementioned pseudo husband, would love hearing how I was the first girl to spit-shine this guy's lamp. Rook would kill Herbert, and I don't mean that in a cutesy newlywed kind of way. I mean Rook would literally end him. He was a death portent, like me. Killing was his thing.

It was my thing too, sometimes, but at least I was conflicted about it.

Through a crack between crates, I tracked Herb's leisurely exploration of the storage warehouse for a major discount clothing chain. While perusing a bin full of thongs, he spun his lamp around his pointer finger. His face split into a grin as he lifted a sheer black teddy off the pile of lace and sateen.

After casting a sly look my way, he unzipped his pants and took his joystick in hand.

No. No. No. This was not happening. "Put that thing away. This is public indecency."

"Don't be mad, sweet cheeks." He flashed me a full-frontal nightmare. "We're private here."

I covered my eyes. I had to. *Please God, don't let that be the last sight I behold.* At nineteen, I wasn't much older than Herb. The gap in our ages was only two years. But for pity's sake. Grow up.

"You wanna see what you're missing?"

Call it morbid curiosity, but vigorous grunting sounds dragged my hand down my face. It took a second for what I saw to register. I admit it, I stared. My mind spluttered *no freaking way*, refusing to process the information, while my eyes screeched *make it stop, make it stop* and begged to be gouged out.

Djinn and their lamps scoffed at the laws of physics. Otherwise, you couldn't stuff a grown man or a woman into a six-inch space, even with magical lubricating mist. So part of me grasped that it was possible for a djinn to cram things larger than the circumference of their lamp spout into its opening.

But I had obviously never considered other possible uses for that hole that would occur to a teenage boy.

Herb's energetic hip thrusting made me wince in sympathy, and I didn't even have dangly bits. Seriously. Wouldn't that much friction chafe? Finally, embarrassment won out, and I managed to tear my gaze from the wannabe porn star long enough to cook up a decent plan.

Reeling in the fine silver chain around my neck, I fished a quarter-sized medallion from inside my T-shirt, the one sporting a heap of cartoon chickens and aptly emblazoned *fustercluck*, and closed my hand over it. My thumb found the familiar grooves where a plain triskele had been stamped into its center, and I worried the slight indention.

The magic-imbued pendant had come standard with the rest of the marshal equipment issued to me by the Southwestern Conclave after I completed the marshal academy. At the time, it had served one purpose. It summoned the Morrigan. But the Morrigan, who was now my mother-in-law, overlaid the original enchantment with a slightly less legal version as a *welcome to the family* gift the last time I summoned her. Now the talisman was a direct line to her—yay?—as well as a pocket portal that linked to the closet in my office.

I raised my left hand, spoke my Word, and the spell holding my glove in place relaxed. The dozens of intricate runes starting at my fingertips and creeping up my wrist cast soft emerald light that illuminated the area around me. I held the design on the tip of one finger against the triskele while picturing a small room with a locked door, a safe place where I could hide what I didn't want found.

With my eyes shut, I imagined myself unlocking the door and reaching inside the room. I rifled through the gloom until I located what I was looking for—the sleek black pelt of a hound—and then I let myself have it. When I cracked my eyes open, dark fur overflowed my hand, pooling on my lap.

Soft footsteps had me twisting around to check on Herb. No sign of him, his lamp or the teddy.

Raising my chin, I inhaled the scents of starch, fabric softener…and Spicebomb cologne.

Time to put my plan into action. I lifted the skin and draped it across my back, tugging the nose over my head until I peered through the shriveled slits where its eyes had been. A few tense heartbeats later, it stuck, making me shudder while the world shifted from full color to muted yellows, blues and grays.

With a shiver, I shook out my fur and trotted after Herb's spicy-sweet scent.

He knew where I had hidden. Whatever game he was playing, I wanted it finished. The guy had low-end tastes. His larcenous grand total might hit a thousand dollars if I included the box of Milk Duds he'd pocketed at the Grab 'N' Go on Hendricks Boulevard.

Herb was misguided, not dangerous. His wasn't a high-priority case, except to me.

Three wishes.

How much of my hot mess of a life could those fix?

I wish I had never met Rook. I wish for an evergreen money tree (grove) that auto-updated portraits, seals, serial numbers, ink, border and paper. Oh yeah, and I wish I had never met Rook.

Padding across the floor, I swiveled my ears, listening for the sound of heavy breathing.

Nothing. Nada. Zero, zip and zilch.

Herb was surprisingly stealthy when he wasn't busy oiling his lamp. Three steps later, I realized why. Hovering six inches above the poured concrete floor while sitting on a cloud of swirling condensation, he sat with his legs crossed at the ankles, looking downright blissful. I curled my lip. *Ick.* He was all afterglowy.

Careful to keep an eye on the levitating lothario, I circled behind him, putting crates between us when I could. Herb drifted across the floor, humming a tune under his breath. My nape prickled when I stepped out into the open. As I drew closer, I recognized the tune as "Pop Goes the Weasel".

I took a step back, but he whirled on me. Tendrils of roiling fog snapped like bullwhips. One rose-scented tentacle dove at me, pulling up short while Herb scowled at the snarling black dog standing where he expected a pissed-off woman. The snakelike appendages writhed while their master's lips quirked.

"Let me guess." His laughter bounced off the walls. "You like it doggy—"

I lunged for his throat, teeth snapping.

He squeaked and toppled off his menacing cloud. The haze vanished with a hiss.

"Look, lady." He backpedaled with his lamp hand lifted. "I didn't do nothing."

Except blast me with superheated mist when I tried to question him. Searing layers of skin off a marshal was not the way for him to earn a get-out-of-jail-free card. No matter how petty his previous crimes, and even though I had targeted him for less than altruistic reasons, assaulting a marshal meant his chances of getting out of this unscathed had vanished in a puff of smoke. Selfish as my motives were, he was unaware of them when he chose to greet me with violence. Still, I wouldn't hurt the guy.

Probably.

A growl rumbled in my throat while I advanced on Herb.

"T-that's close enough." His lamp scraped against the concrete as he crab-walked out of range. "I told you the truth. I can't grant wishes. Not until I'm an adult, in like another two thousand years."

I flattened my ears against my head. He had told me that, and it might be true. I had no one to blame for this situation but myself. I chose to come after Herb. I saw his file, had a selfish thought, and here I was. That didn't change the fact he had decided to up the stakes in his game. Since I hadn't mastered the art of speaking while in this form, not in this realm at least, I chuffed. The guy was terrified and disarmed. I might as well shift back so I could read him his rights.

Almost a full minute passed while I grappled with the hound's skin. Shifting in the mortal realm was much harder than it had been in Faerie. During that time, Herbert experienced a change of heart. It must have been obvious I was struggling. He got his feet under him and called his mist to cloak him.

This was not good. I had little control over my body while in transition, and this skin was stuck like glue. I couldn't rip it off or smooth it back down fast enough to dodge him, so I braced for his attack.

It never came.

A grim-faced man materialized in front of Herb, placing himself between us, and pressed the blade of his sword against the young djinn's bobbing Adam's apple. The warrior's skin was ashen. His sleek black hair hung in a queue past his hips. The somber man was sidhe, an Unseelie, and half of the matched set assigned to protect me during my final year in this realm.

Three hundred forty-eight days left…

Glum as they both were, I couldn't tell my guards apart until my roommate hit on the idea of tagging their light black armor with nail polish. Judging by the olive drab streak on the back of this guy's upper thigh, my bacon had just been saved by Righty. Lefty, who boasted a red crème swatch on his calf, must still be using glamour to conceal his presence, because only shut and locked bathroom doors kept them from breathing down my neck.

Sometimes even then I had my doubts.

Note to self: invest in thermal goggles.

With a shiver, the hound's skin finally released me. I rose on two shaky legs with the pelt in hand.

"Thanks for the save." I patted Righty on the shoulder.

He didn't blink, but I read *you're welcome* between the lines.

CHAPTER TWO

After slapping a restraining Word on Herb, I loaded him into a sedan as old as I was, then headed to the office. Righty and Lefty didn't ride with us. My hand-me-down wheels made them nervous for whatever reason. It was hard to tell if the peeling *A Honor Roll Student* stickers on the bumper or the flaking white paint job I touched up with a Wite-Out brush had convinced them it was a rolling deathtrap.

No skin off my nose. Their fear of an imminent and fiery death gave me room to breathe.

Fifteen minutes later, we reached the outskirts of Wink, Texas. Gravel pinged the undercarriage of the car as I turned up the winding driveway belonging to an abandoned farmhouse. When I reached the yard and parked, I noticed some enterprising soul had spray painted *See Rock City* in chunky white letters on the barn's roof since my check-in last week. Vandalism was a common occurrence. Management practically encouraged it. I doubted they would even bother slapping a fresh coat of glamour over the top.

While I sat there drumming my fingers on the steering wheel, the withered cornfield behind the old house drew my eye.

Less than two weeks ago, I walked into that field as Thierry Thackeray, conclave marshal. I had walked out as Princess Thierry Thackeray of House Unseelie, future queen of Faerie and its inhabitants.

My kingdom for a time machine.

I didn't want a crown, or a husband. I wanted my old life back.

I might have been cut from the same cloth as my father, but I wasn't princess material.

"What is this place?" a nervous voice asked from the backseat.

Clearing my head, I exhaled through the tight knot in my chest. Herb had been so quiet I almost forgot he was there. I killed the engine. "Welcome to the Southwestern Conclave's Texas Outpost."

I stepped into a puddle when I got out, soaking my sock through my sneaker and dampening the frayed cuff of my jeans. I opened his door, grabbed his upper arm and hauled him onto his feet. He teetered while regaining his balance.

A built-in bonus to using a restraining Word was it sapped the strength of the person it bound to fuel the spell. Long-term usage caused fatigue, but Herb had energy to spare.

He blinked, eyes swimming in their sockets, and leaned against the car. "I want my phone call."

"Someone watches too much *Law & Order*." I popped the trunk, selected a dainty jar of orange blossom honey from a wooden crate then slammed it shut again. Herb looked steady enough, so I gripped his shoulder and guided him onto the rickety front porch. "You will be processed and sent to a holding cell to wait while your father is summoned. You're a minor. The best thing for you to do now is sit down, shut up and hope the magistrates don't try you as an adult for assaulting a marshal."

"You're going to summon my dad?" he squeaked.

"Yep." I grasped the doorknob and spoke a Word. "From what I hear, djinns really hate that."

The glamour shrouding the farmhouse sloughed away to reveal a tidy brick building. The office was one of five identical structures encircling the fae equivalent of a maximum security prison.

With the influx of fae leaving their motherland for the mortal realm, the Faerie High Court had made the decision to form the Earthen Conclave centuries ago. Now every country had a branch, and each one self-governed. In the United States, there were five regional divisions with headquarters based in Lebanon, Kansas. Each division was presided over by one

Seelie and one Unseelie magistrate, and they were responsible for maintaining the outposts in each state in their region.

There were two ways of becoming a marshal, a fae peace officer with clearance to use deadly force. You swore a binding oath of neutrality that released upon your death, or you were born into the role.

As the daughter of Macsen Sullivan, the Black Dog of the Faerie High Court, the job was in my blood. As my father before me, I was bound into service by both House Seelie and House Unseelie. I was a faithful servant of Faerie, and once I would have said I was impartial. I wasn't as sure these days.

"You don't get it." Herb jerked from my grasp. "He'll kill me."

"He'll be pissed." I clasped the back of his neck. "I doubt you'll die from fatherly disapproval."

"I haven't passed the Seven Trials." He squirmed. "I haven't earned a lamp."

I stared at him while his meaning dawned. "You're telling me you stole a lamp?"

"My f-father's free." His lip quivered. "It was my mother's third wish."

I shook him by the collar. "You're telling me you stole *your father's* lamp?"

"He hates it, hates what we are. He won't teach me, but I'm manifesting, I've got all this power, and I can't control it. I thought the lamp would help, but it makes things worse. It makes me feed it more magic. I think—I think it wants to devour me." He shook the hand clutching the lamp at me. "I can't put it down. See? It's stuck. My dad quit cold turkey, like thirty years ago, and it's starving."

Some objects did accumulate residual energies as they passed through hands over the years. The older an item and the more powerful those hands were, the greater the charge it collected until it had a power all its own. Some substances were hungrier than others, but metal usually remained latent.

But djinns lived for eons with the metal of their lamps conducting their magic. If any object had a right to gain an appetite, it stood to reason that would be one of them. That didn't excuse Herbert's actions—he had chosen to pick up the lamp in the first place—but I understood the need to push back.

I had my own daddy issues after all.

"I don't know enough about djinns to know if what you're claiming is possible, but I'll ask someone about it who knows before summoning your dad, okay?" Between the lamp theft and his crime spree, I doubted anything I said would help his case much.

His hunched shoulders slumped with relief. "Thanks."

After opening the door, I pushed him through it into the reception area. "Don't thank a fae."

One day he might meet someone with fewer qualms about collecting on that debt than I had.

"Is that a real thing?" he asked as I handed him off to a steward for processing.

"Say it to the wrong person and it becomes a very real, very bad thing," I cautioned him.

"Children these days." Mable tsked from behind her tidy receptionist's desk. "Parents get so worked up over how to hide their mistakes and their pasts that they end up enabling history to repeat itself."

I narrowed my eyes at her, but it was hard maintaining a glare at someone who reminded you of Mrs. Claus. Instead of red, she wore pink. And instead of fur-trimmed boots, she preferred fuchsia snakeskin. But her cheeks were rosy, and she baked a mean cookie.

I rocked back on my heels. "We are talking about Herb's parents and not mine, right?"

Her soft laughter made the room brighter somehow. "Does it matter?"

"I guess not." I reached into my pocket and presented the jar to her. "For you."

She moistened her lips. "You didn't have to."

"I know." That was half the reason why I did. The other half being it was smart to stay on her good side. She was the one who assigned cases, and the more she loved me, the better cases I found waiting for me on my desk.

Better cases meant higher bounties. More money meant increased risk, too, but I had bills to pay.

With a plump hand, she indicated a chair angled across from hers. I dropped into it with a smile while she sampled her bribe. Mable was a bean-tighe, a type of hearth spirit. She would live for as long as the building she was bound to stood, and I hoped hers stood forever. The job wouldn't be the same without her.

While she licked her tasting spoon clean, I dropped Herb's file in front of her and got comfortable.

"Long night?" She lifted a tray of honey oat cookies and offered them to me.

"Very." I snagged one, bit down and moaned. "Have I told you your talents are wasted here?"

"My people exist to tend our homes and care for our families." Mable gazed lovingly around the room. "This is home. You and the other marshals are my family. I'm happiest when you're happy."

I gave her fingers a squeeze.

"Thierry Thackeray," an overhead speaker blared, "report to the magistrates' chambers."

I exchanged a startled look with Mable. "When did we get a PA system?"

"It's always been there, dear, but I think—" The wrinkles on her forehead deepened. "That might be the first time it's ever been used."

A groan pushed me to my feet. "That can't be a good thing."

"It could be," she said cheerily. "Honestly, Thierry, the world isn't all doom and gloom."

Famous last words.

CHAPTER THREE

During the eight years I attended public school, back in the days when I still thought I was human, I never caused trouble worthy of being sent to the principal's office. But if I had, I imagined the walk of shame after being called out in front of the class felt like this.

After trudging up three flights of stairs, I rounded a corner and stopped in front of a heavy door carved from glimmering silver-veined oak imported from Faerie.

My fist rose at the same time a cool voice called, "Enter."

Stepping inside made me do a double take. The room was split down the middle by some unseen line, and every item on the left side was mirrored on the right side. The shelves lining the walls, the bulky silver-veined oak desks—also imports— even the knickknacks and the arrangement of the workspaces were identical. The only obvious difference, other than the magistrates' contrasting appearances, was the crests inlaid into each desk, indicating house loyalty.

"Magistrates," I greeted them.

Evander, the Seelie magistrate, was golden-skinned. His pale blond hair hung in a sheet down his back, and his shrewd lapis eyes appraised me. He stood when I entered, which showed more respect than the scowl Kerwin, the Unseelie magistrate, aimed at me.

Kerwin resembled my guards with his grayish skin and ink-blot hair. His eyes were onyx. Cold, dark and chilling.

"Always a pleasure, Thierry," Evander began. "Please, sit."

I sat when he did, taking the chair in front of his desk since he was the one who offered. I angled myself so I could watch

Kerwin from the corner of my eye. His glower darkened. I had slighted him, and Evander's pleased expression told me the maneuver had been calculated, but switching sides now would only make things worse. Instead of playing musical chairs, I stayed put and faked ignorance of their political maneuvering.

"I believe that we discussed the new terms of your employment in this very room less than two weeks ago." Kerwin leaned forward. "And yet payroll was notified not ten minutes ago to prepare a check for you."

I glanced between them. "You have notifications set on my account?"

"We have taken precautions for your safety," Evander soothed. "You were asked not to accept any fieldwork without clearing the cases through us first."

"I have bills to pay." I struggled to keep my voice level. "Base salary around here is peanuts, in case you haven't noticed."

As if waiting for me to raise the point, Kerwin flashed a sharp smile. "You are a wealthy woman. You have no need of this position. In fact, your attentions are best focused elsewhere."

"Is that caveman speak for I should let my husband club me over the head and drag me back to the cave where I belong?" I barely kept the snarl from my tone.

"Thierry is a modern woman. She wants to pay her own way, to be independent." Evander tsked Kerwin. "The sooner your house accepts that, the easier her transition will be."

I sat up straighter. "Thank you, Evander."

"She refused the crown and abandoned our people for what?" Kerwin swept his hand around the room, no doubt including all my past transgressions. "She apprehended a djinn, a teenager, which makes him twice as volatile. If she wants my respect, she must earn it. Starting with assuming her rightful place on the throne."

My mouth fell open, but none of the biting retorts scrolling through my mind popped out of it. Maybe my brain-to-mouth filter had finally kicked in. Took it long enough.

"You might not want me as your house's princess," I said calmly. "You might hate the idea of me being queen one day.

You might even tell yourself it's not because I'm a half-blood, though we both know better, but consider this." I twisted in my seat to face him. "My mother was kidnapped by a representative of your house. The same man also tricked me into performing fae marriage rites and ensured I took my father's place in the Coronation Hunt. Then, after I won, he went after my crown."

"A crown you didn't want."

"Rook used me. I want to live a quiet life in Wink. I want to pay my bills, live in my crap apartment with my best friend and maybe one day meet a guy and fall in love."

The word *love* furrowed their brows.

Sidhe weren't big on love. Wealth or political gain, now those were Sidhe aphrodisiacs. Exceptional beauty was another. They were stumped as to why I wasn't giddy over the prospect of finding myself married to Rook—who was, I admit, easy on the eyes—when our marriage improved us both financially and politically.

"We find ourselves at an impasse," Evander began. "You agreed to our stipulations in order to continue working as a marshal. Yet you have proven your willingness to disregard those conditions. Do you wish to continue our arrangement or not?"

"I do." I had to work if I wanted to make ends meet until my earthbound year expired.

"All right." He nodded. "What do you think is a fair punishment?"

Fair was the trick question on this oral exam. "I get to set the terms?"

"You are Black Dog's daughter," Kerwin said snidely.

Ah. So this was a test. Too hard, and they would suspect my judgment was compromised. Too lenient, and they would know it was. The trick was in determining proper recompense.

"A two-week suspension..." I swallowed hard, "...without pay."

Two weeks without a check. I would be lucky to afford ramen noodles after my bills got paid.

Kerwin smirked. "Only two?"

"Kerwin," Evander warned.

"Last year a new hire—a transfer from another division—helped himself to a file off Mable's desk. He brought in the collar and was suspended for a week without pay." At their expectant stares, I elaborated. "The case was earmarked for me, so when I showed up to collect the file, Mable explained why I was being reassigned."

Evander made a thoughtful noise.

"Since my word should be worth more, I doubled the amount. Besides, I had Righty and—I mean, my guards with me. I wasn't in imminent danger, or they would have brought me straight here."

Where they would have used the tether between realms to ship me straight back to Rook aboard the *Faerie Express*.

"These are dangerous times," Evander admonished. "Your predecessor's murderer has not yet been captured."

My father was on the killer's trail. That meant whoever offed King Moran was as good as caught. Until then, I was stuck with the guards and with light duty.

"I am well aware." I tried sounding contrite. "Though I do appreciate your concern."

The magistrates exchanged glances.

"We accept your ruling," Evander said.

I pinched my lips together to hold back a whimper. This was going to suck. I had a small nest egg to help during lean times, but Mom's house payment was a drain on my savings, and payments on her new car made my eye twitch.

I ought to woman up and tell her the conclave had cut off her stipend for raising a magically gifted minor after I turned eighteen, but she wouldn't be living in Wink, under the watchful eye of the fae, if not for me. I owed her for giving up her life in exchange for mine. I had given up my right to complain the day I turned thirteen and the powers I inherited from the father I had never met jolted to life and killed five of my best friends.

I had been chasing my tail since I got back from Faerie. Two weeks away from the job might do me good. From here on out, I was calling this suspension a vacation. A much-needed one.

"I'll let Mable know on my way out." I stood on numb legs, flashed them a smile and then got the heck out of Dodge.

CHAPTER FOUR

Mai found me in our apartment hours after the magistrates dismissed me. I was curled up on our old brocade couch wearing Eeyore pajamas with a melting pint of Ben & Jerry's Chocolate Therapy on my lap. She walked through the door as episode fourteen in season eight of *Supernatural* ended, just in time to catch me wiping drool off my chin from watching Dean slide on his Clark Kent-style glasses.

Life didn't get better than this. How had I forgotten Netflix was my soul mate?

Mai stepped between me and the television. She plucked the soggy carton from my lap and set it on the coffee table. "Do you want to talk about it?" She brushed her hands off on her pressed khaki pants.

"No." I leaned around her. "I would like you to get out of the way, though."

"You're self-medicating." She perched on the couch beside me. "What happened? Did Shaw—?"

"No." I cranked up the volume. "I haven't heard from him in days."

"Then what's with the pity party?" She tugged my ponytail. "And why didn't I get an invite?"

I licked the melting goo off the spoon I refused to surrender. "I got suspended."

"For how long?" She hooked her arm around my shoulders and pulled me down until I slumped over her lap. After resting the side of my face on her thigh, she popped the spoon from my mouth. "Tell Auntie Mai all about it. What happened?"

"Two weeks." A tear leaked from the corner of my eye. "Without pay."

"Damn."

"I took a case without clearing it through the magistrates. Consider my wallet—I mean wrist—slapped."

"Double damn."

I sniffled. "Exactly."

She slid the hairband out of my hair and combed her fingers through the tangled strands. "Look at it this way. In a year, you'll be queen and no one will be the boss of you. In the meantime, might I suggest having Righty or Lefty snap off the magistrates' arms and beat them with their own hands?"

I sob-laughed at the mental picture.

"So," she asked casually, "what are you going to do for two weeks?"

I lifted my arm. The tiny Roku remote hung from my wrist on its purple nylon tether. "This."

"Yeah." Mai rolled it—and the topmost layer of my skin— off me. "No."

"Freaking monkeys." I rubbed the angry red line until my healing abilities kicked in and the mark vanished. "Not cool." I rolled onto my back. "You don't mess with a girl's season pass to oblivion."

She tossed the poor remote across the room, where it bounced onto a sand-colored rug and hit the stained-white tip of a bleached cow skull's horn. Don't ask. Mom went through a Western Gothic period after we moved to Wink. Cow hides up on the walls, skulls on the tables, horn coat hangers…

Between Mai's cherry-blossom hand-me-down furniture and my death-to-all-bovines accents, the apartment was clash of floral and macabre. We had a *love blossoms in the desert* theme happening.

"I have a plan," she announced.

"The last time you said that, we woke up in a Minotaur herd's bull pen with no pants on."

She jostled my shoulder. "But we had fun. Right?"

"They pierced my nose."

"Come on." She waggled her eyebrows. "It looked sexy."

"Mom almost killed me."

Leaning over me, she examined my nostrils. "You can't tell it ever happened."

Thanks to my healing abilities, and not my best friend.

I clamped a hand over my nose. "Do you mind?"

"Not so much."

"What's your plan?" I slapped my hands up over my eyes. "Say it fast, like ripping off a bandage."

"You. Me. Daytona Beach."

"That's it?" I peered through my fingers at her. "You want to hit the beach?"

"Why not?" She ticked off reasons on her fingers. "It's hot. We're hot. We're both off work. We both—"

"Back that up." I tapped her second finger. "Why are you off work?"

"You really thought I would let my best friend sulk home alone for two weeks?" She rolled her eyes. "Well, technically, you're on your own for week two. I'm still rocking the wannabe internship thing, so all I could manage was five days off plus the weekends. That gives us nine whole days together."

"How did—?" I levered up onto my elbows. "You acted like you didn't know."

"I wanted you to *confide* in me." She palmed my forehead and pushed me back down. "I swung by your office on my lunch break since you have a tendency to be kidnapped and weren't answering your phone. Mable told me what happened, so I made all the arrangements before I left work today."

"Sheesh." I crossed my arms over my chest. "Get kidnapped once, and you're branded for life."

"You came home married, crowned, with a DayGlo prehistoric cat and two Unseelie guardians."

I mashed my lips together. She had a point. Several in fact. "You are—"

She glared at me. "Don't ruin the moment, Tee."

"I was going to say you're the best."

"Oh." She preened. "Then you may continue."

"Nah." I elbowed her in the thigh. "The moment's passed."

A soft growl rumbled under her breath.

"Two questions." I tilted my head back. "Where will we stay? And how will we get there?"

Fae like me weren't allowed to fly without special conclave sanction, not that I could afford the ticket even if they cleared me, which they wouldn't. Neither magistrate wanted me out of their sight.

"I have an idea about the first." She patted my forehead. "As to the second, I'll drive us."

"No offense, but your ideas usually end in nakedness and/or in tears." I chewed over safer, more budget-friendly options. "We could always hit up roach motels like we used to during spring break."

"Um, no." Mai wrinkled her pert nose. "I'm older now, and wiser. Plus, I saw one of those specials involving a black light and hotel sheets." Her shudder shook my shoulders. "Stop doubting my brilliance and listen. My mostly middle sister, Aimi—" she had fourteen siblings, "—just moved to Kissimmee. Her new husband, Jon, is the reynard of the largest kitsune skulk in Central Florida."

"I'm all for staying with family to cut costs, but that's an hour or so drive from the beach, isn't it?"

"Yes, *but*—" she lifted a finger, "—his family owns a condo on Daytona Beach."

"They won't mind if we crash there?" Given my current predicament, I had my doubts.

"Truth?" She pursed her lips. "Kitsunes are aligned with the Seelie. There's a good chance even for Aimi's sake, because of his position, that Jon would be hesitant to shelter the Unseelie princess."

"I can't blame him." Dreams of condo crashing burst. "This princess thing is a royal pain."

"Ha ha, funny girl." Mai absently wove locks of my hair into tiny braids I would never unravel without her help. "For his sake, I've decided it's best not to tell him *you* are the friend I'm bringing."

Foreboding clouded my thoughts. "Is that wise?"

She shrugged. "Plausible deniability."

I worried my bottom lip with my teeth. "I don't want to get him into any trouble."

"I'm not *totally* irresponsible. I'll tell Daddy. He'll vouch for you if it comes down to it." She gathered my hands in hers. "This might be our last chance for a girls only getaway before you have to go."

Go. As in back to Faerie. Where I would be crowned and have to play house with Rook.

"I know." My heart wrenched. "But I'd be dragging the guards, and then there's Diode."

She glanced around as if she had forgotten he should be here. "Where is he anyway?"

"I haven't seen him since I got home." He prowled the fae parts of town unless I was home to keep him company. "It's got to be hard on a cat used to living in the forest to stay cramped up inside an apartment in the city all day."

She made a commiserating sound before her brow puckered. "The guards don't like cars, right?"

I shrugged. "Not mine anyway."

"What about Diode?"

"He's managed to avoid getting in one so far," I admitted.

"It's just—my car is new and the seats are leather..."

"I'll ask him what he wants to do." I foresaw a feline hissy fit in my future. "So far he's been content guarding the apartment."

"Sounds good." She looked relieved at the prospect of leaving him home. "What about Shaw?"

I picked at the applique on my shirt. "Like I said, I haven't heard from him in a few days."

"Can he last a week without—" she rolled her hand, "—you know?"

"I'm not sure." I tugged on a string. "He's getting stronger now that he's being fed regularly."

Mai popped my hand before I unraveled the embroidered patch. "You can't feed him forever."

But I couldn't let him die, either. Not when I was the one who broke him in the first place. "I'll figure something out."

"You better do it fast," she warned. "He can't follow you to Faerie. Your hubs would gut him."

I rolled my eyes so hard I heard rattling noises. "My husband can suck it."

"Don't give him any ideas."

I snorted, grabbed a pillow and bashed her over the head with it. "Hussy."

"What?" She cackled. "You said he's hot, and you two *are* married."

"We're not that kind of married."

"Pfft." She sighed. "How can I live vicariously through you if you never do anything even remotely naughty?"

"Sorry, sugar paws." I reached up and patted her cheek. "But your future husband will thank me. After a lifetime of suppression, when your soul mate passes your foxy test, he's in for a sexplosion."

"God yes," she agreed. "He'll be lucky if it doesn't kill him."

I grinned up at her. "He'll be lucky either way."

A slight flush pinked her cheeks. "So, and I expect total honesty here, because I will know if you're lying. Tell me, are you ready to give up your ice-cream-gorging ways and embrace the light?"

"Yes." I rose onto my elbows. "I guess I should tell Mom, huh?"

"That's your call. Literally." She considered me. "A trip to the beach is innocent enough even she can't take offense."

"Mai," I said in a warning tone too tired to fool either of us.

"Okay, so, you make your calls. I'll make my calls." She slid out from under me, hopped off the couch and left my head to bounce on the cushions. "Car leaves at seven a.m. Be there or be square."

The goober was backing toward her bedroom, holding her thumbs and index fingers in a square shape, when she tripped over the sneakers I'd kicked off by the door.

"I am so sorry." I jumped to my feet. "Are you okay?"

She held two thumbs up. "I meant to do that."

I was still grinning when my phone's caller ID flashed Shaw's number.

CHAPTER FIVE

My thumb hesitated over the green call icon. As cranky as I was, as bad as my day had been, Shaw would pick this moment to check in. He was the needle pricking the balloon of happiness Mai had inflated for me.

"Well, color me pink and call me a tutu," I answered. "You do know how to use a phone."

His husky voice rolled across the line, giving me shivers. "I heard about what happened."

I groaned and shifted onto my side. "I love her, but Mable's mouth needs an off switch."

"Do you want to talk about it?"

"No." I was done rehashing my stupidity over and over in my head. I didn't want to go for round three out loud.

"Are you sure?" he pressed.

I ground the heel of my palm into my eye. "I forgot I sucked at math and took a calculated risk."

"Are you sure you don't mean chemistry?" Mai chirped. "Since it blew up in your face?"

"Hold on," I told Shaw. To Mai, I said, "I thought you were showering."

"I'm not wearing a towel dress for giggles." She swept her arm over herself, indicating the terrycloth wrapping her body. "Can you snap the reins right quick? I want to be sure I'm showering alone."

Kitsunes, like most shifters, had no problem with nudity. That Mai hadn't waltzed in here naked meant my invisible friends were getting under her skin.

"Tahlil paque." To me.

Two sullen guardsmen appeared behind Mai, close enough their shadows dwarfed her. She whirled to face them and almost lost her grip on the towel.

I was an idiot. The problem was obvious, and I had missed it.

"On second thought…" She paled when she glimpsed my darkening mood and backed toward her room. "Maybe I'll go for a run before bed."

"Go change, Mai." Anger crackled in the order. "I'll keep an eye on them until you're finished."

Once the door to her bedroom shut—and locked—I turned my attention to them. "This is a House problem, isn't it?"

Neither guard answered as they stood tall and defiant in their stiff black leather armor.

"Kitsunes are aligned with House Seelie." Lefty barely suppressed a grimace at my proclamation. "The thing is, we aren't in Faerie. We're in the mortal realm. Things are handled differently here." Righty shifted his weight as if I bored him. "That woman is my best friend. Seelie or not, I value her life above my own. Do you understand what that means?" I waited. "What? No takers? Fine. Let me break it down for you. Don't talk to Mai, and make damn sure you don't watch during her private moments, or I will drain you dry, roll you up and mail your skin back to Faerie in a cardboard tube."

"She is *Seelie*," Lefty seethed.

"And I'm neutral, which means I get to have friends on both sides of the border. Fun, huh?"

"You are *our* princess," Righty roared. "You have no right—"

I clucked my tongue at him. "That's no way to talk to your future queen."

His response was a throttled snarl.

Clearly I wasn't the only one less than thrilled with the High Court's pick for princess.

"Thierry?" a tiny voice called.

Crap. I had forgotten Shaw was on the phone. "Almost done," I told him. Pointing at the guards, I warned them, "This harassment stops now. Go stand in the corner where I can keep an eye on you."

Even without a human upbringing to cue them in, some punishments were universal. They understood they had been disciplined like naughty children. Okay, so it wasn't in my best interest to antagonize my guards in case political troubles in Faerie boiled over onto my life here, but this was Mai's home too. She had to feel safe here, and it sucked knowing my entourage had stolen that comfort from her.

I sighed into my phone, too tired to utter another half-hearted greeting.

"Trouble in paradise?" Shaw chuckled.

"Don't make this worse than it already is."

"Okay." A minute lapsed.

"Really?" I dredged up a laugh. "That's all you've got?"

He cleared his throat. "What are you doing for the next two weeks?"

"I have plans with Mai," I hedged. "I was about to call you, actually."

Expectation filled another awkward silence.

"We're leaving for Florida tomorrow," I blurted.

No response.

"You're stronger now, almost back to normal," I rambled, "so I figured if I topped you off…"

"I would last until you got back," he finished for me.

"Yeah." I winced. "That."

"Who's going with you?"

"Righty and Lefty—" I raised my voice, "—if they can behave. Maybe Diode."

"Righty and Lefty?" His voice strained. "I assume you mean your guards?"

"Yes, my guards." I flushed. "And no, I didn't check to see if the designations fit."

His surprised bark of laughter rewarded me. "Where are you staying?"

I debated my response. "We're staying with Mai's family, at their condo."

"Kitsunes are aligned with the Seelie."

I should have known employing tact was a waste of breath. Shaw knew me too well.

"I'm neutral," I ground out, "so we ought to get along just fine."

"You know they won't see it that way."

Now it was my turn not to answer him. I was tired of the pressure to choose a side. I saw each of the houses in shades of gray. I knew the Seelie weren't as kind as their smiles implied and that the Unseelie weren't as cruel as their sneers warned. There were extremes in both camps, but most of the fae were middle-of-the-roaders. That was what I wanted to go back to being—a line-straddler.

"When should I come over?"

"Sooner rather than later." I rubbed my eyes, which felt gritty and dry from my Supernatural marathon. "You know Mai. She plans on rolling out early, and I'm full of ice cream. I won't be awake much longer."

"Can I bring you anything?" He didn't let me respond. "I can grab Marco's."

"Stop trying to bribe me." I groaned. "I can't say no to their pizza, and it feels slimy trading bits of my soul for pepperoni and onions."

"We could mix it up," he offered. "Go for pineapple and ham."

"You can't see me, but I just shuddered."

Amusement saturated his voice. "I'll grab dinner and see you in a few."

I ended the call and stared at the phone, feeling a little like takeout myself.

Shaw arrived as I finished packing my suitcase. I ignored the jump in my pulse and the way I had to force myself to walk slowly to the door so I didn't seem too eager. As it was, I fumbled the lock, and my expression hitched between an instinctive smile and the cautious frown that materialized when I was around him lately.

"Hi." He leaned in and pressed a quick kiss to my cheek.

My skin tingled. It was all I could do not to reach up and touch the spot. "Hi yourself."

"Can you…?" He lifted a case of ginger beer while the pizzas on his other arm teetered.

"Sure." Our fingers brushed as I grasped the handle. My gaze held his for a breathless moment then fell to his boots. The view there was safer. "You look good." That brief glimpse of him eased my conscience. The wicked gleam to his coppery eyes had returned. His lips were full and pink again. Even his mahogany hair had a healthy sheen to it. "And by good, I mean you look healthy."

His answering tone was light. "My new diet seems to agree with me."

Unsure how to respond, I answered him with a half-cocked grin. "Give me a second, and I'll clear us some room." I shoved a stack of unopened bills off the coffee table onto the floor. "I apologize for the mess." I took the steaming pizza from him. "I was playing creditor roulette earlier."

He noticed the small trash can by my foot. "Winner gets paid?"

"That about sums it up." I tugged on the edge of a manila folder trapped between the two greasy pizza boxes featuring Marco's cartoonish dancing mushroom. "What's this?"

"It's a new lead on an old case." He rolled his shoulders, dismissing the file.

Resisting the temptation to peek inside, I set down the food. "What's it doing in my apartment?"

He could have left it in his truck. In fact, in light of my suspension, he should have left it there.

"The folder must have gotten stuck." He managed a passible impression of innocence. "I hear cheese is one hell of an adhesive."

"Uh-huh." I tapped the file. "What about the wax paper?"

Wax paper came on a roll, in a box with a serrated edge, just like tinfoil, and Shaw *loved* it. He kept a roll in his messenger bag as an aid for his spellwork. He used it as a liner, made funnels for getting ingredients into tight spaces, preserved herbs he picked on roadsides, used the wax as a lubricant and to waterproof temporary workspaces. So yeah, we both knew he had trimmed a length to protect the file from the greasy boxes.

I raised my eyebrows. "It just unrolled and trimmed itself to fit?"

"You're a fairy princess, and you're questioning the existence of self-cutting wax paper?"

"Touché." I huffed out a breath. "I guess this is a working dinner."

"I always loved watching you work."

Startled by his compliment, I ducked my head and reached for the folder to cover my surprise. It wasn't like he had been stingy with praise back when we were partners. He was a good marshal, and that meant he behaved professionally, even when our relationship blurred the line into personal. The shock came from my reaction to his praise. His words sent warmth flooding through my chest.

Rook and I...were complicated. Yes, I had kissed him. Twice. Maybe three times. But I had also been pretty damn sure I wasn't leaving Faerie with a pulse. At the time, making out with a handsome guy didn't seem like a bad way to spend my last night alive.

Having survived, I got the fun of living with those consequences.

"You don't have to collaborate if you don't want to," Shaw said.

"Twist my arm, why don't you?" I grabbed the file before common sense kicked in, and flipped it open to the first page. "A missing person's case?" I skimmed the file. "Female. Thirty-five. She's got fae blood a few generations back." That might explain how the case fell into his hands. "Valkyrie, huh? Those bloodlines are rare."

"They are," he agreed.

I gave him a look. "Is that why you got stuck investigating this?"

He shook his head.

"Then I don't get it." I thumped the file. "This information is months old."

"Considering the person in question vanished ten years ago, it's still recent by comparison."

"Why haven't you followed up yet? This looks promising."

He tapped the file's edge. "Check the bottom of the last page."

"The subject was spotted at a Walmart in— You've got to be kidding me." I scowled. "Orlando?"

"She was on vacation with her husband and their kids in Port Arkansas, about eight hours from Wink, on the Texas coast, when she disappeared." He studied me. "I was given the information while I was…away…but Florida was too far to travel in my condition."

My eyes narrowed. "And now that your food's on the move, you can be too."

"I didn't ask you to go."

"Of course not." I picked at the edge of the file. "You're just making the most of a convenient situation."

His shoulders rose and fell.

"What am I missing here?" I read the topmost sheet again. "This isn't like you."

Sure we had our share of missing persons' cases to work. Fae were hell to find when they didn't want to be found. But those were handed down from the conclave. This case read like freelance work.

"The missing woman, Jenna." He set his jaw. "She was my brother's wife."

"Wife?" My hand spasmed, and papers slid across the floor. "A married incubus?"

Shaw's brother had a wife. He was married. A married incubus. The revelation shifted the world beneath my feet. Or, since I was seated, my ass.

"We are capable of commitment," he growled.

For a day? A week? We had lasted almost a month. Yet here was proof an incubus could choose to settle down, choose to spend his life with one woman. I guess, for Shaw, I just wasn't her. I locked down that line of thought and shut my mouth before the past spewed over my lips and ruined the weird truce we had worked so hard to maintain since I began feeding him. "So this is personal."

"Yes."

"Having had my mother kidnapped recently, I get that you need to look out for your family."

"So you don't mind me crashing your trip?"

"That's not what I said." Mai would kill me if she found out he was tagging along on our vacay. "You're welcome to stay in Orlando. I'll be an hour away, on Daytona Beach, working on my tan." His eyes flashed white, and a shiver rippled down my spine. "That's close enough you can find me if you need to, but far enough away we can each handle business without tripping over the other one."

"Fair enough."

I bent to collect the scattered papers. "We probably shouldn't mention this to Mai, though."

The front door swung open, and Mai sauntered in wearing tangerine-colored biking shorts and a white sports bra under a long, sweat-stained tank top. Its swirling tie-dyed pattern reminded me of a melting Creamsicle. Her cellphone was strapped to her upper arm in an elastic holster, and earbuds hung from around her neck. She stared at Shaw and me expectantly. "Did someone use my name in vain?"

Damn fae super hearing.

"I was just telling Shaw about our vacation plans." I cut him a *back me up here* look.

He made himself comfortable. "Thierry said you're heading to Daytona for a few days."

"We are." If Mai shifted now, her tail would be twitching. "I guess you're here for—" she inserted air quotes, "—dinner."

He swept his arm out to indicate the food he brought. "You're welcome to join us."

"Kinky." She curled her lip. "But I'll pass."

"Mai," I warned.

"I'm grabbing a shower." She pointed at me. "Scream if he gets handsy."

"Will do." I saluted her. "Save you a slice?"

"Or three." She wiped sweat off her forehead. "Why burn calories if not to replace them?"

"Why indeed." I nodded sagely.

"Tee…"

"I'm on it." I snapped my fingers, and the guards reappeared. I cut them each a hard glare. "Remember our little chat, boys."

The glacial looks they returned told me they remembered our talk very well.

After exhaling with relief, Mai edged toward the hall and dipped into her room.

Shaw raised his eyebrows over her hasty exit, and mine rose at his reaction. Hot chick, tight clothes, starving incubus. I expected passing interest. He showed none. No white clouded his eyes. No claws tipped his fingers. No white flesh rippled as hunger settled into Shaw's driver's seat.

It was a stark reminder of my prime view from the top of his food pyramid.

Part of me thrilled to know I was the only woman Shaw— and his hunger—craved, but the hollow spot in my chest kept me honest. It wasn't me he wanted. It wasn't like he suddenly decided to give *us* a second chance. He didn't want to be faithful. He was stuck with me. We were bound together until I figured out how to fix the energy circuit forcing him to feed only from me.

"She never did like me much," was all he said.

Taking pity on him, I confided, "You failed her test on the first day of the academy. That kind of thing leaves a mark."

His eyes widened. "She tested me?"

"She thought you were hot, and I was curious how kitsunes tested their mates." I folded my legs underneath me, settling in to eat my dinner before it got cold. "So I told her she should go for it."

"She asked your permission first?" His brow furrowed. "What if I had passed?"

Another, sharper pang made it difficult to breathe. "Then you and Mai would be a thing."

He took a slow drink from his beer. "You would have been okay with that?"

No. I would have fought for him. Worse, I might have lost my best friend over a guy. But Shaw was Shaw, and Rook or not, I couldn't deal with the idea of him being with my best friend.

"That was then." I flipped open the box, grabbed a slice of pizza and said in my primmest voice, "I'm married now."

"That's not an answer," he said softly.

I felt my guards' eyes on me. "What do you want me to say?"

He opened his mouth, shut it, shook his head and then took another drink.

"I couldn't have said it better myself," I muttered.

CHAPTER SIX

That night, after Shaw left and I forced myself to crawl into bed, I dreamed of Rook. I knew our meeting was more than it seemed, because I "woke" balanced precariously on the limb of the tree where I had briefly slept in his arms.

Sentimental is my husband.

When I struggled against the threads binding his illusion, I smelled my brand of fabric softener and sensed the soft pillow beneath my cheek. It wasn't much, but the knowledge I could end this dream calmed me.

Rook reclined against a knot of staggered limbs, the perfect spacing to make him a backrest while protecting him from taking a nasty tumble. If he had been a human, a fall like that would have killed him. Given his ability to sprout wings, and my apparent lack of feathers, I was more concerned for myself.

If I fell to my death in a dream, would I die in reality?

He tapped the ends of a leaf with his fingertips. "How are things in the mortal realm?"

"As good as they're going to get." I scooted closer to the tree's trunk. "What about here?"

"In dreams," he mused, "all is well."

I reached the heart of the tree and wrapped a companionable arm around it. "I meant in Faerie, and you know it."

"Both houses follow me, for now." His hand dropped. "Neither are pleased with your absence."

Tough. Their pleasure was the least of my concerns. "Have you heard from Mac?"

He shook his head. "No one has."

"So King Moran's killer is still at large?" Not great news. The marshal in me wanted to see the murderer pay for his crime, but his ability to dodge my father actually played out in my favor. If the fae believed I was at risk from an assassination plot in Faerie, they would stay open to keeping me hidden here.

"You could say that."

I scowled at him. "He's either been caught or he hasn't."

"The answer is not so simple."

"Riddles aren't my thing." I stifled a yawn. "Why did you visit me?"

A cunning spark lit his eyes. "Can't a husband want to see his wife?"

I rolled my eyes. "We both know our marriage isn't real."

"It could be." He sat up. "It's not unusual for monarchs to have their spouses chosen for them."

"Except *you* chose *me*. You arranged all of this."

"Not all of it. You played your part beautifully, Princess." He interlaced his fingers. "I believed you were capable of winning the Coronation Hunt, but to watch it... You amazed me, Thierry."

Conflicting emotions wound me up until I didn't trust myself to respond.

He looked serious when he said, "If ever anyone was worthy of becoming queen, it is you."

"It's late, and I'm tired." Another yawn overtook me. "Why are you here?"

"Our bargain stipulated that you would be trained in the ways of royalty." He leaned forward. "I studied alongside my brother. I can teach you what you need to know, as much as anyone can. But you are at a disadvantage. This world, this role, is new to you when others have lived here and coveted it all their lives."

I heard what he didn't say too. I didn't want the position. That meant I wouldn't fight for it.

"You are powerful and clever," he offered, "but both houses are filled with more dangerous and slyer fae than you can imagine. Our only hope of surviving is if we work together, and even then..."

His gaze drifted toward the night beyond us and widened slightly.

"Rook?" I wasn't brave enough to glance behind me and risk falling.

"You must go." He waved his hand, and the dream—or whatever it was—dissolved.

CHAPTER SEVEN

I jolted upright on a gasp then doubled over coughing. My lungs burned from lack of oxygen. It hurt to suck in air, ached as my chest expanded. I stung all over. Stumbling from the bed, I collapsed on the floor as my door burst open and Mai rushed in steadying a baseball bat on her shoulder.

"Tee?"

I groaned.

"Are you okay? What happened? Where are they?" She screamed, "Show yourselves, bastards."

"What?" I arranged myself into a sitting position. "Who is *they*?"

She growled, "Righty and Lefty, of course."

If my mind hadn't been sleep-addled, I'd like to think I would have figured that out for myself.

"They had nothing to do with this." I shoved to my knees. "I had a dream, that's all."

A dream whose fading tendrils haunted me. The way my strange meeting with Rook ended left me cold. How his eyes shot wide when he forced me from sleep. I was worried about him, yeah, but I was concerned for me too. What did it mean for me if Rook got hurt? Being the considerate wife I was, I hadn't given his safety a second thought. I had been too eager to escape Faerie—and get my life back—to consider the mess I left him to clean up.

Of course, it was a mess of his own making, but still.

"Oh." She lowered her weapon, and I noticed the price tag stuck to it. "Want to talk?"

According to my alarm clock, it was four forty-five in the morning. I had planned on waking up at six so I could make Mai's seven o'clock deadline. "Sure." I covered a yawn. "First I need coffee."

"Why don't we get an early start?" She smiled at my groan. "I'll stop at Java Bean, my treat."

Right. Because from here on out, my cash flow was dammed. "Can I get a muffin?"

Her lips pursed in careful consideration. "Blueberry, yes. Strawberry, no."

I pouted. "But I love the strawberry ones."

"Sorry, Princess." She winked then spun on her heel. "I'm on an all-blue diet this week."

I was about to question how that was possible when it hit me I hadn't made travel arrangements for my guards yet. Drawing on all the patience allotted to me at this time of morning, I summoned them.

Both fae appeared, dressed and ready for battle, like five o'clock wasn't the butt crack of dawn.

"Has something happened?" Righty asked, scanning the area.

"No," I assured him. "It's nothing like that."

Lefty kept a hand on his sword hilt. "Nothing got past me—" he glowered, "—except the fox."

I bit my lip and counted backwards from ten. "Leave," I told him. "Right now."

He vanished with a pleased smirk I would be happy to wipe off his face with a two-by-four.

"Am I dismissed as well?" Righty's tone was milder, prickly but not hostile.

I took a cleansing breath. "I'm sure you've overheard me planning for a trip to Daytona."

"Yes." A thoughtful pause ticked past. "Daire and I have made our preparations."

"Daire?" Oh. He meant Lefty. "Ah. Good. I should have thought to ask you earlier."

"It's no trouble." Righty inclined his head. "Where you go, we must follow."

"Still, I should have given you a heads up." His puzzled reaction made me think the direction of our conversation mystified him. "It was wrong of me to assume you had nothing better to do."

Emotions clouded Righty's face, all conflicting and none I could easily identify. "I don't."

Exhaling through my teeth, I accepted that a lifetime of Unseelie brainwashing wasn't unraveled in a day.

"Well, either way, we're about to leave." It felt weird telling him what he must have overheard, but since I rarely saw him or Lefty—*Daire*—without summoning them first, I wasn't ever sure how much either of them knew or how often they pooled their information. "Will you two be riding down with us, or do you prefer alternate means of transportation?"

"We spoke with the cat earlier," he said. "We agreed that he would ride in the car with you and act as guardian until you reach your destination. Once there, Daire and I will resume our posts."

I perked up at that. "Diode's here?" I had been afraid I wouldn't see him before we left.

Righty nodded at me. "He's lounging in the living room."

"Excellent." I plucked at my shirt. "Can I get some privacy to change, please?"

Back in familiar territory, Righty relaxed into his role. "Yes, of course."

He poofed.

The bedroom door remained shut, and I hadn't heard footsteps, but when I inhaled, I no longer scented him. My nose was a hair better than Mai's, but she couldn't pinpoint the guards even when they were standing next to her. For the first time, it occurred to me that might be intentional.

The ringing of my phone distracted me from bounding out to check on Diode. A quick glance at its display showed an unfamiliar number. I wasn't sure it was a Texas area code. It looked more like a Nevada prefix. Still, this was my work line, so I answered. "Marshal Thackeray."

"I must meet with you," a crisp, accented voice demanded. British maybe?

Trying for polite, I didn't snap back. "Who is this?"

"I owe you, Marshal." He sounded less than thrilled about it. "I always pay my debts."

"I'm heading out of town on business," I lied. "Call me in a week, and we'll set something up."

"That simply will not do."

Silence hummed in my ear. The call ended before I could wheedle more information out of him.

I stared at the display. Weird. He owed me? Was that a veiled threat?

Without caffeine to jolt my brain cells, I wasn't sure. He sounded serious about paying his debt, which meant this weirdness wasn't over yet. This guy wanted to meet, huh? Maybe next week wouldn't be so boring after all.

Just what my life needed. More excitement.

After dropping my phone into my purse, I began detangling my hair.

I ditched my pajamas for shorts and a tank top, set my compact navy suitcase on the floor, wheeled it over the threshold and then hesitated. The messenger bag filled with my marshal equipment hung on the doorknob. I had guards. I had Diode. Shaw would be a phone call away. I could go unarmed. Trust I wouldn't need to defend myself.

But my fingers itched for the strap. Being a marshal was the weight keeping me anchored to who I was. All the politics and Faerie drama weren't me. Not yet at least. Trusting my safety to someone else wasn't either.

After snagging the worn satchel, I felt better for it. I didn't need anyone fighting battles for me. Thinking of the strange caller, I grinned. In fact, exercise might do me good.

"Look what the cat dragged in," I snarked at Diode as I entered the living room.

The panther-sized cat made a show of stretching before padding over to say hello with a purr so deep it vibrated my teeth when he leaned against my leg. I sank my fingers in his glossy highlighter-yellow fur and scratched.

"The guards informed me of the situation," he said. "I have taken measures to ensure my own comfort."

"Wow." I was impressed. "Everyone around here is so…efficient."

Haphazard as Mai and I had lived our lives up to this point, I felt disorganized by comparison.

"You are under enough stress as it is." He flicked his tail. "We will not add to it."

I bent down and kissed the top of his furry head. "You're the best cat ever."

His grin bared wicked, sharp teeth. "I know."

"Are we ready to roll?" Mai strolled into the room, wheeling a compact purple suitcase identical to mine. Except mine lacked the designer label. And the fancy color. And the retractable handle that actually retracted.

Okay. Well. They *were* both suitcases on wheels.

"Almost." Diode prowled to the couch and returned with a brown paper bag clasped in his jaws.

"For me?" I accepted the package and waited while he flicked his tongue in disgust at the flavor.

"For me, actually." He sat on his haunches and curled his tail around his front paws. "Open it."

I tore the bag—it had been stapled shut—and pulled out a thin black leather collar. "Um."

"That won't fit you, fur face," Mai said helpfully.

The tip of his tail twitched. "You would think so."

He managed to make it sound like an insult, which amused me. Unlike her animosity toward the guards, Mai had a friendly, if antagonistic, relationship with Diode. Foxes were a part of the *Canidae* family, a fact Diode was fast to mention the first time she tried petting him.

Bam. Just like that, a good old-fashioned cat-versus-dog rivalry was born.

Ignoring their banter, I asked him, "What is it you want me to do with this exactly?"

He looked like I had asked him to bark or something. "Fasten it around my neck. What else?"

"This should be interesting." Mai again.

Afraid of hurting his feelings, I unfastened the buckle. "Yell if it pinches."

His response was to stretch out his neck and wait while I pressed the collar to his throat.

"What the—?" A swirl of sparks blindsided me, and I stumbled forward, tripping over...a housecat.

"Meow." The boxy calico pronounced it the way a person would.

Mai dropped her purse. "No way."

"Yes way," he said smugly.

The voice was right, but what the hell. "Diode?"

The cat arched his back with a purr. "Who else would it be?"

After recovering from the shock, I had to admit it was a neat trick. "How did you pull this off?"

"You didn't think all that late-night prowling was for nothing, did you?"

"You're a tomcat." A jumbo-sized one. "I figured you were out...catting around."

"Not hardly." His whiskers flexed. "A witch lives three blocks over to the east. She spelled the leather for me after the guards informed me of your travel plans. I, of course, will be accompanying you."

Mai whimpered, no doubt imagining those needle-like claws piercing her leather seats, but I was all smiles. "Are you sure it was wise to trust her?"

His gaze dropped to my glove. Point taken. I had used a witch to charm the leather of my glove, but it was necessary. My magic killed people, and I wasn't as proficient at wielding it as I would like to be. Yet. My glove was an extra layer of protection for me—and everyone I came into contact with.

"Okay, well." I glanced around the room. "I guess the gang's all here."

Everyone except Shaw.

"Cool." Mai gathered her things and bolted out the door. "Last one to the car is a rotten egg."

Diode looked alarmed. "What?"

"Relax." I chuckled. "It's just something people say."

He licked a front paw and smoothed the fur on his face. "People are, quite frankly, ridiculous."

"No argument here." I stepped outside, waiting on Diode to saunter out into the hall, trusting the guards had made their exit while Puss in Boots was expressing his catty superiority. Once he strutted past me, I locked up the apartment, grabbed my bags and followed Mai down to the parking lot. When I got there, I pretended not to notice the blue-black truck idling discreetly behind a row of SUVs. Or the fact its driver stared a hole through my thin tank top while I crossed the blacktop and headed for Mai's tiny sports car.

If she noticed the truck—or its ogling driver—she didn't mention it. I felt certain she hadn't, given the fact she wasn't throwing things or stomping her feet. Feeling certain my secret would last through breakfast, I helped Mai finish loading the car and then climbed in and held on tight.

CHAPTER EIGHT

Mai wasn't a bad driver, exactly. Her foot just had a high lead content. I also suspected she was colorblind, which explained why she had blown through four red lights and counting.

While she continued shattering traffic laws at record speeds, I braced my right hand on the dash and pinned Diode to my chest with my left arm. His fur stood on end, and his piercing claws sank into my neck and chest.

Breakfast had been a bad idea. Coffee sloshed in my stomach and the muffin… Oh, the muffin.

"You're not going to hurl, are you?" Mai decelerated by several precious miles per hour.

"My stomach hasn't decided yet," I admitted.

Diode's words were muffled against my shirt.

Mai reached over and patted his back. "I think he said he can't breathe."

I eased my grip, and sure enough, Diode shot from my arms, panting as he hit the backseat.

"Sorry," I called to his retreating tail.

He curled up on the floorboard on the blanket I brought for him and began moaning.

"Poor fur britches," Mai said, not sounding sorry at all.

Then the hacking started.

Panic spiked her voice. "What is your cat doing back there?"

"It sounds like he's getting carsick." I exhaled slowly, trying to calm my own stomach. "This *is* his first time riding in a car."

Flipping on her blinker, Mai jerked the wheel and cut off an SUV behind us to reach the side of the road. Emergency lights flashing, she pointed to the cat and then to the door. "Get him out *now*."

I hopped to it, gingerly lifting Diode and depositing him on the gravelly shoulder in time for him to toss his Meow Mix. He let me help him back onto the floorboard, where balled up in shadow to rest.

The car rocked when I climbed in and shut the door. I grimaced at Mai as I fastened my seat belt. "You're lucky I'm not a sympathetic vomiter."

Punching the gas, she spun us back onto the interstate. "Should I roll down a window so you can stick your head out and—? *Ouch.*"

"Not funny." I frogged her thigh, punching her leg a second time to get my point across.

"Damn it, that's going to bruise," she whined.

"You'll live. I know you packed makeup," I teased. "You've got concealer."

"Which will clash with the tan I'll be working on," she grumbled.

A blast of classic rock music earned me a sharp look from Mai. Even Diode paused in his moaning.

"That would be me." I pulled my cell from my bra. "Don't look at me like that. It's not Shaw."

"I was actually thinking now that you're a marshal, you should invest in a holster or belt clip for your phone." She reached over and tugged on my bra and tank top straps until my breasts jiggled. "A padded cup is nice, but phones are expensive. Yours needs more protection than that scrap of foam."

I looked down at my boobs. "Are you insulting my bra?"

"No." She hummed. "Well, maybe. Would it kill you to upgrade from plain white cotton?"

"I have black too." I even owned a nude-colored strapless number, so there.

Shaking her head, she turned her attention back to the road. "Are you answering that or what?"

"Yeah, yeah." The display flashed the same number as it had this morning. "Hello?"

"I have decided that I will come to you, in Florida."

I spluttered. "How did you—?"

"How is not important. This is an urgent matter, and it demands an expedient resolution."

"Look, I don't know what your deal is, buddy, or what it is you think you owe me, but I can promise you the only way we're meeting up is on conclave grounds with magistrates watching."

Mai cut her eyes toward the phone. "Everything okay, Tee?"

"I have to go," I told the caller. "Don't dial this number again."

"You have chosen to make this difficult," he said. "Be that as it may, I will be seeing you soon."

He hung up on me. Again.

I stared at the phone. "Maybe I picked a bad time to go on vacation."

"Who was that?"

"I don't know." I recapped our first phone conversation while she nodded along.

"That's weird, even for you."

"Hey."

"Sorry, Tee, but you attract headcases."

I arched a brow. "Is that your professional opinion?"

Mai was an intern with a counselor for displaced fae youth, kids without familial support who were struggling to adjust to their manifesting powers. Most of which activated around the time the kids hit puberty, a bad time to mix volatile hormones with burgeoning magical abilities.

All too often young fae harmed themselves or others without the proper guidance. I was glad Mai would be there to help them sort through those feelings before they resulted in injuries. Between counseling and a private fae school system, fewer kids fell through the cracks like I had, and I was glad they wouldn't carry the same scars I did.

She told me once that my messed-up childhood had inspired her career choice.

I guess being called an inspiration was better than being labeled a cautionary tale.

Mai surprised me by answering, "Actually, yes, it is."

"I'll be sure to mention that to Shaw the next time I see him."

"Go right ahead." Her tone chilled. "He's a prime example."

"You used to think he was hot," I pointed out. "In fact, you encouraged me to pursue him."

"I wanted you to get him out of your system." Her palms smacked the steering wheel. "I didn't expect you to be stuck with that—that *parasite* for the rest of your natural life. Believe me, if I had a time machine, I would crank the dial for two years ago. I would stand next to Mable, shake a finger at you and lecture you on the dangers of dating incubi, no matter how sexy they are at first glance."

Mable had never been a fan of my romantic fascination with Shaw, but she respected him.

"He's a good marshal." I amended, "He's a good guy."

"As a marshal, I can't dispute his record or his work ethic." She exhaled. "As a guy? He sucks."

I would have laughed if she hadn't been serious. "Nobody's perfect."

The car swerved. "Since when are you defending him?"

"*I* broke *him*, Mai." I tightened my seat belt. "Not the other way around."

Her answer was a grumbled, "Yeah, yeah."

"Enough talk about Shaw." The last thing I needed was to slip up and for her to figure out he was tagging along on our vacation. "Enough about the creeper on the phone too. I have Diode. I have the guards. Whatever that guy wants from me, he'll have to go through conclave channels to get it."

A small frown puckered her forehead, but she finally nodded. "New topic."

Eager to turn the tables, I grinned at her. "I met a nice goblin at work last week."

Personally, I blamed the eighties flick *Labyrinth* for her goblin fixation. She burned through available goblin men like wild faefire, but unless I met their king and he was a dead ringer for Jareth, I wasn't interested.

She groaned, unable to resist. "Met as in arrested?"

"Well…"

No one was perfect.

Sixteen hours, many drive-thrus and several rest station potty breaks later, my hands were cramped into arthritic claws and my elbows ached from how I had wedged my arms against the dash. I had given up on taking protective measures fifty or so miles back and made myself as comfortable as I was likely to get.

Darkness falling helped. The bright lights from passing cars—or should I say cars Mai zipped past?—did not. The landscape blurred less with night cloaking the world beyond the windshield. Even Diode had forgiven my earlier fervor and climbed back into my lap to be admired.

He practiced his meowing each time I got distracted.

"Sorry," I mumbled, resuming his petting.

"Someone's getting excited," Mai singsonged. "Can you believe how huge these buildings are?"

"They're massive." Some reminded me of the skyscrapers in Dallas. Galveston Island had been cluttered with them, too, but those memories were faded. I whistled when we drove past a complex so tall I had to crane my neck to see the aircraft warning lights flashing at the top. "Jon's skulk must be loaded."

"Mom asked for a credit report and a bank statement before he was allowed to date my sister."

"Are you serious?" I blurted before my brain caught up to my mouth. "Of course you are."

"Mom is Mom," she said with a shrug.

"I hear you."

We drove until a crosswalk stopped us. Teen girls wielding unfastened glow necklaces as whips giggled and swatted at boys who chased them across the asphalt to a boardwalk starting at the opposite curb. A leaning sign staked into the sand read *Public Beach*.

Between the two buildings on either side of the narrow walkway was my first real glimpse of the ocean in years. My throat squeezed tight at all that open sky dotted with winking stars, the black water rippling and crashing under the moon.

Mai surprised me by proving she did know how to decelerate. "What's with that face?"

I poked her side. "The face you shouldn't be able to see because it's dark and you're driving?"

"It's called peripheral vision. Your bottom lip is sticking out so far it could be a speed bump."

I traced the glass over a cresting wave with my fingertip. "It reminds me of home."

Mom and I had lived in Galveston, Texas until my fae heritage reared its ugly head.

"Now that you're a marshal," she said, "maybe you'll get to go back some day."

"Maybe." I had been back, sort of. When Rook had Mom kidnapped, a fae in his employ, Bháin, had cast an illusion to keep her entertained. She was still lounging in her make-believe Galveston the day I arrived to bring her home. Seeing that familiar place again after so long… It was kind of nice.

"You know I meant to visit, right?"

I snorted. "Scared you might lose me?"

"Yeah," she said seriously. "I am."

Galveston might as well have been on the moon, and we both knew it. I was moving to Faerie in a few short months. Earthly accommodations wouldn't matter then. Once I was crowned, I would be bound to that realm for one hundred years. No more visits to this one. That meant no more Mai, Shaw…or Mom.

"Sorry." Mai drummed her fingers on the wheel. "I forgot the plan. No more talk of the future. Deal?"

"Deal." I sighed with relief. I didn't want her sad—I didn't want to *be* sad—not when we had a perfect week planned.

Mai leaned forward, lips moving as she read signs. "Help me look for— Oh! I see it. Hold on."

She jerked the wheel to the left, and my head bounced off the glass. "Gah. *Mai.*"

Diode, whose claws anchored him to my lap, peered up at me. "Are you all right?"

"I'm lucky her hard head didn't shatter the window." Mai cut the wheel again, gentler this time, and nosed up to the curb to park in front of the condo.

"Your concern for my well-being is, as always, touching."

"Let me take a look." She cupped my cheeks and pulled my head down. "It's not even irritated."

"That makes one thing that isn't," I grumbled.

"Sheesh. I'm sorry." She released me. "It's not like you haven't been brain-damaged before."

There were times in my line of work, after subduing particularly brutal fae, that my brain turned as shaky as gelatin and almost as cognizant. My rock-hard noggin had taken a beating, several in fact. That didn't mean I wanted my best friend to finish me off with a glass sliver to the gray matter.

"Let's just go." I grabbed the door handle. "I'm cranky from being trapped in the car for so long."

...with a driver who thinks stop signs are suggestions and red lights are decorative accents.

Outside, the air was briny and warm. A cool breeze off the water sliced through the humidity. Spotlights illuminated the front of the condo, making me squint after our late-night ride.

Mai stepped out and locked up the car. "Let's check in and find out about parking."

I leaned against my door, angled away from the entryway, and tilted my face up toward the moon. "I think I'll wait here."

"Are you still mad?" she grumped. "I did apologize. Besides, your hair will cover the bruise."

"I'm not mad. Sore, yes, but I'm not angry." Diode, who'd leapt onto the curb when I opened my door, flattened his ears against his head. I toed Mai with my shoe. "We'll guard the car, okay?"

Her consideration lasted all of about a second. "Good idea."

"Foul water. Salt air." Diode's fur stood on end from nose to tail. *"Sand."*

"Are you sure you want to be here?" I bent to scratch behind his ears. "You could go home."

"And leave you to be guarded by those—" He decided against whatever slur he had readied.

"They're not so bad." Righty wasn't as diehard as Lefty, even if he put on a good show.

Diode's green eyes narrowed. "You have a kind heart that makes allowances where it shouldn't."

I got the feeling he wasn't talking about the guards now. "My heart isn't the problem."

I didn't love Rook. Though I would be lying if I claimed to be unaffected by his beauty. He was handsome in the way sidhe men were, tall and leanly muscled. His eyes, though, haunted me. I might have dated him, if we had met under different circumstances. Maybe. After Shaw and I disintegrated, the smart thing to do had been for me to date humans. They were tamer than what I was used to, but nice. None of the guys had been forever material, but I wasn't exactly on the market for a soul mate.

I thought I had one of those once, and I was pretty sure now I knew why they were called that. It wasn't some matching of essence, some perfect fit of personalities. A soul mate was the person who wielded the greatest power imaginable over you, the person who cupped your happiness in their hands. If the worst happened and the relationship crumbled, they used the power you so foolishly lent them to crush your dreams under their heels as they walked out of your life. Those same hands that had so delicately held your joy were plunged in your chest as they ripped your heart out by its roots.

Okay. Fine. Maybe I wasn't quite as over what Shaw had done to me as I pretended. It was hard forgiving and forgetting when the men in my life took turns screwing me over. *Not* in the literal sense.

Being raised by a single mom, I had no illusions that all romances ended with happily ever afters, and it was selfish for me to want to be an exception, but I did. Even though my parents never married, Mom must have loved Mac to have been with him in the first place. Now here I was in the same situation, only mine was reversed. Fae law stated I was hitched, but love had nothing to do with it. Honestly? I didn't know which of us I felt sorrier for.

CHAPTER NINE

Flip-flops slapped pavement, and Mai's voice rang out over the dull roar of the nearby ocean. "Did you get into my stash of Sour Patch Kids while I was gone or something?"

Her reappearance dragged me from my thoughts and from my appreciation of the view. "Hmm?"

She stopped in front of me, hands on hips. "The *I French kissed a lemon* face you're making?"

"Why would I—?" I put up my hands. "Never mind. I was thinking. That's all."

"Tee." She sighed. "This is a vacation. No thinking allowed. Stop that right now."

A smile crept up on me. "You're right."

"I know." She flipped her hair over her shoulder. "But it's always nice to hear you say so."

Rolling my eyes, I noticed a guy trailing her. "You picked up a stray that fast?"

He looked to be in his late teens or early twenties. About her height, he had the bronze skin that tanning-bed manufacturers promised their clients. His hair was sun-bleached blond, and his eyes were a soft gray. The wind shifted, and I inhaled discreetly to be sure. Huh. The guy was one hundred percent human.

"Tee." Pink blossomed in her cheeks as she passed him the keys. "This is Matt. He's the valet."

Seconds later, another young man joined the first. Blond-haired and blue-eyed, her favorite combo.

I checked him, and he came up human too. "And who might you be?"

"I'm Tim. I'm here to help her—um, you—" he flushed, "—both of you—with your bags." He elbowed Matt. "Pop the trunk, and I'll take the ladies to their rooms."

The poor guy's expression tightened as his thumb jabbed her key fob. Clearly, Matt was second-guessing his choice to drive Mai's sporty car into the parking deck. His friend might be stuck with the manual labor, but he also reaped the rewards of knowing her floor and room number.

Not that it would help him. Kitsunes weren't human compatible. She wouldn't even test him.

A sharp *ping* had everyone checking their phones. When I reached into my top to retrieve mine, the guys' eyes followed, widening when I accidentally flashed the frilly white edge of my bra at them. Awkward. Maybe Mai was right and I did need a holster of some kind. Since I was still being stared at, like the guys had just registered that there were *two* women present and one's boobs received text messages, I skipped checking my phone and shoved it into my shorts pocket instead.

A sudden snap of sound startled Matt and Tim into action.

"Chop, chop." Mai clapped her hands. "Let's hurry this along, guys. Momma needs her beauty sleep."

Matt lurched into motion, and a screeching yowl filled the air.

"W-what is that?" He stumbled backward, pointing at the ground near my feet.

Diode.

"He's just a..." My mouth fell open. Diode's calico pattern held, but his natural bright yellow color was seeping into his fur. He looked like someone had dumped a lemon ice on his back. When we left the apartment, he had been about calf height. Now the pointed tips of his ears tickled the bottoms of my kneecaps, and he resembled a bobcat more than a housecat.

"Meow," he said in a clipped voice.

The guys exchanged a tense look. Matt recovered first. He jogged around the car, jumped in and peeled out before Tim recovered. At a loss, Tim stared after his friend and wet his lips. "Your bags are still in the trunk." He sidestepped Diode. "I'll just, um, go get them." He slapped an envelope into Mai's hands. "Grab the first elevator on the right in the lobby. I'll meet you upstairs."

"And people say chivalry is dead," I deadpanned.

"Maybe chivalry is just allergic to cats." Mai nudged Diode with her toe. "We might have to get him a leash."

Diode hissed. "I will not be dragged about by a leash like a common *dog*."

I bent down to ruffle his fur. "Keep hissing and spitting and someone will think you're rabid."

"Hmph." He turned his nose up at me. "I am not susceptible to earthly disease."

Of course he wasn't. "Any clue as to why your camouflage is fading?"

He managed to look chagrined. "Stress would be my guess."

"Then take a chill pill," Mai quipped. "We just got here. Don't mess this up for us."

His tail cracked the ground like a whip. "Far be it from me to ruin your fun."

Mai let his snark roll off her back. "Exactly what I'm saying."

I stepped between them, resting a hand on Mai's shoulder. "Let's change and hit the hay."

"It's barely ten p.m., and I downed six cups of coffee in the last hour alone. I can't sleep yet." A grin spread across her face. "Let's go for a swim. That ought to tire us out."

Catching her enthusiasm, I smiled. "I could go a few laps before bed."

"I will stand guard while you two…" Diode almost gagged, "…swim."

"I'll call down to the front desk and check for warnings before we hit the beach." The night was clear, but I hadn't seen the local forecast, hadn't expected to do more than flop into bed on our first night.

"Actually," Mai said on a chuckle. "I have other plans for us."

With the roar of the ocean at my back, I couldn't imagine anything better than the crash of waves and the call of seagulls. Tomorrow I was eager to slather on sunscreen and trudge through the valleys cut between those white sandy dunes.

After reminding myself it was Mai's vacation too, I managed to stop from pouting. "Do tell."

The smile she flashed me was radiant. "I'll show you as soon as we're changed."

Not trusting her mood, I stepped onto the elevator after she was inside, and we rode up to our rooms. Diode was too bulky for me to carry comfortably with the illusion spell weakening. Plus, he had the same hands-off attitude as Mai did when she was in her fox form, so he trotted alongside me. Small mercy, he was used to elevators from riding the one in our apartment building, so there was no screeching or mewling like there had been during my first attempts at immersing him into my world. For a cat that lived in the wilds of Faerie when he wasn't crashing with Mac, entering my home that first time must have been like stepping onto a spaceship for him.

Mai opened the envelope she had been given by the front desk and tugged out several credit-card-sized keycards.

I whistled. "Do you think they gave us enough?"

She spread them between her fingers and fanned her face. "Pick a card, any card."

Rolling my eyes, I tapped one. It didn't work on the door. Neither did the next three. By process of elimination, the fourth card popped the lock. We entered the living room, and I breathed a sigh of relief.

All the other crap faded. Faerie. My crown. Rook. Shaw. All of it.

A wall of glass cast our reflection back at us when I switched on the overhead lights. At night, it wasn't much to look at, but in the daylight? The view would be spectacular. Mai would settle for nothing less. The walls were painted stark white and kept bare, meant to keep the focus on the no-doubt-stunning view. Beige carpet cushioned my feet, and equally nondescript leather furniture filled the room. I caved to the smile tugging my lips.

For the next week, this was my reality. Sun. Beach. Ocean. My best friend.

Diode yowled when the door shut, pinching his tail.

And my psychedelic calico bobcat.

We explored our accommodations while waiting on our luggage to arrive. I was impressed. There were two bedrooms, each with its own bath. We even had a kitchenette, which meant I could buy groceries and skip the tab on eating fast food this week. The living room was cramped, but it had a great view of the Atlantic. French doors opened onto a narrow patio overlooking the glistening sea. This was a lot nicer than anything I could afford even when I wasn't flat busted.

Mai made the rounds, too, wrinkling her nose whenever an item failed to meet her lofty standards.

"This place is great," I said to distract her.

Her hands found her hips, and she glanced around. "We must be paying for the location."

"Stop being a snob." I jostled her elbow. "This is great, and you know it."

She cracked a smile. "Thanks."

"You have nothing to thank me for." I was mooching off her, not the other way around.

"Yes, I do." She turned serious on me. "You call me on being a bitch when Mom's programming kicks in."

"She didn't totally brainwash you." For the most part. "Besides, she just wants you to be happy."

"As long as my idea of happy means settling down and popping out kits, then yes, she does."

"Mai..." I slung my arm around her shoulders.

"No." She shrugged me off and crossed the room. "We agreed. Life can wait. We're here to have fun."

"Yes." I nodded. "Fun."

She snorted. "Dork."

Chimes rang through the room.

"Finally." Mai bolted to answer the door.

While she was occupied, I took out my phone and checked the earlier text I had missed. I darted a quick glance at my bedroom door before I dialed the number on the screen. One ring. Two. Three.

Shaw answered on the fourth ring. "How's the view?"

"Dark and moony. How's yours?"

"It depends." A smile lurked in his voice. "How do you feel about boxers versus briefs?"

A flush zinged up the back of my neck. His question reminded me of the first time I saw Rook in the flesh. There had been plenty of his perfect fae flesh out on display. He had met me at his door wearing nothing but a pair of faded jeans and an enigmatic smile.

I rubbed the sting from my nape. "Did you forget to pack your undies?"

Shaw's chuckle did confusing things to my stomach. I should have texted him instead of calling.

"I'm checking out the store where my sister-in-law was spotted."

"Any reason why you're looking for her in menswear?"

"I'm not. Exactly."

I knew him too well. I could tell he was hiding something. "What is it?"

"Hey, get a move on." Mai burst into the room and tossed a swimsuit at my face. "Oh. Who's on the phone?" She flung a towel on the bed and mouthed, *Mom?*

I nodded, hating that I was lying to her.

She jerked her thumb over her shoulder and pantomimed getting changed.

I bobbed my head again, adding another thumbs-up to the mix. I waited until she left before I shut my door under the pretense of undressing. "I can't talk now," I said softly. "Can I call you later?"

"It's a date."

Click.

"No," I growled at the dead air, "it's not."

CHAPTER TEN

Mai sashayed into my bedroom wearing a strapless navy-blue bikini top that gathered between her breasts. The bottom was white, the pattern a twist on traditional paisley in navy and turquoise with gold accents.

It put my simple black one-piece suit to shame.

I snatched the enormous beach towel off my bed and wrapped it around my waist. I offered to carry one down for her, but she declined.

She cocked her hip and struck a pose. "I can't cover all this up."

"I figured you'd say that." I shouldered an oversized straw bag, my cell, a book on types of blood-drinking fae—a threat realer than any vampire—and other necessities.

Shaking her head at me, she asked, "Ready to go?"

"Yep." A good marshal was always prepared. "Where's this surprise you've been promising?"

She curled her finger at me. "Right this way."

We left our room, but instead of hopping on the elevator, she led me down the hall to a large set of picture windows overlooking the right side of the hotel. She yanked the gauzy curtains aside with a grand flourish then waited for me to step up and check out the view. I approached cautiously and gasped.

A kidney-shaped pool dominated one side of the cobbled patio area. Recessed lights created a path leading straight to the water's edge. But that wasn't the surprise. Shaped almost like a smile, a second pool hugged the first, nudging giant inner tubes striped with glow-in-the-dark paint around its narrow loop. A strip of palm trees wrapped in Christmas lights divided the two areas. Swaying in the breeze, they blasted disco-style lighting from their fronds.

"A lazy river?" I burst out laughing.

She came to stand beside me. "I know how much you love them."

I did love them. I wasn't as big a fan of pools as Mom was, but agitate some water and dump me in a donut-shaped inner tube, and I was in heaven.

I slung an arm around her waist. "Have I told you lately that you're the best friend ever?"

"Not since yesterday." She leaned her head against my shoulder. "But I never tire of hearing my praises sung."

We turned at the sound of the elevator opening behind us, but the booth was empty except for the rich fragrance of curry chicken.

Too bad I was on a strict budget. Takeout smelled divine after our long drive.

"Moment over." I bobbed my shoulder. "Let's head down there."

We bolted for the elevator and rode it down to the lobby. Finding the pool was easy. We followed the pounding bass and flow of the twenty-something crowd, and they led us straight to it.

Like a mini theme park, the area boasted a small bank of lockers with an attendant booth. Behind that, a tower of inner tubes leaned. Unlike a theme park, a long bar curved down one side of the patio. Its thatched roof whispered on the breeze, and dance music poured out of the speakers hanging from its bamboo rafters.

I strolled up to the booth and flashed a keycard at the attendant that did...I'm not sure what...and the guy passed me a brightly colored inner tube.

Mai was right behind me, and she pointed at my float. "Can I get one of those in turquoise?"

"Sure. Yeah." The attendant swept his gaze over Mai. "You can have whatever you want."

Needless to say, he didn't ask her for ID.

She turned and winked, and I scowled. "How do you do that?"

"This—" she gestured down her body, "—is a magic bikini."

I cocked a dubious eyebrow. "It is?"

"No man can resist me when I'm wearing it." She grinned. "It works like a charm. Get it?"

"Oh, I get it." She didn't need magic to charm men. Her natural charisma had them eating out of the palm of her hand. If I didn't know how hardcore the kitsune dating scene was, I might be jealous.

Pulling one of my moves, she tugged a keycard from her top. "Do you want to hold on to this?"

"Sure." Figuring it was safer with me, I stuffed the card into the side pocket of my bag. I rented a locker for the week and got a key on an orange plastic coil bracelet in return. Once I stashed my bag, we found the launching station.

After a few false starts, where I tried to get Mai into her inner tube without her actually getting wet, a pair of lifeguards climbed from their respective towers to lift her and center her on her float while I gawked. Flirtatious laughter trailed after her as her float was snared by the current, and she was swept away from me.

I managed to flip myself—twice—before ringing the hole with my butt instead of my thigh. The lifeguards never batted an eye. They were watching Mai arrange herself as artfully as one can while sitting prim and proper in the center of a giant, inflatable donut while dunking one's ass into icy water.

Trusting she couldn't stir up too much trouble while confined to her inner tube, I arranged my limbs for maximum relaxation potential. I leaned my head back and shut my eyes to block out the glaring lights. Stifling a yawn, I fought the urge to nap. But between the early start and the tense trip, I couldn't resist. I dozed.

"Where are you?"

My head snapped up at the sound of Rook's voice, and my hands scrambled for purchase on the same narrow limb where I woke last time. Heart in my throat, I crept toward the tree trunk and held on.

"That's a damn good question," I snapped.

"We already covered this." He looked bored. "You're in a dream."

I had to ask. "If I die in this dream, will I die in real life?"

"You won't fall." A fierce glint shone in his eyes. "And you won't die. I won't allow it." The spark in his gaze ignited as he studied me. "Where are you?"

I glanced down and noticed I still wore my swimsuit. "Oh. I'm at a pool."

He bolted upright. "You're sleeping in the water?"

"Not exactly." I flushed as I realized he was right. I had fallen asleep in the lazy river. "I'm in a float that protects me from drowning." I hoped. "Plus, there are lifeguards on duty. They watch over everyone."

Especially foxy ladies in bikinis…

Seeming mollified, Rook reclined once more. "This is not ideal."

"Tell me about it." Even if my body was asleep, he was keeping my mind awake and exhausted.

"This is the only way we can communicate." He smiled slowly. "For now."

I glowered at the reminder I would be hauled back to Faerie all too soon.

A thought occurred to me. "Hey, what happened last time? You just vanished."

His smile widened. "Were you concerned for me?"

"No."

"You're a bad liar, Thierry. No matter. I can teach you to be a better one."

I bet you could. "What is the purpose of these dreams?"

"I told you." He rested his elbows on his knees. "I must educate you if you are to survive here."

I had trained one way or another for the last six years. This was familiar territory. "When do we begin?"

He waved a hand at my swimsuit. "Once you're dressed more appropriately."

"This is a dream, right? Can't you just snap your fingers and make it happen?"

"I could," he admitted, staring so intently I crossed my arms over my chest. "But we have time. Besides, I would prefer knowing that your body is safe while I have your mind otherwise occupied."

I couldn't fault his logic. If my inner tube floated over one of the agitators creating the current, those powerful jets could dump me headfirst into the water. Would the shock wake me? I hoped so.

I didn't want to depend on lust-struck teenage boys to save me.

A distant awareness thrummed through the back of my mind, but the body in the pool wasn't as real to me as this treetop conversation. Reality was playing tug-of-war with my consciousness.

"You're struggling." He leaned forward and cupped my cheek. "Eager to escape me?"

Yes. "I'm eager to get back to my vacation."

"Vacation." He turned thoughtful. "I have never had one of those."

A stab of pity kept me from jerking out of his grasp. "Maybe when things have settled down?"

A brittle smile answered me. "Perhaps then."

I searched his face for an answer to his mood. "I get the feeling you aren't telling me everything."

"Let me bear the burden for now." His voice softened. "It will be ours to share soon enough."

I flinched at the reminder, and he let his hand fall away.

"I required these preemptive meetings in order to let you acclimate to the dream state, but the time for idle conversation is over. The next time I summon you, we set to work. Be prepared."

"I will be."

If no loophole could be found for me in our original bargain, then I must prepare for the dangers awaiting me in Faerie. So far, my only way out was to serve my one-hundred-year sentence as queen. By that time, all the mortals I knew would be dead, including my mother.

Serving wasn't an option.

Rook settled back into his spindly-branch chair. "A question, before you go."

"Okay." I made a rolling gesture with my hand.

He crossed one long leg over the other. "Who is with you on this *vacation*?"

"Mai invited me." I shifted on the limb. "The guards are with me." No need to tell him that they hadn't arrived yet. "Diode is here too, but he's not thrilled about it. Water and cats, cats and water."

His toe tapped in the air. "Is that all?"

Sensing he must already know the answer and that lying would get me nowhere, I took a breath and admitted, "Shaw is working a case in a city about an hour away. Since I've been suspended, I'm not involved. He's not doing conclave work anyway. It's a personal matter."

"You're rambling," Rook noted.

"I don't ramble." Much.

"This vacation—it happens far away from your home, correct? That is what makes it exotic?"

Oh crap. He was putting the pieces together. "Yes."

Rook's lips thinned. "I have seen the way he looks at you."

A spark of anger had me clenching my jaw. "Are you spying on me?"

"I have loyal subjects who are kind enough to lend me their eyes from time to time."

That explained the black bird who tapped on my window my first night home from Faerie. I thought since Rook was across realms, his hold on his flock would wane. No such luck. If he was still using their eyes to watch me, then he had a stronger presence in the mortal realm than I had realized.

"I have less than a year of freedom left," I growled. "Can you not stalk me during that time?"

He looked puzzled by why I wouldn't want his beady-eyed subjects following me everywhere I went. "How else can I know of your life until then?"

Pinching started in my temples, working across my forehead. "You could ask me."

"Fine. I will ask you now. Do you have feelings for that incubus?"

My throat constricted, but the denial I intended didn't come.

"You share a past with him." Rook demanded, "Does he understand your future is mine?"

That earlier spark burst into a rush of furious anger. "My future is *mine*."

In a flash, I was gulping chlorinated water and thrashing. My inner tube, which I had flailed out of, flipped over and bopped me on the head. I stood, and the chilly water barely hit me at waist level. Spluttering, I shoved the limp curtain of hair from my eyes and looped an arm over the float to keep it from escaping. Once I gained my bearings, I oriented myself and searched the spinning inner tubes for Mai.

She was nowhere in sight.

CHAPTER ELEVEN

A firm—yet unseen—hand gripped my upper arm and began guiding me around the last bend, toward the steps leading from the pool. Reflex tightened my muscles. Only the abundance of humans kept me from decking my would-be escort. Chlorine and the remnants of sunscreen on my fellow swimmers dampened my ability to scent, but I had a good idea of who this was now that I was recovering from my visit with Rook.

"Warn a girl next time," I said to the presence on my right.

"I thought you were in distress." Righty's voice almost blended with the babbling water.

"Well, I'm not." I stared where he ought to be standing. There were ripples in the water from all the jets and splashing, but no eddies gave away the fact my guard stood there. "You can let go now."

He did, and I waded toward the submerged steps.

"I apologize," he said. "I should not have interfered."

"You're fine." I craned my neck. "I was on my way out of the pool anyway."

No response. No sign of Mai, either.

"Are you guys just arriving?" I reached the stairs and climbed them, hiding a smile when Righty cupped the inner tube to relieve me of its weight while allowing me to appear as if I was carrying it.

Sometimes I really wanted to like that guy.

"We've been here since you left your apartment this morning, securing the area."

"How did you manage that?" I teased, "Do you have a portal in your pocket?"

He didn't deny it.

Okay then. "Is everything as it should be?"

"For now. I will keep you abreast of any further developments."

That sounded ominous. "I don't suppose you've seen Mai?"

"No." He volunteered, "Daire is with her."

My gut did a little twist. "Why?"

"As the location appears to be secure, I thought you would appreciate us extending our services to your friend."

His voice was calm, reasonable, and I didn't trust it for a minute.

We returned the float, then I set out for the crowded bar. "Let's see what they're up to."

Sure enough, Mai sat on a stool with a ring of admirers around her. Kitsunes may not have lures per se, but the girl had wicked mojo when it came to the opposite sex.

When she spotted me, she waved and hopped off her perch. "See you later, alligators."

A tall man wearing a linen suit cut off her retreat. "Let her wait a while, crocodile."

When he grabbed her arm, I tapped him on the back.

He swung around, teeth bared, snarling a challenge from one predator to another. It took a split second for the threat to register because my brain stalled. The guy was gorgeous. Black hair styled in a frohawk. Skin darker than the night at the patio's edge, and his eyes... They reminded me of how Rook's had looked the first time I met him. Empty. Cold. Eternal.

No, I didn't like this guy one bit.

"You should let go of my friend," I told him.

He arched a dark eyebrow. "Would you take her place?"

"I'm already married." I flashed my megawatt smile. "But thanks for asking."

Ha! Score one for faux marriages everywhere.

When he didn't budge, I leaned in closer. "Let me introduce myself. I'm Marshal Thackeray—"

"—with the Southwestern Conclave," he finished for me.

I didn't ask how he knew. I didn't want to give him another advantage over me when he already had one. I had no idea who he was, but I didn't have to let him know how much my ignorance bugged me.

"My reputation precedes me." I grinned. "Since you know who I am, you also know I don't play nice." Fair, yes. Nice, no. "My friend here doesn't look eager to continue your conversation. I would let her go if I were you. There are plenty of other women who would be flattered by your attention."

His eyebrows rose. "You think so?"

"Sure." I pried Mai's hand from his tight grip with a decisive yank then shoved her behind me. "Nice meeting you." I placed a guiding hand on her shoulder and called out "Enjoy your night" on our way past.

His expression made my knees weak, and not in a good way.

"Oh." He tenderly caressed his hand where my fingertips had brushed him. "I will."

My shoulders twitched under the tangible weight of his stare. Slowly, so as not to provoke any of his predatory instincts, we retreated a safe distance away.

"We need to leave the area," a cool voice said to my right.

Thinking of the handsome-yet-creepy fae, I nodded. "Where's Daire?"

"Making sure we aren't followed."

His calm made me curious. "I notice you didn't step in back there."

"The fae appeared oblivious to our presence. I saw no reason why I should announce myself unless the situation escalated." He exhaled. "I was unable to sense what type of fae he is. His power barely registered until you touched him, then it surged. Could you scent him?"

The suggestion stunned me so much I stopped walking. "The thought never occurred to me."

Righty made a thoughtful noise.

"He was using glamour to conceal himself with a side of compulsion mixed in for good measure." I followed that line of reasoning. "Otherwise, I would have spotted him—" a threat who was obviously fae, obviously dangerous, "—scented him or demanded he declare himself."

Mai rested her hand on my arm. "Is it safe to stay here?"

"He is Unseelie," Righty answered. "He would not dare strike against our future queen."

Mai and I shared a look that conveyed our doubt. Faerie had been teetering on the brink of war for a long time. King Moran's death and my controversial appointment could very well be the straws that dislocated the camel's back. Rook was working to diffuse the situation, but our subjects were almost as fond of him as they were of me. Both of us were half-bloods, and few pure-blooded fae were eager to bow before a half-human sovereign. Especially not one who had killed both the Seelie and Unseelie candidates for the crown.

"I'm hungry." Mai rubbed her arms. "You want to hit one of the fast-food joints?"

"That would be unwise," a fourth voice entered our conversation. "Your admirer just left."

"We don't want to risk bumping into him on the sidewalk." I nodded. "Gotcha."

Beside me, Mai shivered. "Delivery?"

"That sounds perfect." I hooked my arm through hers. "We'll eat and rent movies to watch until we fall asleep."

After collecting our belongings from the storage locker, we headed up to our room. There we found Diode in a compromising position on the carpet in the living room. He didn't pause his grooming session to acknowledge us, but he did swivel his eyes to watch our grim procession.

He hacked once. "What happened?"

We told him, and he began pacing. The more I watched, the more certain I was he was growing before my eyes.

Like sands through a flip-flop thong, our perfect vacation was slipping through our fingers—toes?

"Beaches are a favorite hunting ground for predatory fae," I said to anyone listening. "They prey on the drunk and drugged-up humans who wash ashore every summer." I bent to rub Diode. "It's not like this guy, whoever he is, set out to find us in particular. It was probably a wrong-place, wrong-time deal." I raked a hand through my damp, stringy hair. "That doesn't mean I agree with what he's doing, I don't." The conclave accepted fae had to feed and that humans were on the menu, but I didn't have to like it. "I'll see if I can get him removed through official channels." Shaw could coordinate a fae removal with the Florida conclave outpost without dropping my name. "He'll come back when he gets hungry, though. They always do. Hopefully we'll be gone before that happens."

A month ago, this wouldn't have been an issue. I would have spotted the guy working his mojo in a condo filled with humans and kids, labeled him as high risk, and then gotten rid of him. I would have done it alone, or if I was desperate, I might have called for backup. Now? Forget about it.

Being a princess meant examining all things dangerous and then determining what threat, if any, was posed to me. I hated feeling targeted. I hated having my work taken from me. But I knew the fae were unsettled, and I was an obvious target. Kill me and they got the war so many clamored for.

Before someone lowered the doom-and-gloom hammer on my evening, I addressed the room a second time, hoping for better results. "Food and a movie." I raised my hand. "Who's with me?"

Mai lifted a timid hand.

"Good enough." I headed for my room. "I'll grab my laptop, and we'll check out delivery possibilities on the strip." The rumble in my stomach convinced me dishing out for fast food was a great idea. I would shop for groceries to stock the pantry tomorrow. Tonight, there was a plate of curry chicken calling my name.

CHAPTER TWELVE

Rook was waiting for me when my eyes closed. He greeted me wearing extravagant black-and-white regalia, some fae cross between a tux and a suit of armor. His pitch-black hair hung in a single braid down his spine. His pale skin luminesced, and his sharp eyes mocked my slack-jawed reaction.

We stood on black-and-white checkered tiles made from polished marble. There were no walls or ceiling. Beyond the floor lurked an abyss. Over our heads, stars twinkled in unfamiliar constellations. I awarded bonus points for the enormous moon hanging overhead, so round and bright it lit the room.

I stood before him in a T-shirt, panties and fuzzy yellow socks. "I was wearing pajama shorts when I went to sleep."

His tone was all kinds of innocent. "Were you?"

I concentrated very hard on wearing jeans, and they appeared. "Why so formal?"

Rook scowled at my wardrobe choice. "To be treated as a royal, one must look the part."

"Okay." I gestured around us. "What's all this?"

He snapped his fingers, and classical music filled the air. Narrow white bars snapped into place, creating four walls that boxed us into a square-shaped room. As the song—a waltz, I think—played, each note popped into existence on the corresponding line. Music was being written before our eyes.

"Your coronation ball will be the likes of which Faerie has never beheld," he promised.

"That's not necessary, really." I spun in a slow circle, watching the progression of the song. "I'm not much of a dancer."

"That's what all this is for." He held out his hand. "I want you to shine, Thierry."

I walked up to him and slapped my hand into his. "By shine, you mean not embarrass you."

"You could never do that." He delivered the line with such sincerity, I almost believed him.

Up close Rook's wood-smoke-and-embers scent enfolded me, and my belly tightened pleasantly.

He reeled me closer, until six inches separated our chests, and beamed at me with such pride, I let myself imagine what our life might be like as a couple. Though his political aspirations had brought us together, Rook was not unaffected by me. And, if I were honest, I wasn't immune to his appeal. He was a beautiful man. I also suspected he had a decent heart hidden underneath his ambition, but being railroaded into marriage and the whole kidnapping-my-mom thing meant I spent more time dreaming of strangling him than making out with him.

Of course, that could be said about most men in my life.

"What were you thinking about just now?" He peered down at me. "You were smiling."

"I was thinking of how often I daydream about strangling you."

"You're passionate." He decided, "There are worse attributes in a wife."

He slid his arm around my waist. His fingers grazed higher, leaving trails of warmth in their wake, until his broad palm rested confidently between my shoulder blades.

"Follow my lead," he said.

After a few false starts, he taught me a basic box step. Putting those new moves to the music left me muttering counts under my breath and curling my toes out of fear his quick steps would crush my feet through my socks.

"You're overthinking it." His grip on my hand tightened. "Focus on the music." His voice turned persuasive. "On me."

Against my better judgment, I did as he asked, falling into his dark eyes, following his lead as he hummed along with the music. The longer we danced, the easier we moved, until my legs were sore and my breathing labored. Color splashed his cheeks, and his devilish grin widened.

"It can be like this every night once we're together." He sounded wistful.

I misstepped, almost tripping us both, and spun out of his arms. "Is that what this is?"

He stood there, chest heaving, eyes shining, saying nothing. It was answer enough for me.

I shook my head. "I thought you were supposed to be teaching me how to survive Faerie."

"You will learn, but until then, you have me."

"That's been your plan all along." I felt like an idiot for not seeing it sooner. "The consuls think you're here, teaching me how to rule Faerie while you're really here trying to seduce me through my dreams." When would I learn that trusting Rook never ended well for me? "You want to keep me dependent on you, even if my glaring ignorance gets me killed."

Muscles leapt in his jaw. "I would never let you be harmed."

Bitter laughter spilled over my lips. "Oh, that's right. If I die, so do your dreams."

"Thierry…"

"No." I backed away from him. "I'm out of here."

I woke in my bed, fists clenched in the covers and heart racing with anger. Then, to compound a frustrating situation, I did the one thing even dumber than falling for Rook's shenanigans. Yet again.

I called Shaw.

Shaw picked up just as I was getting nervous he might not. I should have taken the cosmic out I had been given, but no. I hung on the line, counting the rings until they almost put me to sleep.

"Hey."

His graveled voice jolted me as I drifted halfway between sleep and wakefulness.

"Thierry?"

"Sorry." I shifted onto my side. "I'm here."

"You're up late. Are you keeping night hours?"

I worked dusk until dawn most times because the hunting was easier, but there was no point now.

"Not so much." I rubbed my eyes. "How about you?"

"If I hadn't forgotten to turn off my ringer, we wouldn't be having this conversation."

"I shouldn't have called so early." A guilty twinge hit me. "I'll let you get back to sleep."

"You called for a reason." He sounded more alert. "What's up?"

I reflected on the details of the dream and decided to make this about him. "How's your case?"

Maybe too alert. "That's not why you called."

Damn him for knowing me so well. "It's complicated."

"You should print that on business cards." Amusement saturated his voice. "Do you really want details?"

"Spill." As I said it, I realized I meant it. I hoped his trip wasn't a bust like mine had been so far.

"I exhausted my best lead." He exhaled. "One grainy security feed placed Jenna in the area, but now I don't know if I can trust myself to be objective. It looked like her, but not like her. She was rail thin for one thing. Jenna was always curvy, especially after she had the kids. Her walk was all wrong, her motions jerky and uncoordinated. Things change in ten years, but that much? I'm not convinced it was her."

I sensed he wanted to say more and gave him time to force out the words.

"All this time I figured she was gone," he said softly. "That was the only thing that made sense. She wouldn't have left my brother. She loved him, and Ian worshipped her." He paused. "Being with an incubus is hard long term, but she made it look easy. He was her Ian, and that was that. Even if things got rough between them, she never would have left her kids. Not in a million years."

A familiar pang rocked me. *A wife and kids.* Some scrap of hope that should have been stamped out last year lit up at the possibility. Longing in Shaw's voice tightened my chest. Had his attempt to date me been proof he wanted what his brother once had? Maybe. It hardly mattered now.

I cleared my throat. "Anything I can do?"

He mulled it over a moment. "Not from an hour away."

I smiled at his dejected tone. "Is that an invitation?"

"It is if it gets you here."

I sounded skeptical when I asked, "You're that desperate for help?"

"I'm that desperate to see you."

I held the phone out at arm's length, stared at the screen, then placed it back against my ear. "Are you *flirting* with me?"

He laughed, and heat twined through me. "After all this time, do you really have to ask?"

I bit my lip to keep from blurting *yes*. Even if Rook wasn't a factor, our relationship was one hot mess. Shaw might like the idea of fidelity, but he had already struck out once with me. Did he covet the idea of a *Happily Ever After: Incubus Edition* enough to retry committing to me now that he had no choice but to be faithful? Did I want that kind of relationship? One born from necessity instead of love?

No. I didn't. I couldn't do that to either of us. I deserved to find a guy who was genuinely crazy about me, and Shaw deserved the chance to find a woman who could drive him crazy. In a good way.

I kept my tone light. "I can't exactly sneak over there and back without Mai noticing."

Another sigh from him punctuated the frustration we shared. "I know."

We lapsed into a tense quiet filled with things both of us knew better than to say.

He broke the silence first. "Are you sure you don't want to tell me why you called?"

Admit to him how conflicted I felt about my husband? That I had been having tender feelings for Rook before he smashed them? Another, safer option surfaced. "We had some excitement tonight. A fae—I'm not sure what kind—manhandled Mai at the pool. I broke up the altercation, but I got a bad vibe off him."

"Where were your guards?" He bit off the words.

"They were with me," I said primly, "but they trusted me to handle it."

"In other words, they were afraid revealing themselves would mark you as a person of interest."

I growled in response.

"You couldn't scent him?" Shaw pressed. "What about the guards? What did they sense?"

I explained my glamour-compulsion combo theory. "All we know for sure is he's Unseelie."

Some of the tension bled from his voice. "That gives you a wild card to play if you meet him again. It ought to keep you safe enough."

Unless he was a member of the Anti-Princess League who would be happy to dispatch me, but I didn't say that. The guy knew my name. I was betting he knew my title too. So was our new friend a half-blood hater? A Raven loyalist? By engaging with me, was he thumbing his nose at the conclave? Or Faerie? Or both?

I didn't know, but Shaw was right about one thing. If there was a next time, playing the princess card would accomplish one of two goals. Put the guy in his place or green light the guards to use deadly force in his removal. Either outcome was a win as far as I was concerned.

I tried not to think about the various factions eager to see my crown put back in play. They could keep the thing. They could keep Faerie, too, but first I needed a workaround that didn't involve loyal subjects lopping off my head to retrieve the aforementioned crown.

I was happy to hand it over, no guillotine required.

Shaw asked no less than what I expected. "What do you want me to do?"

"I was hoping you could mention the guy's choice of feeding grounds to the marshals at the Florida outpost."

"I see."

"They know you're in the area." Marshals with threat-level-four designations, like us, had to announce themselves when traveling across state lines. I hadn't for obvious reasons, but Shaw would have. "It makes sense someone would mention it to you."

He drew out his response. "Someone who isn't you."

Damn he caught on fast.

"Exactly," I agreed.

He continued, "Because they don't know where you are."

Maybe too fast.

I debated fudging the truth, but lies had a way of biting me on the ass. "Not exactly."

He groaned my name.

I shot into defensive mode. "I'm being careful."

"You say that, and yet here you are, calling me in the middle of the night."

"Hey," I snapped, "you didn't have to answer."

"Yes, I did."

"No, you didn't."

"What if you had been in danger?" he demanded.

"I would have figured something out."

He grunted, unconvinced. "What if something had happened to you?"

I struck a low blow. "Then you wouldn't be able to feed?"

His anger was a palpable force. "You know a food source isn't all you are to me."

I wasn't sure who I was reminding when I said, "It's all I can be."

"And yet..." he pointed out again, "...you made this phone call."

Damn incubus. His brain must run on moonbeams, because mine was out of gas. I had to end this before I said something I really regretted. "If you're going to be an ass, forget about it."

I hung up on Shaw and tossed my phone across the bed. Then it hit me. *Crap.* No wonder he was pissed. I was supposed to call him earlier to finish our conversation about his adventures in menswear and forgot. I bet he sat there, staring at his display, debating whether to pick up before a sense of duty won out and he finally answered.

Guess this was a night for making bad decisions all around.

CHAPTER THIRTEEN

"Rise and shine."

"No." I groaned and pulled the covers over my head.

"I made coffee." Mai hummed. "It smells so good and fresh and delicious and—"

I lowered the cover in increments. "You're the spawn of Satan."

"Aww." She mimed wiping tears. "I'll tell Daddy you said so. He'll be so flattered."

A snort escaped me as I pushed upright and squinted at the sun. "What time is it?"

"Noon." She passed me the warm mug. "You were out cold. How late did you stay up?"

I covered a yawn. "I don't know."

After visiting with Rook and calling Shaw, there hadn't been much time left for rest.

"I would have let you sleep, but Diode got a burr in his fur about making sure you were alive."

I fashioned an excuse from Shaw's assumption. "Switching from third shift to first is always tough."

"Tell me about it." She covered her mouth. "I've been on first for what—a week? I hate it."

"Foxes are nocturnal." I laughed. "You should tell your boss working first shift goes against your nature."

"That's not a bad idea." She plucked at her bottom lip. "I wonder if I could get away with it."

"Check with Dr. Row in the med ward. If she writes you an excuse, it might work."

She gave me an appreciative nod. "You're kind of an evil genius when you first wake up."

I blew on the coffee in the hopes of not blistering my tongue. "Thanks, I think."

She flopped onto the mattress. "Now that you're awake, what do you want to do today?"

I held the mug away from me so the scalding liquid wouldn't splash down my chest. "Swim? Sunbathe? Play beach volleyball?"

Her voice took on a mischievous quality. "There are gray men in the shallows."

"Selkies?" My voice cracked. "I've never seen one."

"Apparently, it's mating season."

Suspicion pushed me out of bed, the better to tower over her. "How do you know all this?"

She rolled onto her stomach and scissored her legs. "I might have gone snorkeling earlier."

"Are you serious?"

"As a heart attack." She propped her chin in her hands. "They'll rent anything to anyone these days."

I glowered down at her. "Rental availability is not the point, and you know it."

She stuck out her tongue at me. "It's not like I was floating around testing all the males."

I relaxed a fraction.

She winked. "Just the cute ones."

To keep my opinions to myself, I chugged coffee until I gulped air. Damn it. We were on vacation. This was not the time for me to lecture. I should go with the flow, meet some nice selkies and check out life under the sea via rent-a-flippers and a snorkel.

I studied her flushed cheeks. "Did you have any luck?"

"There was this one guy." She groaned and rolled onto her back. "He's gorgeous, Tee."

Fae beauty was definitely a selling point. It was their teeth and claws you had to watch out for.

Her glow made me a touch jealous. I hadn't felt all lit up inside in a long time. "Did you test him?"

Mai's buoyant mood sank. "No."

If it were anatomically possible, I would kick my own ass for dragging her down. I should have kept my mouth shut. Mai *was* passing out tests like handshakes lately, and it worried me. What used to be the ultimate test was becoming more of a pop quiz. She had been burned. A lot. As her friend, I shouldn't make light of what stood between her and her future mate, even if I thought it was archaic.

It was just that selkies were, in my opinion, a bad place to start. They had a bad reputation for knocking up women and then stealing their offspring to raise among their own kind. So, yeah. Not the best fae to look to for a relationship.

Says the girl who dated an incubus...

"You do realize you can enjoy a man's company without expecting a lifelong commitment?"

"I know." She rested her forearm over her eyes. "I don't see the point. Why invest myself in a guy who isn't *the one*? I mean, that's what the test is for, right? So what if it has to be widely administered to be effective?" She thumped her head on her arms. "I saw what it did to you. When you and Shaw split up, it was bad. You were wrecked. Even your mom called me to ask what was really going on with you. She wanted *details*."

My mother had wanted details? "You never told me she called you."

"She made me promise I wouldn't tell you about it." Mai sighed. "I should have kept my mouth shut, but I want to put this into perspective for you. Love is catastrophic, cataclysmic—and other *c* words I can't think of right now. It destroys people. So why suffer when I have a predestined mate?"

So this was it. The truth at last. She was afraid of falling in love without using the test as a safety net. A predestined mate was safe. The whole preordained thing meant he was made for her and her alone. Love guaranteed. Best sex ever, all covered in the fine print.

I envied her that.

For years I had built Shaw up as this ideal man in my head. In hindsight, I could admit that was part of the problem. Place someone high enough on a pedestal and you're asking for them to fall. Shaw's incubus nature had given him a push.

"Losing Shaw didn't wreck me," I lied through my teeth. "I kept both hands on the wheel."

"Tee, your hands might have been on the wheel, but you stomped on the gas and played chicken with oncoming traffic." She rolled toward me. "You were written up five times for excessive force during the first month alone. Oddly enough, those were all instances involving incubi. Huh. Almost like you targeted them."

Heat swept up the base of my neck. "I could have handled things better post-Shaw. Happy?"

Neutrality apparently only extended so far, even if impartiality was in your blood.

Mai studied me. "I don't think you believe that."

"Stop shrinking me. I'm not your patient. Legally, you're not even allowed to have patients. This is not about me and Shaw." Thank God. "This is about you."

"You used the s-word." She clutched her chest. "That hurts."

Classic Mai. Land her jabs, let me vent, let her vent at me, and then diffuse the situation.

"So," I said, wrapping my hand around her ankle. "Are we flirting with gray men or what?"

"Thierry," she warned.

She kicked out. I caught that leg and tucked it under my arm, returning my attention to her other foot.

"I'll give you rabies if you do it."

I snorted. "You don't have rabies."

She bared her teeth and squirmed. "I didn't say I would do it personally."

"It's a simple question." I tickled the bottom of her foot. "Yes or no."

Mai thrashed. Promises of reciprocation were gasped. My anatomy was threatened which, being a girl, wasn't as effective as it could have been if we had dragged the guards into the fray. I kept on until she couldn't breathe and her legs went noodly, until our worries faded and we were just two young women with nothing better to do than to see who could make the other pee their pants laughing first.

Dressed to thrill, Mai sashayed into the living room wearing a silver bikini. This one I had seen crumpled on her bed earlier and almost tossed it, thinking it was tinfoil left over from our delivery. Three small triangles covered her important bits, each held in place by string and a prayer. A mesh cover-up hit her mid-thigh. Its metallic-gray color reminded me of chain mail. Her sleek hair was French braided across the top of her head like a woven hairband and finished off in a sloppy bun behind her right ear.

Feeling slouchy in my simple black tank, hair in a loose ponytail, I trailed the resident fashion plate to the front door.

Diode barred our path. "This is a bad idea."

"We'll be careful," I assured him. "I'll bring the guards and my bag."

All my ward-breaking and minor spell-casting ingredients were in there, along with knives and a few poisons. Some snacks. Lip balm. A bottle of water. Sunscreen. With that bag, I was prepared.

Marshals weren't taught much in the way of magic use until they had adequate field experience. I knew bare-bones castings from working with Shaw, who had a knack for spellwork. Compared to his skill, I was still in training wheels. But he had fifty-three years on me and practiced more often than I did.

Diode's ears swiveled. "Have you thought this through?"

"Yes?"

Sensing a weakness, he pounced. "Ah-ha. There it is. Doubt."

Mai shifted from foot to foot. "What is your problem, fur face?"

He lifted his chin. "Have you seen how much water is out there?"

She slapped her forehead. "Hello? It's the ocean."

"Ocean. Pah." He flattened his ears. "It's unnatural."

"We're in Florida." She threw up her hands. "It's a peninsula, as in, land surrounded by water on three sides."

"There is something unsettling about this place." He sniffed. "She should not be left alone in it."

I walked over and knelt beside him. "Is this a cat-and-water thing, or can you sense a threat?"

"The spell on the collar is dampening my abilities," he said, tail bristling, "but something is prickling my fur."

I stroked down his back, and he rose on tiptoe, arching under my hand. "I'll stay if you want."

He stopped mid-purr and speared a corner of the room with his vibrant gaze. "Well?"

Righty materialized with Lefty behind him. "Selkies are aligned with the Seelie, but they aren't a threat. They're here to mate, and one call from Thierry can get them banned from Florida's coast. I believe they're given a three-day window, and if they lose Florida, they've lost their chance for the year."

I frowned at him. I hadn't known about a three-day window. No wonder sightings were so rare.

The tip of Diode's tail curled thoughtfully. "Would they obey the orders of an Unseelie noble?"

"No." Righty shook his head. "But they would have no choice but to honor a conclave edict."

"Very well. Go have your fun." Diode batted my thigh with his paw. "Be careful."

"I will be." I patted his head. "Can I bring you anything back?"

He sauntered toward a patch of sunlit carpet. "I have all I require here."

Before he changed his mind, Mai grabbed my upper arm and hauled me down to the beach.

"I hate to say this, but your cat is neurotic."

"He has water issues. He's a cat. He's allowed."

Her lips twitched. "Have you ever been around a cat long enough to know this isn't normal?"

"No," I admitted. "I'm not a cat person."

"Then take my word for it, as someone who has a sister who breeds Sphinxes, he's a weirdo."

I bumped my shoulder against hers. "Be nice. He saved my ass in Faerie. He's good people."

"I'm not saying he isn't. I'm just saying he's eccentric, even for a cat."

I shrugged. "As long as he's not hurting anyone, I don't care what he does."

Her laughter tapered into a low whistle of appreciation. "My God, Thierry. Look. Slabs of abs."

My mouth got a tad dry. "Those are the gray men?"

She bit the nail on her pointer finger. "Mmm-hmm."

"Wow."

Hang around fae awhile and their beauty starts to blur. Nothing was blurring here. Twelve men, all tall and tan with swimmers' bodies, lounged on the beach near a multicolored umbrella that popped against the white sands. Neighboring rental lounges with their navy-blue fabric never stood a chance. The umbrella's bright colors and its slight spin drew the eye straight toward all of those surfer-god bodies. A clever marketing campaign executed to perfection.

All the women stared openly, and the gray men ate the attention up with a spoon. Otherwise, why wear skintight black swim briefs more at home in Europe than in Florida, where the boardshorts style was the norm? Oh yeah. They knew what those skimpy briefs did to women. Between a grunting selkies-versus-selkies volleyball game and guys evening out their nonexistent tan lines, I was shocked that no one had drowned while gawking.

I bet these guys knew CPR. They were probably certified in mouth to, well, everything.

Mai's voice was dreamy. "Why would they ever cover up those bodies with seal skins?"

The same reason they removed them. They were of each world and belonged wholly to neither.

I could relate.

"Legend says if you hide a selkie's skin or take one from the sea, they die of broken hearts."

"I bet I could kiss it and make it better."

"They're half seal, Mai. You don't kiss away half of someone's identity."

She bumped her hip into mine. "Don't ruin my love-conquers-all fantasies for me."

I dusted the conversation off my hands. "Fantasize away."

Let her imagination run wild, as long as I didn't have front-row seats for the sappy movie playing out in her head.

"They aren't mingling much," I observed.

Gray men sightings were rare, and rarer still in warm waters. These outings served a purpose. The kind of purpose best served by endless supplies of bikini-clad humans with lowered inhibitions.

The crowd of gathering women was ripe for picking, so why weren't they being plucked?

"Now that you mention it, they were flirting earlier, but I didn't see any, um, you know."

"Splashing and dashing?" I supplied. "Reeling and dealing?"

Her mouth fell open like I didn't have her to thank for half my repertoire of immaturity.

I tapped her chin, and her teeth clicked. "Watch out. They might take it as an invitation."

She rubbed her cheeks to hide her blush. "I can't even with you right now."

"Back again?" a paper-thin voice rattled.

My gaze hit on the umbrella, and I noticed a stoop-backed man sitting underneath it.

"Now, now," Mai chided. "You boys don't have a monopoly on the beach."

His hand gripped the thick pole and twisted. "Don't we?"

Mai cut me a confused look. Clearly, this wasn't the welcome she expected. I jerked my head toward the hotel. She lifted a finger, asking for a minute.

"Did I misstep before?" She circled to stand in front of the man. "If I did, I apologize."

The mesmerizing spinning stopped. "You brought *her*."

I stepped forward. "*Her* has a name."

"You should not have come back, little fox." He shifted his grip higher on the pole. "The others will scent your friend. Death is not welcome in our midst."

"In that case, we'll be on our way." I waved at Mai. "Come on."

The man shook his head. "It's too late."

The Adonises we had admired earlier converged on us while we chatted with the elder.

Fingertips brushed my elbow, a reassurance from Righty. A reminder he could get me out if I wanted to go. Good to know, but no way was I leaving Mai trapped behind the wall of agitated man-seals. Instead, I waded through muscular bodies and stood by her side, placing us between the old man and the sea.

"This is not a defensible position," Lefty hissed in my ear.

To keep his presence our little secret, I ignored him.

From this angle I could see the elder's face, and I had to admit the guy must have been hot in his day. He still had bone structure that drew the eye and radiated an alpha vibe that cowed his followers.

So of course I stomped on social etiquette rather than dance around it. "What's your problem?"

He examined the waves behind us. "You are."

"I get that, but why? I haven't hurt you or threatened you." I added, "I'm here on vacation."

His lips curled. "Death takes a vacation?"

"No, it doesn't," I answered truthfully. "But I'm not death. I'm just me."

I might be a portent thanks to my father, but his legacy didn't define me.

"Can you prove it?" His gaze lowered to the sand and refused to meet my eyes. "Why should I believe you?"

A dangerous idea sparked, but I filed it under *last resort*. "I have nothing to prove to you or anyone else." Nudges at my elbows told me both of my guards were ready to intervene if necessary. "We're leaving now."

The man flicked his wrist as a wave crashed behind us. Cool water teased the backs of our heels and sucked us lower into the sand. Shadows loomed over us. Reinforcements. Great. The one nearest Mai wrapped a casual arm around her waist, but when she struggled, he brought her hard against him in an embrace she couldn't wriggle out of.

"You really don't want to hurt her," I told him.

"We won't harm the kitsune," the old man replied. "If you prove yourself, then you may go." He pointed to another selkie.

"Invoke the perimeter spell. We don't need humans seeing this."

I cocked an eyebrow at their preparedness. "What did you have in mind?"

"A race," he said with a flash of white teeth. "The winner decides the loser's fate."

I ran every day. Okay, so every *other* day. I was in good shape, better since the princess thing began making me paranoid. Terrain would be key. Sand would bog me down and cost me the advantage. Assuming they didn't opt for a swim-off, which if I were half-seal, would be my pick. Either way, it was a lose/lose proposition for me.

This losing thing was getting old.

I squinted at the elder. "The kitsune goes free either way?"

"Yes." The old man inclined his head. "She is welcome among us."

That was one point in my favor at least. "What are the rules of this race?"

"You are the challenger, so you may choose either the weapon or the location."

Freaking monkeys. This was not the harmless afternoon of flirting I had planned, damn it.

With a smug grin hitching his lips, he asked, "What is your preference?"

I smiled blithely at him. "I defer the first choice to my opponent."

"Thierry…" Righty warned in my ear.

"Let us end this now," Lefty murmured.

"I would prefer to part ways without violence," I said to them through tight lips. "We wait."

"An interesting choice," the man allowed. "Kynon, step forward."

Possibly the most handsome man present came to my side and tipped his head.

"Kynon is the swiftest among us," the elder bragged. "The challenger has given you first choice. Take it."

"I choose location." His voice was surprisingly soft. "I choose the Mother."

I shook my head. "Surprise, surprise. A selkie choosing sea over land."

"It is a mercy I offer you," he said. "I will end this quickly."

My heart stuttered. "This is a race to the death?"

"You are death." A pucker appeared between his eyebrows. "There is only one end for you."

"Kynon has chosen," the instigator called. "Choose your weapon."

A slow grin spread over my face. "I can have any item I want to protect myself?"

His nod was regal. "Yes."

Last resort, here I come.

I lowered the boom. "Then I choose your skin."

For the first time since I'd arrived, he looked right at me. Horror shone bright in his eyes. I wasn't sure what his hang-up with death was, or how he sensed I was a portent, but his shock told me I had reaffirmed his worst fears, proving myself evil beyond measure and in need of being put down.

Jerking his chin up, the elder gestured toward Kynon. "He will retrieve my pelt from the vault."

My opponent strode toward the waves, dove into the water and disappeared.

Mai, who had stopped resisting her attack-hugger huffed. "Now what?"

"Now we wait."

The man reached out beside him and began twirling the umbrella.

CHAPTER FOURTEEN

Kynon took his sweet time. Left unprotected, my skin began to burn. I had a bottle of sunscreen in my messenger bag, but the gray men had taken that an hour ago after they caught me arguing with Righty under my breath and decided I must be crazy or was activating a pre-mixed hex.

They gave my paltry spellwork skills way too much credit.

"How are you holding up?" I called to Mai.

The old man had taken pity on her and allowed her to share in the shade of his umbrella.

Not a euphemism.

"You're going from lobster to fire hydrant." She glared at the elder. "Can I bring her water?"

He shook his head. "She will soon have all the water she desires."

I flashed him a nasty smile. "Salt water that will dehydrate me more if I drink it."

He spread his hands in a helpless gesture.

A frustrated growl jerked the nearby gray men into high alert.

Oh.

That was me.

"When you are finished being stubborn," Righty said, "we will handle the situation."

"You say handle, but what I hear is slaughter." I sighed. "You can't kill this many Seelie."

As precarious as my position was on the throne, a misstep of this magnitude would topple me. If a murderous faux pas got me off the queenly hook, I would consider taking a header, but it wouldn't. The only thing it would earn me was a knife in the back once Rook dragged me to Faerie.

"You are learning," Lefty remarked. "That response was almost diplomatic."

I stuck my tongue out at him, which meant I was mocking thin air.

Smooth. Real smooth.

Behind me, waves slapped the shore, and cooling waters frothed around my ankles.

The old man's spine stiffened. "You brought it, then?"

"I did." Kynon's voice rose from over my shoulder.

From his seat in the sand, the old man made a gesture in the air. "Let it be done."

Kynon came to my side, clutching the fur tight in his hands. "What will you do with this?"

A knowing smile curled my lips. *Sweet confirmation.* He had no idea. Not who I was or what I was about to do. These guys picked up on my portent vibes somehow, but his ignorance was proof they hadn't specifically targeted me. Good. That made this business.

Business I could handle.

I wrested the gray lump from his grip. "Why don't I show you?"

Exhaling through my teeth, I focused on the skin and let myself sink inside its residual memories. With my hold on its identity secured, I draped the skin down my back, pulling its eye slits over mine. Magic shimmied over my body, twisting me into a more compact shape. Down and down I went, until my soft belly rested on the hot sand. Thick whiskers flicked when I twitched my nose. Shifting side to side, I thumped my meaty hind flippers and barked at Kynon.

His head swung between me and the old man, who shot to his feet.

"What manner of creature are you?" he demanded.

I barked again. Speaking while shifted was still a work in progress.

He shook a gnarled finger at my face. "Do not mock me."

Mai rose slowly. "She can't talk once she's shifted."

The elder spun on her. "Is she a shifter, then?"

She extended a hand and wobbled it. "Not exactly."

"What manner of creature is she?" he repeated.

She leaned around him and looked to me for permission. I made a strangled cough.

That must have been enough for Mai. "She's the Black Dog's daughter."

This time the strangled noise came from his throat. "Macsen Sullivan's child?"

"He's the only Black Dog I know of." She huffed. "Well, except for Tee."

His knees buckled before they gave, and he hit the sand near me. "You're the princess."

Cough-bark-cough.

Mai plopped onto the sand near me. "I think she's wondering if the race to the death is still on."

"I offer my humble apologies, Princess Thierry." He bowed low before me. "I only sought to protect my people. I meant no offense, Highness."

Figuring it was safe to let go of the skin, I did, or tried to. I had sunk so deep into its memories, I was loath to be parted from the Mother, the sea, reluctant to walk as men did in this hot, dry place.

Mai stroked the length of my spine and whispered, "It's safe to come out now."

Her touch, her voice, shocked my own memories to the forefront of my brain, and I released the skin with a shudder, peeling it off while magic crackled and stood my hairs on end.

"Next time—" I coughed into my fist, "—have a reason before you attack someone, okay?"

"Death has not been kind to us." His lips flattened. "We are picked off, one by one, year by year."

"If you're this aggressive to outsiders, I can see why." I passed him his pelt. "I have never seen gray men, but legends of your people's beauty lured me down to the shore. I was curious." I paused when his papery hand brushed mine. "I offered you and yours no insult, and yet you challenged me."

"We must protect ourselves against your kind."

"Wait." I rubbed my forehead. "You thought because I was a death portent that I would, what, kill you? For no reason?"

He returned my frown. "It is the nature of a portent to announce death, is it not?"

I couldn't fault his logic. That was how the portent business worked. Back in Faerie, if you saw Mac coming for you, you knew you were as good as dead. My presence wasn't as commanding or as damning. I didn't know my father to comment on his intentions, but I approached each situation with hope I could leave with a suspect in custody. Not dried out, rolled up and tucked under my arm.

Magic like mine fed on death, on the souls of the condemned.

Hungry days were good days. They kept me honest.

The burn in my gut had increased since returning from Faerie. Maybe because I was using more magic these days? The non-lethal kind. The skin-walking trick was cool, but it would get me killed if I didn't get a handle on it and soon. My transition time sucked, and without my runes, I was just a half-fae girl with a nifty parlor trick. If Righty hadn't intervened with Herbert, the perverted djinn might have dry-humped me to death—or worse—before I sprouted hands to fend him off.

And I did *not* want to die wearing a dollar-store thong and the dried sweat of a teenager.

Swaying on my feet, I wobbled as one of the pelt's memories surfaced until the hazy images coalesced into one crystalline remembrance.

"When I wore the pelt, I saw a giant black bird swooping low over the sand. It poached the skins from your people when they come ashore to shift and mate." Other flashes of insight followed. "The bird can't catch them at sea," I said dazedly. "Selkies must shift to human on dry land. It waits until they're pink-skinned and helpless. Then it snaps their fragile necks in its crooked beak."

The elder glanced at Kynon then back to me. "I— Yes."

Not just any black bird, either. "The Morrigan."

Frail as he appeared, the old man's voice raged with the force of his anger. "Yes."

"I have to ask." Though I wasn't sure I wanted the answer. "Can you sense her in me?"

"Yes." His forehead creased. "You carry something of her magic in you."

For a panicked second, I thought he sensed some cosmic marker Rook had implanted in me, and I was primed to scratch off the topmost layer of my skin to remove it at any cost. *I am not his.* Then it hit me, and my hand shot to my throat.

"Not in me." I lifted the silver charm I never removed. "On me."

Gamely, he held out his hand. "May I?"

"Sure." I leaned forward so he could inspect it. It was too valuable to remove. I couldn't risk losing it.

Wrinkled fingers tapped the triquetra stamped into the metal. "What is this?"

"All marshals are issued these pendants," I explained. "They allow us to summon the Morrigan. When arrests go bad, we call her to consume the remains so there's nothing left for humans to find."

"Are all of them so strong?"

I bit down on the inside of my cheek. No, they weren't. Not even close, but I wasn't about to tell him that.

An ear-piercing yowl shifted his attention off me, and I used the distraction to reclaim my necklace.

I shielded my eyes from the sun and peered toward the boardwalk leading from our condo onto the beach. "What is he doing here?"

Mai shielded her eyes from the sun. *"Diode?"*

My bobcat-sized kitty stiffly picked his way across the sand, swiping at anyone who dared look his way twice. His neon gaze collided with mine, and his ears swiveled backward.

Uh-oh.

His splotchy fur stood on end by the time he reached us. His whiskers shot forward, and he spat at the sea.

"What is that?" the old man asked.

"He's a friend," I said, stretching out my hand toward Diode.

"Don't touch him." Mai popped my wrist. "Any more stress and—"

"—he'll explode to regular size like a feline piñata," I finished.

"You have been standing on the shore, surrounded by these gray men for several hours now." A snarl curled Diode's upper lip. "I must assume, therefore, that you have seen all you came to see and that you are ready to return to your rooms?" His tail bristled as he squared off with the old man. "It's a mercy that her guard alerted me when he did. Had she been harmed by your hand, I would have peeled the flesh from your bones and gifted her with both your skins."

The old man's spine stiffened. "I will not be threatened, Old One."

Old One? I glanced between them.

"I have threatened you. Offend me again, and words will fail to suffice." Diode picked his way to me on dry pockets of sand and swatted my bare leg. "Carry me to our rooms."

The old man gaped.

"It's all right." I grunted as I lifted Diode, bringing him in front of my face and rubbing our noses together. "Who's a cute widdle kitty cat? Who's my special wittle boy?"

His claws flexed. "I should have let the selkies take you."

"Eh, they would have given me back." I addressed the small gathering. "It was nice to meet you all, and I'm glad we will part as friends." I hated playing the game, but I rolled the dice and made my first promise using the power awaiting me in Faerie. "Once I am made queen, I will speak to the Morrigan on your behalf."

"You have our gratitude, Princess." The old man bowed. "It will change nothing, but we appreciate the gesture."

"It can't hurt to try."

He didn't respond.

Diode sank his claws into my arm. "We should be going."

With a tight nod to the pod, I braved the sizzling sands and began the walk back to our condo.

Mai fell in step beside me. "Sorry."

"For what?" I jerked my chin toward the gray men. "You couldn't have predicted that."

"Still." She stared ahead. "We have to be more careful. You're an Unseelie royal, and we can't keep pretending you're a neutral who's welcome to crash all the parties like we used to. It's dangerous."

I counted backward from ten before answering. I was doing that a lot lately.

"My views haven't changed." *I* hadn't changed. "I'm still me."

"I know that, but people who have never met you..." She shrugged. "All they hear is the title."

As much as I hated it, this was a wakeup call for me. We had escaped unscathed, thanks to a quirk of mine, but would I be so lucky the next time? Would my friends? She was right. I had to be more careful. Even if I had no special love or loyalty to my house, the others expected it from me.

Walking into this situation with the gray men, I could have gotten myself killed or had to kill to protect myself, and it would have been my fault. I wasn't on the clock. No official duty had brought me here. I was on my own time, and I was mingling freely the way I always did, a luxury I could no longer afford.

"Princess?"

I glanced over my shoulder and spotted a gray man, a teenager, and barely that. Thirteen if I had to guess. He was easy on the eyes, as they all were, but his movements were less fluid as though he was still growing into his height. Unlike the elder, he met my gaze and held it. He wasn't afraid. I bet he thought he could take me if he had to.

I liked him already.

Despite Diode's grumbling, I turned to face the boy. "You can call me Thierry."

His gaze plunged into the sand. "I can't do that."

The kid was coiled tight and ready to burst. I quirked an eyebrow at him. "Do you need something?"

"My great uncle—our pod elder—has a touch of foresight. It's why we beached earlier than usual." His cheeks reddened. "He wasn't sure why we had to be here, only that we did."

"Okay." Intersections of fate made my skin crawl. "What is it you need from me?"

"Some of the others—my parents—worry he will think meeting you was the reason for his vision. He will think you were sent to us as a sign that better times are ahead for our pod, but please," he begged. "Don't mention us to the Morrigan."

Interesting. "Is there a reason why I shouldn't?"

A hard glint sparkled in his eyes. "If she thinks we asked for help, she'll kill us in one fell swoop instead of picking us off one at a time."

My temper combusted in a scalding, choking blast of anger.

That right there was the reason why the Unseelie mantle weighed on me. Seelie weren't always sparkling rays of light. Just as Unseelie weren't always as dark or sinister as their reputation intimated. Either might take exception to something another faction did and make their lives a living hell in payment for it, but this burned my biscuits.

I didn't expect cuddle time with the Morrigan. She wasn't that kind of mother-in-law. Heck, she wasn't that kind of mother. Her reputation was hard won, and she was proud of it. But now her notoriety was rubbing off on me, and I didn't like it. It bred expectation. Doors that once opened to me were now slammed in my face. I got that. I understood. Mac's legacy stuck me with baggage too.

The difference being my father's legacy challenged me. His standard gave me a rung to grasp, a name to live up to. I didn't want to be *Black Dog's Daughter*. I wanted to be Marshal Thackeray, the best marshal in my region. I wanted to outshine my father on my own merits. All the Morrigan's name lent me was grief. Fear was as easy to inspire as pain was to inflict. I could hurt people. I could kill them. I was good at it, and God knew some days I craved it. But I wanted to be my best self, not my worst.

My tone was calm, even. "What does the Morrigan have against the gray men?"

The youth rocked back on his heels. "My great uncle, he stole something from her. And then he lost it."

I frowned. "What could he have taken that would piss her off enough to murder an entire pod?"

"My great aunt…" His voice blended with the churning sea. "She was the Morrigan's daughter, and no one has seen her in centuries."

CHAPTER FIFTEEN

Back in my room, I collapsed face-first onto my bed with a groan. The mattress dipped when Mai sat, and I rolled against her. Seconds later, Diode strolled up my spine. I grunted as vertebrae popped under his hefty weight.

When he reached my head, he leapt onto the pillow. Batting aside the tangles obscuring my face, he peered at me. "What does the selkie elder running away with the Morrigan's daughter mean for you?"

I would have ignored him if he hadn't placed a persuasive paw—claws out—on my hand.

"Back this train up." Mai shoved me onto my side. "Why do I get the feeling you two already knew about this?"

Guilt welled in me. "Back in Faerie, Rook confided in me that he has a missing half-sister."

She jabbed a finger in Diode's face. "You told the *cat* before you told me?"

He batted her hand—claws in. "The *cat* was in the room when the confession was made."

"Why does it mean anything?" She threw up her hands. "I get why Rook would want to know where his sister went, she's family, but if she's missing here too… I don't know. Will telling him change anything?"

"No." I exhaled. "It won't."

She patted my thigh. "What's with the face?"

Diode rumbled thoughtfully. "She was going to use the sister's location as leverage with Rook."

Mai popped my leg. "Smart."

"It was an inkling." And that was being generous. "Not a fully formed plan."

"It was a good inkling," Diode allowed.

I closed my eyes. "Yeah, well, my twenty-four-karat leverage over Rook just turned copper."

I felt green thinking about it. Information on his sister would have been invaluable.

Mai palmed my forehead and peeled open my right eye. "So they ran away together, the Morrigan found them, and she started picking selkies off for revenge?"

"It looks that way." The selkies had chosen the wrong nest to rob. "The Morrigan is unique among the fae. She's allowed to cross realms regularly to collect tithes. She could have made any number of side trips. The conclave must have eyes on her, but only the higher-ups would know about it."

"You are a higher-up." She pointed at the ceiling. "You're a princess."

"A princess of Faerie," Diode interjected. "At worst, Thierry ranks as a junior marshal. At best, she is viewed as a visiting dignitary seeking asylum. She poses a security risk, actually, now that her loyalties will be seen as lying with House Unseelie and not with the conclave or its neutral views."

Hearing that, my molars were in real danger of being ground into powder.

"So what she doesn't already know, they aren't inclined to tell her," Mai surmised.

"Exactly." I sat up and crossed my legs. "Whatever the Morrigan is doing, I can't interfere with it. Yet."

There would be plenty of time for confrontations later. One hundred years of endless days filled with politicking awaited me. Until then, the blood she shed was on my hands.

"I don't like this." Diode leapt to the floor, reared up on the windowsill and gazed out at the shore. "We should not be here when the gray men are here. The Morrigan hasn't struck yet, or even your title wouldn't have protected you. We should leave before she attacks, before she finds her next victim."

"What do you propose?" I hated tossing the idea out there. "Do we go home?"

"That would be the wisest course of action." Diode tipped his head.

"Never let it be said I was incapable of making wise decisions." Even when they sucked. "We go home."

Mai flopped backwards and flailed her arms. "Could fate not kick us in the balls this once?"

"We have balls?" I glanced between my legs. "Weird. I never even knew they were there."

She snorted until I grabbed one of her legs and lifted it. "Whose are bigger?"

"Size doesn't matter." Her squeak pierced my ears. "It's the swing in your schling that counts."

The door shattered, and my guards burst into the room, swords drawn and teeth flashing.

Mai startled, twisting and flopping onto the carpet on all fours.

Righty grasped the situation first. "I assume you're well?"

"There was screaming." Lefty was slower to read the signs. "Why was there screaming?"

"I didn't scream. I squeaked. Big difference." Mai stood and straightened her top. "Thierry conducted a surprise anatomy lesson on me. She caught me off-guard, that's all."

Both men raised their eyebrows, or tried to. Righty had the motion down, but Lefty's did a tiny upward twitch, which might have been the most expression I had ever seen on him.

"We're leaving Daytona," I told them.

They nodded in concert and left, shutting the door behind them.

I sat there, gazing through the window at the glittering waves. "I wish I had more time." I rested my elbow on my knee and my chin in my palm. "I want to talk to the old man again."

Diode dropped his front paws onto the floor, sounding heavier than he had earlier. "That is inadvisable."

"I'll do it," Mai volunteered.

"If it's too dangerous for me, it's too dangerous for you."

"I'll take one of your guards."

"Not an option." I shook my head. "I'm not risking you for my own curiosity."

She blocked my view. "Will the information help you with Rook?"

"I don't know." There were too many variables. "Maybe."

She dusted her hands. "Good enough for me."

"You're worth more to me than any *maybe*." I went to my feet. "You're worth more than anything that elder can tell me. Without Rook's sister in the flesh, the information's value is questionable at best."

"Look, there's too much history between the selkies and the Morrigan and the Morrigan and you for him to confide more than he already has. But I—" she fluffed her hair, "—spent all morning with them. They liked me until you came along—no offense—and I can win them over again. Even if I can't get information direct from the source, I bet I can get the young one to talk. I'll use the bikini."

Lord help them. "The magic bikini?"

"Nope." She tugged the chain-mail cover-up over her head, retied her strings and plumped her breasts. "How do I look?"

"Like you couldn't afford the entire roll of tinfoil so you tore the corners off a sheet."

Eyes narrowed, she snatched my pillow off the bed and walloped me in the face until her nails poked holes in the case and down stuffing leaked into the air and into my mouth.

"Truce." I spat out a feather.

Pausing with the limp case held over her head, she considered the flurries swirling through the room and lowered her weapon. "I accept your surrender." She walked over and pressed the deflated pillow into my hands. "Don't sweat it, Tee. I've got this."

Too late for that. Beads were forming on my spine the longer her plan pinged around in my head.

"One more thing." She backed into the hall, doorknob in hand. "Make me a promise."

"Sure." I drew out the word. "What did you have in mind?"

"Promise me while I'm gone that you'll have some fun." She winked. "Do something reckless."

"I thought the whole point of you going to meet the selkies was for me to avoid being reckless?"

Pointer and thumb held an inch apart, she narrowed her eyes. "Just a splash of recklessness."

Expecting the worst, I inhaled then exhaled slowly. "Tell me what I've gotten myself into."

"I want you to get your ass downstairs and float in that lazy river until I fish you out of it."

Swimming. Danger all around us, and she wanted me to go tubing. "Why?"

"This was supposed to be your big send-off, Tee. You and me, sand and sun and surf. A big, fun week of...big, fun things." She went serious on me. "Instead, we got a phone stalker, some freaky guy with a god complex, sulky selkies, and to top it all off, we ran straight into the one thing I wanted to get you away from most. Your new family." Her fingertips drummed the doorframe. "This whole trip has sucked ass so far. It's okay. You can say it."

Tell the truth? Or lie convincingly? "It hasn't sucked ass."

Mai wasn't fooled. "I picked this hotel especially for you, because of that lazy river. The least you can do to thank me for my considerateness is to make a few relaxing laps—while you're actually conscious."

I must have had water in my ears. "You *picked* this *hotel*?"

Her face blanched.

"Gotta go." She ducked out of my room. "Bye."

The door slammed behind her.

I pointed after her. "She lied to me."

The whiskers on Diode's face flexed. "It appears so."

Why that little *grrr*. "Guys, I don't care who, but someone go keep tabs on her."

After stomping into the bathroom, I snatched my slightly damp beach towel off the counter and stormed past Diode into the living room. I had one hand wrapping the doorknob when he and Righty caught up to me.

The cat stepped forward. "Where are you going?"

"For a swim."

Condos were to my bank account as permanent markers were to toddlers: forever out of reach.

When Mai said her brother-in-law's skulk owned a condo, I pictured a fancy hotel-like property people visited once or twice a year for vacation. The lack of personal items was explained away by a commercial I saw once mentioning how you chose your week and then were assigned your room.

A quick visit to Google on my cell set me straight and made me feel like an idiot. Mai said *condo*, but I heard *timeshare*. I was embarrassed by how easily she had wielded my ignorance against me.

While nursing my injured pride, I stashed all my necessities in my locker, then snagged a jumbo inner tube from the attendant and headed for the submerged stairs. Lefty had gone with Mai, and boy had he look thrilled to be loaned to my Seelie bestie. I took the delegation as confirmation that Righty had more seniority and therefore also had his choice of charges.

Technically, as a conclave employee, Mai was neutral. It was a job requirement. But Lefty didn't want to hear that. He seemed content nursing his anger, so who was I to dump a bucket of ice-cold truth over his hot head?

After flinging my tube in the pool, I waded into the water and belly-flopped onto the float with a grunt.

Righty was nearby. I was getting good at sensing him. Once I rounded the bend, I heard startled gasps and spotted two humans staggering from where he must have knocked them out of his way. He stuck near the pool's edge, following my trek around the watery loops and bends while I studied my reflection.

I decided I didn't look like a sucker.

Not that it stopped people from treating me like one.

Shaking off my weird mood, I closed my eyes against the girl I saw in the water, the one whose mouth sagged at the corners and who sported dark smudges under her eyes.

Mai knew me better than anyone. Well, almost anyone. If I had to be duped, at least it had been by a worthy opponent and one who kept my best interests at heart. My ignorance wasn't her fault.

I don't know how long I drifted like that, allowing my mind to wander, before Righty materialized nearly on top of me.

"We need to go." His voice grated near my ear. "I sense old magic here."

My mouth went dry. "The Morrigan?"

"No." His grip steadied the inner tube while I climbed off. "Something else."

I inhaled on reflex but came up empty. "Our fae friend?"

Being slapped with an eviction notice from the conclave must have pissed him off.

"It's difficult to explain."

"Try." I grabbed for him, but my hand closed over air. "Mai's still out there."

"Mai is at the bar." He clamped down on my arm. "Daire is watching her."

Jerk better protect her too, if he knew what was good for him.

Righty led me to the steps, hauled me out of the pool and flung my inner tube toward a lifeguard station. He barreled through alarmed humans, who quickly locked their glares on me as though I had pushed them out of my way. It wasn't until my arm started throbbing that I realized he had never let go. For Righty to hurt me meant he was on autopilot. He had one mission: protect his ward.

He jerked me forward. "There she is."

"Mai," I called.

She spun on her barstool, both arms waving in the air as she swayed to music. "Hey to you too."

I winced, but we kept going until Righty cleared me a path straight to her. Once I got close, she slid into my arms. Her pupils were huge, and her eyes weren't tracking.

"Hey." I patted her cheek. "You okay?"

Rapid-fire giggles answered me.

Under my breath, I told Righty, "I need help."

"Stay put," he said. "Daire and I will handle this."

To my left, an unseen force knocked partiers aside. A fight broke out between two guys too drunk to do more than slur in each other's general direction. They shut up fast enough when a buzzer sounded. The crowd gasped as the lights flickered. Squeals and cheers erupted when the patio went dark.

"I have Mai," Righty called over the chattering voices. "We need to get moving if we want to be first in line for the elevators."

As if on cue, emergency lights popped on, emitting a dull, red glow. I spotted Righty's leather-clad back and Mai's limp form hanging from the cradle of his arms a few steps ahead of me. I jogged to get in front of them and wedged open the automatic doors leading into the poolside area.

A frisson of magic near my left elbow relieved me of the strain, allowing me to cradle Mai's head to protect her while Righty squeezed through the tight gap made tighter by the swimsuit-clad masses following our lead. Herd mentality indeed.

"What happened?" I looked to my left. "She was supposed to be schmoozing with the selkies."

"We explored the beach first. It took a while for us to locate the pod. They had moved onto another hotel's property. When the gray men saw her, they asked her to leave. She refused, and the elder was called. She caught the young one's eye and managed a word with him before we left. The boy agreed to meet her here." He grunted as the crowd swept us forward. "I left her sitting at the bar with a glass of ginger ale while I performed a perimeter check. I reported to Odhran, and when I returned, I found her like this."

Odhran? Righty had a name after all. I filed it away for later. "How long ago was that?"

He paused to consider. "Ten minutes at most."

Ten minutes from sober to shit-faced meant drugs or a spell or both.

"I assume we have you to thank for the blackout." I grimaced. "What did you do?"

"I tripped the breaker." He grabbed my arm and jerked me toward the elevators. "It's a quick fix even humans can't botch."

Acting casual, Lefty and I flanked Righty. We stood shoulder-to-shoulder before the chrome doors and waited for the moment we could step onboard and end this. Twenty minutes lapsed, counted down by the glow of my cellphone's screen, before a hum filled the air and lights flickered on in a burst that left me squinting and folks in the lobby cheering. Being first in line, we hustled into the booth as soon as the elevators got the all-clear and rode it up to our floor.

Mai earned a few sympathetic looks from partygoers in the crowd. As for the guards, well, there was a reason no one else braved the trip up with us.

At the door to our room, I growled a curse. "I left my bag."

"Here." A rough, braided handle brushed my hand. Lefty urged, "Take it."

I did, and when he released it, the illusion masking my bag vanished. "This was in a locker."

"I broke the lock." He sounded totally fine with that. "They will probably keep your deposit."

I didn't pay one, so if I was blamed for the lock, it would get charged to the room.

At least that meant it was coming out of Mai's pocket and not her brother-in-law's. It would be easier for me to pay damages that way.

Still, I was impressed Lefty had thought to grab the bag. "You're good at this."

"I know," he answered in complete seriousness.

Shaking my head, I palmed the keycard. I never swiped them right on the first try, but when the red light flashed a third time, Righty made an impatient noise and Lefty plucked the card from my fingers. He was poised to try his luck when a chime made us turn. Packed as the scene downstairs had been, I expected cranky guests to pour out and break for their rooms. Instead the elevator doors opened on an empty booth. I inhaled but scented nothing out of the ordinary. Just a whiff of spicy takeout.

I drew in a longer breath. "Do you remember smelling that on the way up here?"

Lefty tensed when he noticed my hand had gone automatically to my glove. "No."

"Get us in that room," I said quietly.

He slid the key through the slit, and of course it worked for him on the first try.

We hustled inside, and Righty hurried Mai into her chosen room and stretched her across the bed. Lefty locked the door behind us and bolted it. "What did you scent?"

I explained how the elevator had pulled the same trick on our first night here. Heck, I had tried to order curry chicken takeout because of it. Too bad there were no Indian restaurants on the strip.

I peered through the peephole, but the hall remained empty.

Righty reemerged wearing a stiff expression and dusting off his arms. "She's sleeping."

"Good. Keep an eye on her." I held up a finger and made a beeline for the balcony. "Give me a minute."

Righty moved to follow me.

I wagged the finger. "Alone."

His expression pinched. "Stay where I can see you."

"Will do."

On the balcony, I stood with the room at my back, facing the crashing waves, and pulled out my cell. Mai would smother me in my sleep if she knew, but I hit my first speed-dial combo and waited.

Shaw answered with my name. "Thierry?"

"We have a problem."

The pleased tenor of his voice hardened. "What's wrong?"

"The list is too long."

"Okay, we'll start simple. Where are you?"

"We're at the condo—hotel—whatever."

"What's the immediate threat?"

My mouth fell open. *So many options.* "My guards say there's old magic here."

"That's a little broad." He voiced what I had been thinking. "Can they narrow it down?"

"They can't be more specific. It's just a feeling they have."

"Tell me everything."

Everything was too big for over the phone, but I gave him the highlights.

"Are you heading home?" He sounded hopeful I would say *yes.*

"I don't know if that's wise." I had a twofold issue here. For one thing, some nebulous evil was hanging out at a condo frequented by humans. As a marshal, my duty was to ascertain whether there was potential for the situation to expose fae to said humans, and to neutralize the threat if I deemed it necessary. The second issue was more personal. Mai wasn't well. Moving her in her condition wasn't ideal, but better sick and uncomfortable than dead. "It's a long drive back to Wink for her."

"I'm an hour away." His tone was firm. "Come to me."

I bit my lip to keep from telling him how perfect that sounded. Shaw already held enough power over me. We might not be on the best terms now, but I used to think he was invincible. I once idolized him, and no matter how painful our past might be, I still trusted him absolutely. With my life, if not my heart.

As soon as he offered his protection, I felt the safety of his arms banding around me.

"I'll reserve a room and send you the hotel information," he continued, not bothering to wait on an answer. "I'll make some inquiries and see what my contacts can dig up about the Daytona area."

I held out for thirty seconds. "Are you going to investigate?"

"You know the answer." His voice held a smile. "The question is, are you helping me?"

I hung up with a quick "Bye" and a matching grin. We really did make a good team.

While Shaw made his preparations, I made mine. I headed back into the living room and clapped my hands once to get everyone's attention. "Pack up. We're leaving for Orlando."

The guards exchanged a long glance before Righty faced me. "That is inadvisable."

"No, staying here while Mai recovers is inadvisable." I anchored my hands on my hips. "We're leaving."

"I cannot allow you to put yourself in danger." Righty eased between me and the door, and Lefty flanked him. "We should stay the night and depart for Wink in the morning."

Diode strolled to my side and sat. "Thierry has decided it is in our best interest to go." He lifted a paw and licked the delicate claws he unsheathed. "I believe, as she is your princess, you must obey her orders."

"Short of physically restraining me, you're not keeping me here." I cocked an eyebrow at them. "It's not safe for Mai, and protecting her is my top priority."

Lefty stepped forward, but Righty put a hand on his shoulder. "We will honor your wishes, for now."

"That's all I'm asking for, guys." I flashed them a smile then nudged Diode with my toe. "Want to help me pack?"

His ears swiveled toward me. "I would be delighted," he said dryly.

With a chuckle, I set off for my room and shut the door behind us.

He leapt onto the mattress. "What's bothering you?"

"Really?" I cast him a look. "You have to ask?"

"Point taken." He curled his tail around his front paws. "Was there something specific you wanted with me?"

"Other than your sparkling company?" I grinned at his moue. "I just wanted to give you a heads up that I'll be driving us to Orlando in Mai's car."

The skin around his eyes tightened. "Is taking the car necessary?"

"How else are we supposed to get there?"

His head swung toward the door. "I might have an idea about that."

I straightened and eyed his thoughtful expression warily. "What does that mean?"

"It means…" he stood and shot his tail straight up in the air, "…I'll meet you there."

After hopping to the floor he strolled to the door, waited for me to open it for him then sashayed into the living room, leaving me to wonder how he was going to manage that, and how on earth he could possibly think I could be a worse driver than Mai.

CHAPTER SIXTEEN

My palms sweated against the leather steering wheel the entire sixty minutes it took to reach Orlando. For a girl used to driving a hand-me-down, Mai's car intimidated me. If I dinged my car, so what? No one would notice. Probably not even me. One hairline scratch on her celery-green baby and Mai would throttle me. *Then* demand I file a posthumous insurance claim.

"That guy..." Mai slurred. "He...slipped me...somefink."

"What guy?" I waited. "The bartender? The selkie? The fae?"

I could see the gray men drugging and ditching when confronted by a female they couldn't disarm by flexing their tight abs or flashing their retina-searing smiles. But to do that to Mai? Knowing who I was and what I was capable of? What I would do if she was harmed?

The old man was smarter than that.

Left unable to defend herself, drooling from the corner of her mouth and propped up alone at the bar, she had been a sitting duck for any predatory fae still hanging around the hotel. For unscrupulous humans too.

There was more than one kind of monster. My job had hammered that point home very well, thanks.

Being a tourist town, Orlando had almost as many hotels as it had red lights. From its perch in a docking station on the dash, my cellphone's GPS app directed me farther from the main drag and all the mouse-eared tourists toward the outskirts. Hotels here glittered less and slouched comfortably on the curb. This was where the theme-park veterans went to escape the marked-up lodging and themed dining.

"Turn left and arrive at your destination," my phone announced proudly.

I did, and once the car was safely parked, I palmed my cell and stepped out of the car to call Shaw.

"I saw you pull in," he said by way of answering.

"Hello to you too." My gaze slid over the lit-up windows, wondering which one framed him.

A whirring sound drew my attention toward a set of automatic doors.

Shaw strode out of the hotel lobby, paperwork in hand, his gait tight and his shoulders tense. Black jeans encased his legs. His T-shirt wanted to be black but managed navy. Black boots clicked on the pavement when he crossed to me. Copper eyes flashed in the dark. Humidity had stripped his rich mahogany hair of its slight curl, and it hung limp around his ears. The intensity of his scowl made the night cower, but I was smiling.

He waggled his phone by his ear. "You can hang up now."

Never to be outdone, I waggled right back. "After you."

He snorted a laugh and disconnected. Feeling magnanimous after my victory, I did the same.

The car rocked when I braced against it and struck a casual pose. Inside, Mai snuffled.

Shaw walked right up to me, leaving a foot of space between us. "You scared me."

"Hunger makes me cranky too." I nodded. "No worries. Your food supply is safe and sound."

His harsh exhale told me several things he wouldn't say outright. Mostly that it was late and he was tired, but also that I was the only thing standing between him and his comfy bed.

Thoughts of Shaw and a bed could derail the swiftest of thinkers, and I wasn't one.

His palm hit the car door beside me, and he leaned in close. "I don't like being scared."

"I have a teddy bear you can borrow." I molded my spine to the metal. "His name is Garlic."

A half smile flashed the dimple in his cheek. "Do I want to know?"

"It's a perfectly respectable name." I feigned indignation. "I had a thing for vampires as a kid."

Though I hadn't known I was half-fae back then, I had always been fascinated by things that went bump in the night. Mom had been too. Right up until she realized she had given birth to one of them.

His gaze slid over every inch of me, assessing. "How's Mai?"

I checked on her through the window. "Drowsy. Woozy. Queasy. Not much fun in a car."

A flicker of attention on her, then the full weight of his stare settled back on me. "I mixed up a tonic to flush her system of toxins."

I traced the door seam behind me. "I appreciate you letting me drag you into this."

He rolled his shoulders. "What are friends for?"

I kicked up the wattage of my smile in answer.

Friends. Sure. Me and Shaw. Practically BFFs. Buddies who knew how a morning-after kiss tasted. Partners who knew the precise geography of each other's bodies. Colleagues who knew how much pressure to apply and where to make the other come undone. Two people who knew how to say *I love you* with a touch.

Friends. Sure. Why not?

Shaw's face dipped closer. "Where are your guards?"

"They're probably scouting out the place." I swallowed. "We didn't travel together."

"Makes sense." His tone was all too reasonable. "Not like it's their job to protect you."

"I can take care of myself." I notched my chin higher. "You have the scars to prove it."

A twitch of his lips, a flash of that cursed dimple. "You were trained to be a marshal, and you're a damned good one, but no one could have prepared you for this. Half of Faerie is calling in favors. I heard the bounty on you is up to fifty million dollars for any Seelie who cashes in your head."

"Fifty million...?" I felt my eyes go wide. "Tell me you're joking."

He sighed. "You're joking."

I shoved him. "You're serious?"

"I'm not sure." He didn't budge. "Why don't you tell me?"

I leaned forward, resting my forehead on his chest. "Do you think whatever was wielding the old magic Righty sensed was after the bounty?"

"No." His breathing hitched. "Old things don't care about money."

That was a small relief. Or not. I couldn't decide. Was it better to kick the bucket due to topping some ridiculous hit list or going out as collateral damage for a nebulous entity's ambiguous purpose?

Shaw's hands found their way to my hair and combed through its length. "Where's Diode?"

"With the guards, wherever they are." I straightened before I melted at Shaw's feet. "Officially, he decided to investigate their method of travel and report back to me on its legalities. Unofficially, the trip to Daytona was his first time riding in a car, and you know how Mai drives. He lost his cat food off the shoulder of I-10 and wasn't eager for a repeat performance."

Shaw let me go but kept a lock of my hair wrapped around his finger. "How do the guards travel?"

I had a good idea, but he wouldn't like it. "I'm not sure."

He gave a short tug. "Not sure as in you don't know, or not sure as in I won't like the answer?"

"I have my suspicions." I scuffed my shoe on the pavement. "I haven't asked outright."

"Ah." He released my hair. "You're the one who doesn't want to know."

"I can't change it." They were acting on orders handed down from above me. "There's only one way I figure they can do it, and it's not good."

Much like my portal-charmed necklace, personal portals were illegal. They might be rooted here in the mortal realm, but they brushed Faerie's underbelly to draw on that kind of magic, and it was unacceptable. Seeing my failure to report my suspicions through Shaw's eyes, I felt the world lurch under my feet.

First the necklace got a pass "to make things simpler" and now the guards got off easy because "I don't know". Weak. Those flimsy excuses wouldn't have tracked with me pre-princessdom, and they weren't tracking with Shaw now. He was standing tall in the middle of the road, right where he should be, while I was veering through lanes of oncoming traffic.

I was so afraid of hearing the answer I wouldn't even ask them the question.

Shaw shook his head. "You don't know what you can change until you dig in and do your damn job."

I recoiled as if he had slapped me. Honestly? I would have preferred to take the hit.

He was around the car and opening Mai's door before I recovered. I grabbed the essentials while he lifted her against his chest. After locking her car, I followed him. We bypassed the office and circled to the rear of the building. I wasn't not convinced it helped us look any less like kidnapper/murderers when he proceeded to carry Mai's limp body up a flight of unlit stairs, but I wasn't going to argue method of delivery with him when I couldn't have hauled her upstairs alone.

After swiping a keycard, Shaw kicked open a door beside a vending machine alcove. He carried Mai inside the room and arranged her comfortably on one of the two queen-sized beds.

With her settled, he snatched a notepad off the desk and scribbled on it.

"My room number." He tore the top sheet off and slapped the paper into my hand. "Night."

"Night," I called to his retreating back.

I jumped when he slammed the door. Crumpling the paper in my fist, I curled up in bed and waited for the others to arrive.

A roar jolted me out of a dreamless sleep. I bolted upright, tossed aside my covers and swung my legs off the bed. Righty sat in a chair pulled beside the door leading into our hotel room. He pointed at the foot of my bed where my now-panther-sized cat twitched his whiskers and flexed his paws in the throes of some phantom hunt.

According to Diode, the guards' magic had scrambled his charm in transit. No loss there. It had almost petered out on its own anyway. As to their method of travel, he summed up all I needed to know in two words: plausible deniability.

A shadow slanted across the curtains, and my heart stuttered.

"It's only Daire," Righty said. "You should sleep."

No, I shouldn't. Rook waited for me in dreams. Only he hadn't been up to visiting lately. I wasn't sure how I felt about that. For the sake of making my next one hundred years more bearable, I kept cracking open the door to friendship with him. That lasted for a few hours, days. Then he found a new way to betray me, and I shut it in his face. Had life in Faerie twisted him until even his best intentions were doomed to fail? Did he even know what honesty was? Was he capable of putting another's welfare ahead of his own?

I didn't know, and that warped curiosity kept me doling out second and third and fourth chances.

I slid to my feet and checked on Mai. Sleeping soundly. "I'm going to get some air."

Righty gave me a tight nod.

The balcony here was longer than at our previous digs, but just as narrow. I stepped out into the humid night and shut the sliding glass door behind me. Inhaling brought the smell of dumpsters and a burger joint. I sneezed the pollutants from my nose then propped my elbows on the railing and gazed up at the stars.

Another scent hit me, earthy and spiked with hints of citrus, but I chose to ignore it—and him.

"It's late," a low voice rumbled on my left.

"Really?" I faked surprise. "For your next trick, maybe you can explain those dots of light in the sky."

Shaw emerged from the shadows wrapping his balcony. "Street lamps or stars, take your pick."

I thinned my lips in answer. "What are you doing out here?"

His eyes glinted. "Think about it."

"One guard covering the front entrance. There are windows, so a second guard positioned inside the room." I straightened. "That makes you the guy guarding the exit. Are we in that much danger?"

He speared me with a look. "You tell me."

"The gray men aren't a threat. They wanted us gone, we're gone. I don't see them caring one way or the—"

"Selkies." He bit off the word. "There were selkies in Daytona? They threatened you?"

"Yes and yes." I blinked innocently at him. "Didn't I mention them?"

"No," he snapped.

"Huh." I started braiding the ends of my hair. "I could have sworn they came up."

"Why would a pod of selkies threaten someone like you? They're a peaceful people."

This was the part I dreaded. There was no way to fudge the truth, it was too dangerous, and he needed to know all of it. "Well, that particular pod is being hunted to extinction by the Morrigan."

Shaw rocked backward. His palm slapped the railing on his balcony and then he was vaulting onto mine.

My hip bumped off the opposite railing before I realized I had taken the first step back. Shaw landed in a tense crouch. His head shot up, narrowed eyes shining white, bronze complexion waning under the moon.

"The Morrigan," he snarled up at me.

"Yes." My foot slid between the metal bars as if trying to escape.

Apparently, he wasn't a fan of highlight reels.

He straightened to his full height. "Did you offer to help them?"

"I did." I tightened my grip on the railing. "They told me not to interfere."

He prowled closer. "Will you interfere?"

Unsure where this crazy train was headed, I told him the truth. "Yes."

"Why?" he breathed down on me.

"No one should have to pay such a high price for making one mistake."

The answer must have satisfied him. His skin darkened by degrees, almost back to normal.

He canted his head. "So you believe in forgiveness?"

This answer would bite me on the ass, I just *knew* it. "Yes."

Shaw leaned forward and braced his hands on top of mine, trapping me between him, our grips and the railing. "If that's true..." the hunger in his eyes made breathing impossible, "...forgive me."

"For earlier?" I waved him off like I thought that was what he meant.

"For months earlier," he clarified. "I want to hear you say it."

Panic dumped adrenaline into my system and left me shaking. Was this some attempt at absolution before the end? I examined him for signs his condition had worsened, but health radiated from him. "Where is this coming from?"

"Thierry." He rubbed his cheek against mine, his lips brushing my ear. "Say the words."

The scent of his skin, the tone of his voice, made my knees wobble. "You're using your lure."

"No." He drew back to look at me, and smug satisfaction wreathed his face. "I'm not."

Anticipation cramped my stomach. Sweat beaded on my skin. Clothes that fit fine when I fell asleep felt too tight. I wanted them off, wanted to feel his bare skin slick beneath my palms, wanted to lick the salty drops from his collarbone.

No. He wasn't using his lure. Simple lust wasn't this dangerous.

The jagged edges of the heart he had broken were digging into my ribs, slicing through my common sense. Part of me would always love Shaw. I accepted that. I just didn't know what to do about it.

"Are you sick?" I reached for his arm. "Is your condition worse?"

"Are you scared?" His copper eyes held pinpricks of white. "Does my nearness bother you?"

I shook my head. "No."

"There's your answer."

"You're not making any sense."

"Nothing has made sense to me since the first time I saw you."

"Why are you doing this?"

"I hurt you, and I'm sorry." His jaw flexed. "I should have explained myself...but I didn't."

"I don't want to have this conversation." *Understatement of the century.*

"Tough." His warm palm cradled my cheek. "You ran into Rook's arms at the sight of me. That tells me you still feel something for me. Other than pity. I want to know, Thierry. Tell me the truth."

The truth. *Ha.* Because there was so much of that going around.

"Rook tricked me." I wet my lips. "It had nothing to do with you."

"You're going to leave in a year." Shaw's hand slid from mine and clenched around the railing. "You're his *wife*." A growl entered his voice. "How do you think it makes me feel? To see what he's turning you into? To know that you're his?" Metal groaned behind me. "Losing you would kill me."

My lips parted, ready to spout some offhanded feeding comment, when his mouth crashed into mine. He pinned me with his hips, with the flex of his arms and the tilt of his head. His taste was hot, familiar. *I was home.* Dreams tasted this way—ambrosial—and then they shattered.

A year later I didn't have enough of my heart patched together to risk this. Losing Shaw... Mai was right. It had wrecked me.

At most, we would have a year together. Probably a good year. Sex. Laughter. Fun. Danger. A year when I would wonder every single day if he was with me because he loved me or because I was the only thing keeping him alive and he was scared of losing it. I could stand feeding him because it was my fault he was broken. I couldn't stand to love him again, not the way the press of his mouth or the grinding of his hips encouraged me to. I had to know this was real, but I couldn't tell if it was anymore.

"You're not kissing me back." His body trembled. "Is it Rook? Do you have feelings for him?"

Saying I didn't have feelings for Rook would be a lie. I felt *something* when I was with him. He was likable when he wasn't being a lying bastard. Was that forever material? No. But I didn't need a husband forever. Just for the next century.

Could Rook and I sustain a platonic marriage? Or would I grow to care for him in time? Love him?

What did it matter? Unless I fixed Shaw before I left, he would die. Even if I did manage to get our lives untangled, it's not like I could ask him to wait a mortal lifetime to be with me.

Shaw had cheated when I was a phone call away. When I was a realm away, with another man, what would he do then? And what right would I have to say anything about it?

"I see," he said softly. He turned, jogged five or six steps, and then leapt back onto his balcony.

Once I heard the *snick* of his sliding doors close, I turned. The railing was warped with the imprint of his fingers. I placed my hand where his larger one had been, soaking up his lingering warmth while I wondered how the hell I had ended up on the run in mouse country.

Short bursts of rock music yanked me from the balcony. I darted inside the room, found my cell and checked the caller ID. My weirdo stalker. *Crap.* I had filed his threat to find me under *things to worry about later*. I rejected the call, noticing Righty had made himself invisible for my comfort—or so he could spy on my conversation with Shaw—then I muted the phone and hit the hay. Tomorrow was a blink away. Reluctant as my eyes were to shut, I couldn't fight sleep long.

CHAPTER SEVENTEEN

Morning sucked. Rook hadn't visited my dreams, probably because two hours wasn't enough time to get me into an REM state of mind. I shifted onto my side with a grunt and found Mai sitting upright in bed. Pillows were crammed behind her back. An assortment of junk food and soda cans were spread across her covers, and a bucket of ice sat on her side of the nightstand. Someone had hit the vending machines. Hard.

The Spanish soap opera she had been watching on mute flickered as the screen went black.

"There she is. I was starting to wonder if you were ever going to wake up." Mai tossed a packet at me. "Are you sure you're not the one they drugged?"

"What—? No." I scanned the wrapper through blurry eyes. "I'm not eating chocolate for breakfast."

"You're saying *no* to chocolate?" She wiped a smudge off her lips. "Sounds like drugs talking to me."

I pushed off the mattress and locked my elbows to force myself to stay vertical. "Where did you get all that?"

A snap of her fingers and an orgasmic scent wafted past my nose on a gust of AC-churned air. "Can you deliver it for me, pretty please?" She fluttered her eyelashes at dead space. "I would do it, but you heard the doctor's orders."

I stopped salivating and wiped my mouth. "What doctor?"

"Dr. Shaw." She flicked crumbs off her covers. "Ever met him? Tall? Dark? Broody? Apparently he gets off on force feeding girls laxatives."

Lefty appeared at the edge of my bed, holding a greasy paper bag away from his body.

"For me?" I snatched it out of his hand and stuck my head in the opening. That first long inhale made me believe in God. Wait. Was I really equating proof of a higher power with the existence of bacon?

Yes. Yes, I was.

"You better stand back before she bites you on accident," Mai warned.

Crunching down on a slightly burnt strip rescued from the bottom of the bag, I shut my eyes in bliss. "Was this your doing?"

"No." He turned his back on us and resumed his post. "It was Shaw."

At the sound of his name, my appetite vanished, and I crumpled the bag.

"Hey." Mai made grabby hands. "That is a perfectly good extra bacon, egg and cheese biscuit. I was just kidding about the laxatives. Mostly."

"There." I snagged a napkin and then tossed her the bag. "Enjoy."

"What gives?" She froze with her hand in the sack. "He didn't take a bite out of it, did he?"

"No." I wiped my fingers. "He wouldn't do that."

He knew how seriously I took crimes against pork products.

"Then what is it?" She examined her prize. "I thought you'd be happy we were playing nice."

The two of them would have to forge a truce the second he and I broke ours. "I am happy."

"That's not your happy face, Tee." She took a tentative nibble. "That's your marshal face."

I rubbed the grit from my eyes. "I have a marshal face?"

"You have several, actually." Food garbled her words. "This is your pissed-and-yet-professional look. I've seen you whip it out at work when a suspect is lying but you don't have proof, and you can't just break his face. Well, I guess you could, but you won't. You're all about being aboveboard."

At least someone still had faith I would do the right thing. Too bad the Morrigan's gift weighed more this morning than it had last night. The chain cut into my nape, and the pendant felt cold as the grave against my skin. My fingers were at the clasp before I stopped myself, and that slight hesitation was telling.

Shaw was right. I was compromised. Even with the burn of shame fresh in my mind, I fumbled. The old me would have yanked off the necklace, logged it into an evidence locker at the office, and then reported the Morrigan to boot.

The new me advised prudence. The charm provided me with instant access to my skins and to a powerful ally. Old Thierry's morals might be looser, but new Thierry was staring down the barrel of a hundred-year sentence. Without allies or weapons, when Faerie aimed and fired, I was the one poised to go *boom*.

"We need to make plans." I tossed aside my rumpled sheets. "Are you well enough to travel yet?"

"Well…about that." She picked at the rubber buttons on the remote. "My dad is on his way to get me."

Mai was a daddy's girl, so her announcement didn't surprise me. "That's okay. I'll mooch a ride home off Shaw." I hadn't spotted his truck last night, but he had to get here somehow.

"Sure you don't mind?" She glanced up. "Daddy's flight lands in an hour, and he's already announced his plans to have me driven home."

"I don't mind, really." The last thing I wanted was to be cooped up with Mr. Hayashi for sixteen hours. "I'll help Shaw for a few days to earn my keep. It's not like I have a job waiting for me. I might as well do something productive while I'm counting down the days."

Her relief was so palpable, I became suspicious. "What happened when you called your dad?"

She had volunteered him to be our voucher if the Daytona skulk took issue with me. Maybe he had stomped on that idea.

"He wasn't as supportive as anticipated." She scrunched up her face. "He refused to back you."

The rest of her scheming clicked together. "That's why you booked us into a hotel."

"Yeah." Her expression darkened. "Dad called Jon and warned him off letting us crash there."

"Let me know when you pay the bill." My wallet whimpered before I made the offer. "I'll cover half."

"This was my treat." She rummaged through her chocolate stash. "Our one big chance to hang out, to go out with a bang, and I was happy to supply the dynamite."

I climbed off my bed and plopped onto hers. Wrapping Mai in a big bear hug, I kissed her cheek with a resounding *smack*. "Thank you."

"Not so tight." Her stomach made a gurgling sound, and she pushed me back. "Oh. Oh, no. That's not good." She blanched. "Shaw's concoction gave me a case of the fox trots. I can't get more than six feet from the toilet."

She shot to her feet and bolted to the bathroom, slamming the door shut behind her while I mentally adjusted the sixteen-hour drive home to Wink to thirty-two hours.

"Has she been like this all morning?" I asked Lefty since Righty was MIA.

"Yes." He wrinkled his nose. "Unfortunately."

The quiet of the room hit me, and I turned a circle. "Where's Diode?"

Lefty raised and then lowered a shoulder.

Buzzing in the vicinity of my bed had me searching for my cell. My stalker again. Great. I thumbed the ignore icon then turned the ringer on and noticed the time. "How long ago was Shaw here?"

"A half hour or less." He indicated the door. "Odhran joined him outside to discuss security measures."

"We're under lock and guard." I frowned. "How much safer can you get?"

His face smoothed into a mask of innocence. "Shaw mentioned concerns about access from the balconies."

Fire leapt into my cheeks and would have singed my eyebrows off if I hadn't chugged some of Mai's ice water. So much for pretending last night was all a dream. Why would Shaw discuss our interlude with Righty? Did it mean Shaw was trying to protect me from himself? That wouldn't work. I had to feed him. Soon. He was due up any day now.

Mentioning the balcony was moot. All four of us had security training. My guards would have noticed the balcony and assessed the risk before I stepped foot inside the room.

They already knew it was a weak spot. It was obvious. That was why Shaw covered it last night.

The only reason he would bother mentioning it to Righty was if…

"Daire." My use of his name shocked him more than me. "Where is Shaw now?"

He stared at me, unblinking. "He left."

I squeezed my cell until the plastic ridges cut into my palm. "*Left* as in went to work his case or *left* as in gone and not coming back?"

"I didn't ask."

My feet were two steps ahead of my brain. I was out the door before Lefty got up from his seat. Five strides later, I bumped smack into dead air and knew I had found them.

I jabbed somewhere in the vicinity of Righty's chest. "Where is he?"

"Packing," the invisible man answered.

Relief flooded me. "Which room is his?"

A door opened a crack. "This one."

Scenting to make sure both guards were outside because Lefty was hot on my heels, I backed into the room. "Don't budge an inch."

The slamming door brought Shaw darting out of the bathroom in a pair of skintight boxer briefs.

My gaze flashed to his, and my mouth went dry. "We need to talk."

He set his hands on his lean hips and waited. "So talk."

A sleek, black suitcase sat open on the bed. Its hinged lid held a change of clothes for after Shaw showered. Otherwise, his room was picked clean and packed tight.

Leaving without saying goodbye.

Hurt made it easier to resist the temptation of his bare torso. "Where are you going?"

"My leads have dried up here. I called my brother with the news last night." He rocked back on his heels. "While I'm local, I might as well go check out whatever the hell is happening in Daytona."

He still planned on going then. "I'll go with you."

"No, you won't."

"But you said—"

"That was before Mai filled in the blanks for me."

"What blanks?"

"This is a routine call," he said firmly. "Sometimes old things get the idea in their heads that they aren't bound by conclave laws. Usually, a reminder visit from a friendly neighborhood marshal is all they need." He lifted his index finger. "It's a one-man job. I'll handle it." He pointed at me. "You get to stay here with Mai."

"Why does it feel like you're punishing me?"

"You're suspended. You can't be present while I conduct official conclave business."

"Official business?" I pried at his weak spot. "So you called Mable and got this approved?"

He didn't reply, which was answer enough.

"This is so official that you called the Southeastern Conclave and got permission to crush the toes of their organization, right?" I walked up to him. "What gives? We were going to investigate together."

"That was before Mai got hurt." He dealt a low blow. "She needs you here."

"Mai is propped up in bed, eating junk food and vegging out on telenovelas. Besides the fact her dad is on the way. You can wait a couple hours, Shaw."

His stance shifted. "Why does this matter so much to you?"

"If I still had my badge, I would have left to go back and fix the problem just like you're doing now." The time on his clock caught my eye. "Except I would have slept later."

"This is a delicate situation." He shook his head. "I can't take a bull into a china shop."

My hands tightened into fists. "What's that supposed to mean?"

He turned away from me. "You've changed."

"No, I—"

"The Thierry I knew wouldn't have gone in guns blazing to bag a djinn kid. Mai said the boy claimed you assaulted him when he refused to grant your wishes. Her office got tagged in the arrest report. What the hell were you thinking?"

I circled around until he had to look at me. "Mai told you that?"

"She's worried about you too."

"Why would she confide in you?" Unless he hit her up while she was drugged. "She hates you."

"Mai and I have never seen eye to eye, but we both…" He bit off the word. "She loves you, and she's worried. You haven't been yourself in weeks. You're being reckless and lashing out. It's like you're hell-bent on finding a way out of going back to Faerie, even if it lands you in a body bag."

I crushed my eyes shut and swallowed my denial. All the pent-up righteous indignation I came here ready to spew at him bled out of the soles of my feet into nothing. My voice, when I found it again, came out little-girl soft and trembling.

"I'm scared."

Two words. One heartfelt admission. That was all it took. I exposed a chink in my armor, and my white knight charged.

Shaw swooped down on me and gathered me against his bare chest. He settled us on the foot of his bed with me in his lap and banded his arms around me so tight I couldn't breathe. I didn't care. It felt so good to be held. I was so tired of being alone with all my fear and anger.

Mom had no idea what had happened to me in Faerie. Partly because she had been under Bháin's enchantment and partly because I was a coward. How did I tell her that after everything she had given up to be my mom, the universe had demanded one more sacrifice from her? I couldn't do it. It was bad enough to have Mai dogging my heels, afraid I might vanish in a puff of smoke if she took her eyes off me.

I had outlined the events for Shaw the night I returned from Faerie, because he had a right to know. But I'd clutched all the ugly details to my chest, unwilling to share them.

I thought I was holding myself together better than this.

I guess I was wrong.

Shaw's voice was warm at my ear. "We'll figure a way out if that's what you want."

"I don't want to be a princess." My tears dampened his chest. "I don't want Rook—any of it."

"Last night I was out of line." He palmed my cheek and made me look at him. "I thought if I knew you loved him, if this was what you wanted, then letting you go would be easier."

I blinked my vision clear. "I don't love Rook. I barely know him." I coughed up the rest before it strangled me. "I don't love him, but maybe I...want me to?"

His arms tightened around me. "You should have told me sooner."

"I can't get out." I wiped my face. "I'm trapped."

"There's always a way out," he said against my hair. "Let me think on it."

A sigh blew past my lips, and the heat of my breath on his chest made his nipple pearl. My thumb swiped over the taut bud, and he shuddered beneath me.

My name was a hot sigh over his lips that warmed me to my bones.

"I'm sorry." I scrambled off his lap and turned my back on him. I raked fingers through my sleep-tangled hair, and my hands were shaking when I screwed up the nerve to face him. "I shouldn't have unloaded all over you."

He laughed, and the weary sound shook his shoulders. "You don't do vulnerable well, do you?"

In drying my cheeks with my shirt hem, I had exposed my soft underbelly to him. Literally.

"You have snot on your nipple." I tugged my shirt down. "It doesn't get more vulnerable than that."

Another man might have grimaced or at least cleaned his chest, but Shaw sat there wearing my tears like some warped badge of honor.

He shifted on the bed and indicated I should take a seat, so I nabbed the task chair tucked under his complementary desk.

I sat and waited while he scratched his five o'clock shadow thoughtfully.

"All right, partner." He gave me his full attention. "Let's start at the beginning. I want the unedited version, deal?"

A smile lit me up from the inside. Work I could do. It was so much better than the waiting or the worrying. I picked up my story where I left off the first night, after the fae confronted

Mai, and I told Shaw every detail I remembered. This time I held nothing back. I gave him everything I had. When I finished, he was wearing a hard, contemplative expression.

He folded his thick arms over his broad chest. "Let's start with Mai's drugging and work our way back."

"Best I can figure, one of two things happened." I relayed what Mai had mumbled during the car ride to Orlando. "Either the selkies drugged her to get her out of their way while they traveled farther down the coast, or her predator pal paid the bartender to mix her a special cocktail."

His lips compressed. "You don't think the gray men are responsible."

"No, I don't." Their fear of the Morrigan extended me some protection, and they knew hurting Mai risked bringing us both down on them. "There's no reason why they would have risked retribution by drugging Mai when they could have swum away from the confrontation. They have one powerful enemy. I doubt they're eager to make another."

"Good point." He nodded. "From what you told me, the last thing they would have wanted was a reason for the Morrigan to get involved, and dragging you into the fray made that a possibility."

"Exactly." I exhaled. "They're terrified of her."

A pause lent weight to his next question. "Are you planning on reporting this situation to the conclave?"

"No." I held up a hand to stave off his scowl. "For me to pursue the claim past the filing stage, I either need an eyewitness to her crimes or sworn testimony from one of the victims. The selkies would have to be willing to press charges, and they won't. All it would do is tip her off that a reckoning is coming, and I don't want to risk her killing them off to avoid the fallout."

"They could seek protected status from the conclave," he insisted.

"The Morrigan is a *goddess*. The selkies can't beat her in a fight—fair or otherwise—and the law can only protect them so far. A piece of paper isn't going to stop her. Not after all this time."

As much as her predation disgusted me, my hands weren't any less bloody. I didn't have a single stone to toss. She might pick the meat off fae bones, but that was after I had devoured their souls.

"She will pay for what she's done," I promised. "She will be answerable to me one day." *Soon.*

Under his breath, he murmured softly, "Not if I can help it."

Doubting I was meant to hear it, I let his comment slide and focused on our problem.

"The most likely candidate is the predator." Whoever and whatever he was. "He left pissed off and hungry."

"Finding Mai alone at the bar would have been tempting." Shaw expanded that line of thought. "He either drugged her or had the bartender do it for him, but then you and your entourage showed up and spooked him. He had to let her go. Again."

Meaning I had made myself a new enemy. Great.

"He didn't know about my guards." I fidgeted. "They were cloaked."

"Are you sure the predator wasn't playing along, pretending not to know they were there?"

"No." The thought Mr. Linen Suit had played us worried me. "He didn't acknowledge them, but fae being fae, that could mean he didn't see them or they were beneath his notice. I don't get why he would go after us at all, especially if he could see the guards. Unless he viewed our presence as a challenge?"

"Maybe." The gears were turning in his head. "He may have been curious why you were there, why you stood up to him without flashing your badge. Maybe he thought you were working undercover and it made him nervous. Maybe he's just that stupid and goes around challenging unknown fae in his territory blindly. I don't know."

Option two sounded good. Too good. "You don't think he's stupid."

A half smile twitched his lips. "Do you?"

"No," I grumped. "Idiots don't live long enough to amass the kind of power the guards sensed."

"You didn't sense anything from Linen at all?"

"No, I didn't." The lack of sensation still bothered me. "Not even a blip."

"Huh." He turned pensive. "Odhran must have logged Linen's magical signature when he sensed it the first time. It's like a fingerprint some fae can recall and use to recognize or identify a person. It's a rare talent, and it was probably his ticket to princess duty." He palmed a towel off his bed. "That means Linen either stopped shielding himself, which seems unlikely since you didn't notice him, or he expended enough energy to register with Odhran. If he was feeding in the vicinity, it might have caused a surge large enough for Odhran to notice."

Feeding. The word made my skin crawl. All of us preyed on someone, but I stuck to fae. Humans reminded me too much of Mom, helpless against the strength of creatures who were centuries older than humanity, monsters who wielded their deadly skills with merciless precision.

"Did you phone in the issue to Mable?" I wondered.

Shaw's interest shifted to the nubs on his towel. "Not yet."

"Why not?" It hit me. "Ha! You're not supposed to be down here either."

"One of the terms of my return was that I can't leave the region without express permission from the magistrates." He eyed me pointedly. "I couldn't get that without first explaining why I was suddenly free to travel—" which would implicate me, "—so I decided to risk it."

Small wonder Linen wasn't afraid to show his face again. The conclave hadn't rapped his knuckles for reaching into the cookie jar after all, because Shaw couldn't report him without tattling on us.

Only the tightness of his expression kept me from laughing.

His scowl sharpened. "You think this is funny."

"It's a little funny." I snickered. "Did the fall off your high horse hurt?"

He growled.

I was not intimidated.

"After all the grief you gave me over not telling the conclave where *I* was, and they don't know where *you* are." I clicked my tongue. "Marshal Shaw, I am shocked by your sudden moral decline."

"Hang around you long enough..." he started.

"Hey." I narrowed my eyes. "You're the one who made googly eyes at an underage cadet."

The dimple in his cheek winked at me. "What you're saying is my moral decline isn't sudden. It was gradual and brought about by continual exposure...to *you*." He stood and looped a towel around his neck and approached me. "Incubi don't have strict age rules about feeding. Food is food. My brother never agreed with that stance. I don't either. I never lost sleep over a missed opportunity until you."

Seeing as how my sitting position put my eyes at crotch level with him, I clambered to my feet.

"The first time I saw you, you were terrified. Magic dripping from your fingertips. Your soul glowing with the lives you had taken. You were a scared kid who had made a terrible mistake. At thirteen, you should have been too young for me to notice. But I did. The incubus saw easy prey where I saw a child." He clenched the towel in his hands. "If I had been a good man, I would have transferred to a different outpost first thing the next morning."

Shaw was responsible for so much of my education, my self-worth, my restraint. No other creature could have understood the hunger coiled in my gut the way he did. Only someone as willing to fight their own nature as he was could have taught me where the line between black and white turned gray.

Unsure what else to say that wouldn't crack open my heart, I said nothing at all.

CHAPTER EIGHTEEN

Two hours later, Daddy Hayashi stepped out of a rented town car wearing a tailored suit that matched his sleek, black ride. As if familiar with the hotel's layout, he took the stairs with a bounce in his step and walked straight to the room I shared with Mai. Two beefy guys kept a few steps behind him, their shoulders so wide they collided trying to take the stairs at the same time. The taller guy fell back and let the shorter one close the gap on Hayashi.

"Is that Mr. Hayashi?" Shaw's voice drifted over my shoulder.

I was hiding out in his room since Mai felt it was best to keep her father and me separated. At the moment, I was kneeling on top of the boxy air-conditioning unit in front of the window, being careful to keep the curtains shut except for a slit.

"Yep." I widened the gap. "Snazzy dresser, isn't he?"

"He looks like a mob boss."

Heat from Shaw's body warmed my back where he leaned close. He had showered and dressed, but the scent of his damp skin filled the room and distracted me from my snooping.

"Mai says he watched *The Godfather* one too many times." I glanced at Shaw over my shoulder and then back at the window. "Her dad is the reynard of one of the larger skulks in west Texas, maybe even the whole state. His kitsunes breed like bunnies."

The Hayashis had money, but most of it was tied up in keeping so many tiny furry mouths fed.

"There are better ways to amass power that include changing fewer diapers."

"Maybe, but they take too long." I laughed under my breath. "He has gorgeous daughters, and I bet each of his ten eldest married into ruling families. His last kit who got hitched is the reason Mai and I ended up in Daytona. She married the reynard of a large central Florida skulk, who owns a condo."

"Hmm." He withdrew, taking his citrusy scent with him. "What about their tests?"

"All I can figure is the Hayashi girls fudged their answers." I tugged on the coarse fabric of the curtains. "Otherwise, the odds of them all landing rich, influential *and* fated mates are pretty slim." No family was that blessed. "Mr. Hayashi hasn't pressured Mai—yet—but she's his baby. He spoils her rotten. Makes her sisters crazy jealous."

"I bet." He lowered his voice. "No one wants to be forced into marriage. Mai's lucky she's avoided that fate."

"So far," I said.

"So far," he agreed.

Afraid he might be wearing a tender expression to match his voice, I kept my back to him and avoided peeking at the sliver of his reflection in the glass.

Fifteen minutes later, Daddy Hayashi escorted Mai down the stairs to his waiting car. The taller guard slid behind the wheel. The other turned toward Mai's coup with a grimace. It would be a long ride for a big guy like that. His legs would have to fold like origami to squeeze into the driver's seat.

I jerked the curtains shut and spun around on the AC unit to hop off the edge. "And they're off."

"We should be leaving soon too." He checked his cell. "We can't wait much longer for Diode."

"Give him a few more minutes." I stretched out my back. "He's been acting strange lately."

"You've only known him a few weeks," Shaw pointed out. "This might be normal for him."

"I know that. It's just…" I bit my thumbnail. "I feel connected to him somehow."

"He was your father's pet." He shrugged. "It's natural for you to want that connection."

"He wasn't Mac's pet." Diode would shred Shaw to ribbons for insinuating otherwise. "They were *associates*."

He shot me an indulgent look. "That sounds like something a cat would say about his master."

I laughed out loud because he was right, and because cat jokes never got old.

A burst of music from my pocket had me reaching for my phone. I checked the ID and rejected.

"Who was that?" Shaw asked oh so casually.

"A wrong number."

"Don't lie to me. You didn't hesitate. You recognized the number."

"Fine." I warned him, "You aren't going to like it."

Explaining the odd calls made his face turn so red I expected smoke to come pouring out of his nostrils.

Oops. Guess I had forgotten to mention those during my purge earlier.

After drawing a calming breath, he began pacing. "You have no idea who's calling you?"

I bumped my cell against my lips. "None."

His steps slowed. "This guy knew you were in Florida how?"

"No clue. Mable wouldn't have told him or anyone else. If he showed up in person, someone might have told him I was on vacation or out of the office." I doubted any of my coworkers would use the *S* word with a civilian. Gossip about a suspension could discredit a marshal in the eyes of the public. "How this guy connected *vacation* to *Florida*, I have no idea."

"Did he mention Daytona?" He paused for my answer.

I thought about it. "No. He sounded confident he could find me, but he never got specific."

Shaw rubbed his jaw. "Is it possible some crackpot with an ounce of psy magic got your number?"

"Anything is possible." The calls didn't feel random, though. "I do pass out my number sometimes."

Shaw pulled up short, and a white sheen frosted his eyes. "Why?"

"Informants. Victims. Coworkers." I smothered a grin. "Hot guys who dig chicks with badges."

He growled in response.

Still fighting a smile, I waggled my cell at him. "How do you want to handle my gentleman caller?"

"You will stay in my sight." He jabbed the air in my direction. "If your mystery caller does have a way of locating you, I want to be there when he shows up. Otherwise, we focus on Linen."

The slow shake of his head when he said *Linen* this time made me blush. My habit of nicknaming people amused him. These days, he just went with it. To me, *Linen* rolled off the tongue smoother than *the guy who probably drugged Mai* or *freaky hotel guy*.

"There's one more thing I should mention." I scrunched up my face. "I'm pretty much broke."

"Still paying your mother's bills?"

The way he said it, calm and without inflection, I could have ignored him. He would have returned the favor if I had, but he knew me, and he knew I wouldn't let a comment like that slide. Not about Mom.

"That's low, Shaw."

"What will she do if you go to Faerie? Are you going to warn her that the gravy train is ending? Or will she keep her seat until it smashes headfirst into a wall? Will you even tell her where you're going?" With visible effort, he reined in his tirade. "All I'm saying is, you see her as a victim—as *your* victim. You think she sacrificed everything for you, and maybe she did, once, but you're missing the big picture here. She's your mom. You love her—"

"You think?"

His voice softened. "She was scared, of you, of me, of all the things she didn't understand. She did good by you. She brought you to folks who could help. But she never bounced back. She never tried to. She lives in a bubble where she feels safe again, and you're so damn scared of bursting it you're tightrope walking over a bed of needles to support her."

"She's my mom."

"And you're her daughter."

"It's my fault—"

"No." He cut me short. "She had a relationship with your father. You're the product of that. The result can't be the fault of the actions preceding it. It's a calculated outcome, one she was well aware of when she chose to be with your father. You don't owe her anything. She's an adult. She made her own choices. You've paid her back a hundred times over. She needs to know the truth. All of it."

My lips pressed together until they startled tingling.

"Say it." He studied me. "Before your head explodes."

"She didn't know who Mac was—what he was." My chest ached. "Their whole relationship was a lie because if she had known the truth, Mom never would have been with him. She would have…"

I couldn't say it. It hurt too much to bend my lips around those words.

She would have stamped out the spark of my life before it ignited.

Shaw's expression gentled. "How is it your fault he lied to her?"

"It's not," I snapped.

"Exactly." He dropped a kiss on the top of my head. "Talk to your mother."

He gathered our things and headed for his truck, tugging the door shut behind him.

Anger clamped me in a chokehold. Even if I had had a comeback ready, and I didn't, I couldn't loosen my fury to spit it out. After a full minute, I gasped for air and shouted, *"Armchair psychologist."*

I found Diode lounging on the shady limb of a bitternut hickory tree with branches overhanging the back half of the parking lot. His furry butt was exposed where anyone looking could see him. I walked under him and yanked on the end of his long tail.

Yowling ensued as Diode tested that whole cats-always-land-on-their-feet thing.

He did, by the way. Land on his feet, I mean.

Morale on the drive back to Daytona hit rock bottom. Forced to cram his long, lean body into the tight space behind our seats, Diode overflowed the extended cab compartment of Shaw's truck. I let him get away with draping his right front paw and tail over the back of my seat because I figured Orlando had seen stranger and dealt with it just fine. From a distance, Diode could pass for a lifelike movie prop or a plush toy won at a carnie booth in any one of the theme parks. Not that I told him so.

Shaw coasted to a stop at an intersection packed with bikini-clad women carrying yoga mats rolled up under their arms. "Is that the right hotel?"

"Yep." I hauled my messenger bag onto my lap and groped around the bottom. "That's it."

He leaned forward to appreciate its height. "How tight is security?"

"Think muumuu." Loose was putting it nicely. "It's a busy hotel in a beachfront town in summer."

"New faces arriving daily." He picked up my thought. "Hard to track who is and isn't a guest."

"The stock rotates and the pantry replenishes itself." No two ways about it. "It's an ideal hunting ground."

"It's early." He spared a glance at Diode. "We need to get a room and stash the cat."

For once, the cat didn't argue. He did add, "I'm hungry. There's nothing to hunt here."

I twisted around to face him. "You should have mentioned it earlier."

His claws flexed in and out. "You are traveling light. I don't want to be a burden."

"Light? I have you and two guards and… Oh." I reached behind me to ruffle the fur on his head. "You heard me talking about money." Apparently, when Mom was handing out life advice, I missed the part where you didn't talk finances in front of your children *or* your pets.

"At home, I care for myself." His chin jerked higher. "You shouldn't be responsible for me."

My mind jumped to Wink, but home to him meant Faerie.

"Rook agreed to let you come with me. He's been here and knows the landscape. He knew there were no hunting grounds and that I would have to provide for you." I popped his front paw before he sank claws into Shaw's supple upholstery. "As far as I'm concerned, that makes your needs his concern."

"Are you going to ask him for money?" The steering wheel groaned beneath Shaw's hands.

"No." Diode rumbled a laugh. "That pretender is living on the future queen's coin. She is saying she will do for me what she would not do for herself. She will use Faerie gold to finance my needs."

"Yeah, well, don't let it go to your head." I let him butt his huge furry face against mine. "This is probably the first time that gold has been used for good since it was minted." I spat neon fur stuck in my lip balm. "I'll talk to the guards when they arrive, then you three can hash out all the details."

"Now that we have that settled," Shaw said as his foot tapped the gas, "let's find us a room."

"Rooms," I corrected.

"I thought you were broke."

"I am."

"I'm not exactly rolling in green here, either."

I narrowed my eyes, not believing him for a minute. "Let me guess. You're offering to share?"

"If you're nice to me, I might request two beds instead of a king."

"Hold that thought." I palmed the phone I had unearthed from the depths of my bag, then called Mai. Eighteen minutes later, I hung up with an update on how she was feeling— better—and a reason to smile. "Well, that's one less thing. We've got ourselves a room." Shaw's eyebrows lifted expectantly. "Mai was in no condition to check out yesterday, so as far as the hotel knows, she and I never left. She paid for the week online through one of those bargain travel websites, so the money is gone. At least if we stay, it won't be wasted. Besides, we know that's the area where Linen hunts."

"I can't argue with that logic." Though it was clear he wanted to.

I patted his thigh. "Just think, now we won't have to worry about that pesky bed situation."

He grumbled.

"You can take Mai's room." I clasped my hands together. "We'll have locking doors between us and everything."

Behind us, Diode chuffed with amusement, but beside me, Shaw wasn't laughing.

No matter. I chuckled enough for the both of us.

Sneaking Diode into the bustling hotel this time around was harder. I sent Shaw ahead to secure a baggage trolley from the front desk and had Diode crawl onboard. We used our luggage to hide his paws then draped a couple of shirts over the top of him. It would have to do. With the guards in the ether, we were on our own. Besides, if someone stared too hard at the trolley, Shaw could use a whiff of his lure to draw any unwanted attention onto him.

Even without his lure, he drew more looks than our wobbly cart.

Once the elevator doors closed with a *whoosh*, I exhaled and relaxed against the cool metal wall.

A warm hand enveloped mine, and Shaw interlaced our fingers. For a minute, I expected the stinging tug of magic as he fed. Palm to palm was less intimate than other ways, and he had to be starving. But the pain never materialized. He stood with his back flush to one wall, and me with mine on another. The corner between us stood empty and significant as our hands stretched across it to touch.

Breaking the silence, I stared up at him. "Working on our cover story?"

"Husband and wife?" His lips twitched. "Newlyweds? Honeymoon or vacation?"

I yanked on my hand, wanting it back with a fierceness that startled us both. Surprise transformed into need on his face. The heat in his gaze faded to familiar stark, gnawing hunger that echoed in my gut. "Hungry?"

"Starving," he replied in a rumble I felt clear to my core.

I held perfectly still, staring into his frosty eyes so I could gauge when the danger had passed.

The man who taught me fledgling control of my powers was losing his iron grip on his.

It terrified me. Almost like a ghost from the past had held up a mirror in front of my face and shown me a reflection of my history. Of that circle of dead teens, their glittery pink nails shining, their hands still linked from the silly game we had been playing.

That first terrible, magical current had exploded out of me and raced through them, snatching their souls and stuffing all their raw power inside me until my pores bled with energy.

Even with Shaw standing in front of me, when he got like this, I saw too much of myself in him.

Maybe that was what frightened me the most.

"There are cameras in here." I used a low, nonthreatening voice. "We have to be careful."

"Thierry?" Diode made my name both question and warning.

"Need to feed," Shaw grated out. "Should have done it in Orlando."

A *ting* signaled our stop.

"Our room is right over there." I jerked my chin toward it. "You can hang on that long."

He nodded and shut his eyes, throwing his arm out to catch the doors before they shut.

The task of wheeling Diode down the hall and into the room fell to me. Shaw kept hold of my hand, so I made steering a team effort. I shoved from behind and used Shaw's body as a guide. I don't even think he noticed.

The room door locking behind us he registered, because he pinned me against it by our joined hands and wedged his knee between my thighs. I had trouble moving air through my lungs when his nails extended, their razor tips nicking my knuckles. Color slid from his skin like paint washed down a drain. Hunger peered at me from his face. Its expression of endless craving—for *me*—hit me hard, made my body soften and my brain fog. I remembered how it felt before necessity drove him to obsession with my taste. I recalled the exhilaration of his complete adoration being channeled into me.

If I was death in spirit, then Shaw was rapture incarnate.

No one I killed would have thanked me for it. It was a brutal way to die. But seeing him this way breathed life into the old lore, stories where incubi feasted on their victims' souls as well as their flesh, draining the spark from their lovers, leaving behind an empty shell with a smile on their lips.

Diode's weight leaned against my leg. "I can restrain him."

Tightening his grip on me, Shaw bared his teeth.

"I can handle him." I wiggled my hips to get his attention off Diode. "Are you hungry or what?"

His head whipped toward me. *"Yes."*

With a hungry growl, Shaw's mouth sealed over mine, and all polite dinner etiquette flew out the window. His first draw brought power tingling into my lips. The ant-bite-like stings made my eyes water. Pain was there. The soreness in my chest was more than bruised feelings. It was a loss of self as Shaw devoured fragments of me. The way he broke me down, left me empty and aching, appealed to me more than it should have. I could get lost here, beneath his urgent lips and strong hands. I could forget all that I was or would be, and become his.

The hand not pinned to the door grasped Shaw's belt buckle, and a tentative finger dipped inside the waistband of his jeans. His groaned response melted my knees until I sagged astride his thigh. He teased his hands under the hem of my shirt, claws grazing my rib cage. With a startled grunt, his warm weight vanished.

Without his support, I hit the floor with a gasped *oomph.* The burst of pain in my tailbone cleared my head.

Three feet from the toe of my outstretched leg, Diode pinned Shaw beneath him to the floor. His muzzle hovered less than an inch from Shaw's nose, and his ears flattened against his broad skull.

"That is enough, incubus."

Shaw bucked under him, head turned toward me, clawed hands grasping. *"Mine."*

The cat flexed his paw, and his claws pressed into Shaw's throat. He leaned forward until Shaw's face burned scarlet.

"Get off him." I scrabbled toward them and jerked the cat's tail. "You're suffocating him."

"Good." The yellow tail flicked. "Let him experience the panic you feel when he doesn't stop."

Panic had been the farthest thing from my mind, but telling Diode that might shorten his fuse.

"I should have made him feed earlier." I shouldered my weight into shoving him. "I knew he had to be getting close."

Whiskers stood on end. "Are you a goddess like the Morrigan?"

"No." Even the comparison made me ill.

"Are you omniscient? Or omnipresent? Or omnipotent?"

Two-thirds of that sailed right over my head. "No?"

"Then why do you shoulder so much blame? Why are you responsible for the actions of others? In all my long life, I have never met another being so determined to be at fault for every wrong thing that happens to everyone around them." He shook his head. "You have your father's best traits, and his worst. You share the same fire, the passion to protect those weaker than yourself, and I admire that."

I let his tail slip through my hands.

"I will share with you a concept it took him centuries to grasp." Diode shifted his weight. "Your actions are your choice, just as the actions of others are theirs. You lay no blame at Shaw's feet, even though he is decades your senior—" a dismissive whisker flick, "—and well aware of the limits of his self-control and that being with you tests them. You find no fault with your mother's behavior, though she is as much of an adult as you are."

With his attention on me, he rocked back, applying less pressure to Shaw's windpipe. I bit my tongue and let him speak his mind.

"Thierry, you must learn not only when to lift a burden, but when to set it down." He patted Shaw's lax face with his paw. "Otherwise, your back will break under the strain, and everyone who depends on you will be left as sheep without their shepherd. Do you understand?"

I nodded that I did. "Did you stage this as some kind of intervention?"

"No." Diode slinked away from Shaw and found a patch of sunlight on the carpet to warm himself. "Staging implies effort to bring about a series of events. It was only a matter of time before this occurred."

I leaned forward and pressed two fingers to Shaw's pulse and counted. Strong and steady. "Out like a light." I traced the shadows beneath his lashes. "Sleep tight."

Diode turned a circle, kneaded the carpet and lied down. "You should rest while you can."

"I think I will grab a nap." I stood with a groan. "Can I trust you to play nice with him?"

The great cat blinked. "I haven't killed him yet, have I?"

"I'll take that as a *yes* to the good-behavior thing." Opening my senses, I scanned the area for an indication my guards had arrived. No scent of them. "Keep an eye out for the guards' return too."

"They know their way in." His eyes shut, and he settled. "Now go to bed before I bite your nape and carry you to your room myself. Nothing will happen until nightfall. You can rest for that long."

Knowing he was right, I turned on my heel. "I need to check in with Mom first."

Odds were slim, infinitesimal really, that Mom would cross paths with Mai. But if she did and I wasn't with her and hadn't called Mom to explain where I was, her momma-bear switch would flip.

"How is your mother?" Diode's voice sounded far away.

"She's recovered from her *vacation* in Faerie." Sarcasm dripped from the word. "It's like it never happened."

His head bobbed once before he lowered it to the carpet and resumed his sunbathing.

Phone heavy in my hand, I went to my room and called my mother.

I lied, told her that Mai had food poisoning and went home but insisted I finish out the week. Mom, who enjoyed sand and sun more than anyone else I knew, agreed wholeheartedly. She signed off with an *I love you* and a wistful note in her voice.

Guilt had me dragging a pillow and blanket into the living room to make Shaw comfortable. By the time I had wrestled him into position, I was so tired I curled up beside him and shared his pillow. His unconscious mind must have sensed me. He rolled onto his side, tucking my back against his front. His arm draped over my waist and hauled me closer, until his nose buried in my hair and his even breaths hit the back of my neck.

Safe in his arms, I teetered on the brink of falling asleep. That's when Shaw sighed. A contented huff. The sound a man made when he was right where he wanted to be.

Sleep eluded me after that.

Maybe that was the reason Rook didn't visit, though I was starting to wonder.

CHAPTER NINETEEN

Stiffness in my back woke me. I rolled over and found myself lying alone on the carpet. I pushed onto my feet and stretched while a yawn popped my jaw. No one had turned on the lights after it got dark, but Shaw's laptop screen illuminated his face. I made my way toward him then peered over his shoulder at the grainy surveillance footage playing on a loop while he scrawled notes on a legal pad.

Onscreen, a slight, beautiful woman shopped for toilet paper. "Is that your sister-in-law?"

He glanced at the screen instead of me. "Yes."

Hello, post-feeding awkwardness. "Will you go back to Orlando when we finish up here?"

"No." The snap of his pen hitting paper emphasized his response. "I've seen what I needed to. The trail is too cold. There's nothing I could do from there I can't do from home. Besides, I have cases waiting."

An offer to help him parted my lips, but first things first.

I plopped down onto the closest chair. "How do you want to play this tonight?"

The pen got threaded between his fingers. "Both times Linen went after Mai, she was alone?"

"As far as he knew…" I turned the events over in my head. "Yeah."

Shaw's head lifted, gaze zeroing in on a spot at the far corner of the room. "Ask if there's anything to report."

Righty materialized next to my arm, and I startled. "How long have you two been back?"

"Hours." He bit off the word. "We let you sleep."

The implied, *with Shaw*, I heard loud and clear. "So is this a recap?"

From the shadows by the door, Lefty materialized. "We report to you, not the incubus."

Touchy, touchy. "We're all on the same team here."

"No." Distaste curled Righty's lip. "We are not."

A feline yawn gave Diode a spot in the conversation.

"What am I missing?" I glanced from face to face. "Did everyone wake up on the wrong side of the bed?"

"You didn't make it to the bed," Lefty said under his breath.

"Oh." I drew out the word. "I get it now. This is you two judging me."

"You are wed to Rook." Righty stared down his nose at me. "Consorts must be approved."

I snorted so hard my nostrils burned. "Sorry, guys, but no. Just no."

Lefty stood straighter. "I fail to see what amuses you so."

"I didn't agree to be Rook's wife. It just happened. Like walking through a mountain pass and a boulder falling on top of your head." I pushed to my feet. "The person squished underneath the rock doesn't have to ask it for permission to keep breathing. The person can fight to get free all they want, and the rock can stuff it where the moss don't grow."

Judging by the blank looks, my analogy had gotten away from me. They did that sometimes. "I support monogamy. I won't share a straw in my milkshake, let alone share the person I plan to spend the rest of my life with. The consort thing was skeevy even before you mentioned my husband getting to approve my choice of lover."

The furrowing of Righty's brow amused me until he said, "It is the way things are done."

"We aren't in Faerie, and those rules no longer apply." I scrubbed my face with my palms. "The thing with Shaw isn't what it looked like, but even if it had been, it's none of Daire's business or yours."

"A closed door does wonders for preventing such misunderstandings," Diode rumbled.

I pointed at him. "You are not helping."

"I want you to be happy—" his luminescent gaze cut to Shaw, "—and safe."

My hands dropped, and I almost choked. "Are you implying Rook is a safer choice?"

"No." The big cat bowed into a deep stretch that unsheathed his claws. "You value honesty in a relationship." He sat on his haunches and showed Shaw all his pointy teeth. "You couldn't be with someone who lied to you, even if they had your best interests at heart. You would rather face an obstacle with a partner as equals than be coddled like a child. Trust matters to you, and honesty is its cornerstone."

I got the feeling these two had talked while I was sleeping. Obviously, I had been the topic. Which meant the guards had monitored their conversation. Maybe that—not finding me with Shaw—had bunched their undies. Too bad the guards were too tight-lipped for sharing gossip.

"If that was an elaborate way of calling Rook a bastard," I said, "then I wholeheartedly agree."

Neither guard met my gaze after that. We had been making such progress too.

"You two were absent when we arrived," I addressed them. "I assume you swept the grounds?"

"We did." Righty's clipped tone had returned.

I made a rolling gesture with my hand. "What did you discover?"

"There was no trace of the entity." Lefty always sounded snappish. No real change there.

Diode studied his claws. "The magic he's using to camouflage himself has fooled you before."

"It has fooled *all* of us." I jumped in before the guards' wedgies went atomic. "So we agree there's a chance even if we don't sense Linen, he might be down there." I plucked at my shirt. "I should change before we go. Both times he approached Mai she was..." I considered and rejected several word combinations, "...*scantily clad*. He might have a thing for skin. My swimsuit isn't as flashy, but it will have to do."

"He has your scent." Shaw didn't look happy about it. "I don't think the swimsuit is necessary."

"I agree," Righty said. "If, as you say, he has a thing for skin, the less you show, the safer you will be."

Lefty threw his weight behind the motion for me to stay covered up. Diode graced us with a kingly nod in agreement. *Motion carried.*

"Okay. The swimsuit's out. I still need fresh clothes." This outfit was linty from my nap on the floor. "But I'll keep it casual."

"I assume you mean to use Thierry as bait." The cat sounded displeased.

"The guards will be with me." I shrugged off his worry. "I'll be fine."

"I won't let her get hurt," Shaw promised.

"Don't let the boobs fool you." I smirked. "I'm trained for this."

A slight grin crooked Shaw's lips. "Yes, you are." The look I cut Diode was smug. Shaw continued, "But that doesn't mean any of us want to see you—or your boobs—get hurt."

Utter mortification swept through the fluorescent-yellow cat and turned him sallow. "Her—" He strangled on the word, unable to cough it up. "Her *anatomy* is not up for discussion."

Wrong of me, I know, but I laughed at the prudish crinkle of Diode's nose. "I'll hit the bar and see what happens."

"Don't drink your order," Shaw warned. "We don't know how the drugs got into Mai's drink."

"Well, shucks," I drawled. "This here's my first rodeo, Mr. Incubus. Are you sure you ought to let this little filly run wild?" I lowered my gaze to the vicinity of his belt buckle. "If I need emergency wrangling, how good are you with your…lasso?"

He ignored me, my twang and my lasso reference.

Spoilsport.

The cat's whiskers flexed in thought. "The bartender might be fae."

"If he is, we'll get him relocated." Shaw's expression darkened. "There are kids here."

I could have pointed out that children didn't belly up to the bar, but some fae preferred the young and had no qualms mashing herbs into lollipops or mixing spells into chocolate bars. For now we would focus on the pattern we knew, the option that would give me fewer nightmares later. Linen liked sexy fae women. Sexy wasn't happening. I wasn't that girl. But I was half-fae.

Two out of three ain't bad.

"I assume you're going to hold down the fort?" I asked the lounging cat.

"Not that I have much choice with my charm nullified," he said dryly.

I walked over and scratched under his chin. "If he comes up here looking for trouble, don't hog all the fun."

He leaned into my palm. "You and I have very different ideas of fun."

If I hadn't seen him shred those hounds in Faerie into confetti, I might have believed him. "No." I kissed his nose. "We don't."

His playful swipe at my legs with his sheathed claws made me grin.

After dancing out of his reach, I spun on Righty and Lefty. "Did you see any signs of the gray men?"

Both guards shook their heads. "The beaches are clear."

No surprise there. "Did you sense any other fae in the area?"

"No," they said in unison.

Fae weren't as common as humans, but in a resort this size, this time of year, and so close to the ocean, we should have had company. "So, either there *are* fae here and someone, maybe Linen, is concealing them, or this area has been claimed by something dangerous enough to run off visiting fae it views as competition."

And if Linen was the *something dangerous* claiming this as his territory, how powerful did that make him?

"It doesn't matter much," Shaw finally said. "If Linen is powerful enough to hold territory here, we're going to have a fight on our hands removing him. As tight as the competition is for beachfront hunting grounds, I doubt he leaves his home unguarded. That's assuming he isn't working for someone else."

"Four to one are good odds." Between the guards, Shaw and me, we could hold our own. "We can test his defenses if nothing else."

"I want you to wear this too." He tossed me a small leather pouch on a string.

I caught it, and cold magic rolled up my arm. Then the smell hit me. "*Phew.* What's in this?"

His lips twitched. "Do you really want to know?"

Spellwork was his forte, not mine. But I had a good nose, and I trusted what it told me. I also trusted I didn't want the specifics.

"Let's go the willful-ignorance route, okay?" I tightened the drawstrings. "What does it do?"

"It defuses spells and enchantments cast in your vicinity or on your person." Grim lines hardened his expression. "It won't last more than two hours. Three max."

The spell was active. That meant the clock was ticking. "Then we better get started."

The bar scene spawned a migraine. Lights flashed. Drinks splashed. Half-naked women jiggled while guys filmed their next YouTube upload on their cells. Much to my surprise, the desk clerk told me the hotel serviced two bars.

One was tucked in the corner and strained to exude elegance amid the sandaled masses. Maybe that explained why I had missed it each time I passed through the lobby. The lighting was low, which made for ideal hunting conditions, but there were no singles in sight. Only married couples. Paired with the *Parents After Dark* vibe it had going for it, I ditched that bar and focused on the poolside hangout where Linen had made his first appearance.

A quick check of my phone told me thirty minutes had passed. Time to get noticed.

I ordered a Bahama Mama from a suitably flirty bartender and started making the rounds. Most guys grinned when I cut between them and their partners. The women, not so much. A few men offered to refresh my drink, which I made sure to splash onto the ground while dancing. Not that I wanted to start a drunken catfight over a guy I had no interest in, but hot tempers and loud voices attracted a certain kind of attention.

"All this for me?" a dark voice purred near my ear. "You could have called."

Chills dappled my skin. "You didn't leave a number."

"You left in such a hurry." Linen clicked his tongue. "I'm pleased to see you're not a coward."

The accusation rankled. "I'm surprised you noticed. You liked my friend, remember?"

"I liked her well enough," he admitted, "but she was never the prize."

Meaning he had targeted me all along, through Mai. A fissure of unease shot through me, but he was here now, and I couldn't very well hold up a finger and beat a hasty retreat after telling him this new information meant I had to consult with the fae extraction team I had on standby in the shadows.

His hands landed on my shoulders, and he whirled me around to face him. "Thierry Thackeray."

Following his lead, I spun again, part flirt and part self-defense. I wanted his hands off me.

"That's me." No harm in confirming what he already knew. Besides, it wasn't my Name.

"I am Balamohan." That same flat, black gaze as before drilled into me. "I am Makara here."

Makara. My brain stalled on my rusty Hindu mythology. "That makes you Ganga's pet, right?"

The dark skin covering his jaw tightened as he ground his teeth. "I was once in her service."

From what I remembered, Ganga was a goddess of rivers. Her mount was a Makara, and for the life of me I couldn't remember what that meant. A half-terrestrial and half-aquatic mishmash of a creature maybe?

Having a goddess as his patroness explained how Linen maintained a low baseline, easily concealed, while being able to tap into so much raw magic. Mixing energies also explained the muddied power signature.

Though the way he phrased his answer made me wonder if Ganga was still among the living gods. "Who do you serve now?"

He forced himself to relax into his laid back façade. "That would be telling."

"You do realize as a conclave marshal, I could force you to state your allegiance."

"You could try." Now he was smiling. "The conclave means nothing to me."

"Well, that's where you and I are going to have to disagree." I attempted contriteness. "We have rules in this realm, and everyone has to follow them. If you don't—" I spread my arms, "—you get a visit from someone like me. And no one wants that. So why don't we refresh your memory, okay?"

Those black pools set in his face sparkled. "What if I wanted this visit?"

The thought sent a shiver through me. "Now, now. Flattery won't unbreak the law."

"This is going to be fun," he said with a laugh.

A stinging sensation in my arm made me glance down to where a filament from the jacket of his linen suit stretched over to me, like it had unraveled and a loose string grazed me. Only I couldn't brush it off. It had latched on to me, and the worse it hurt…the less I cared about the pain.

"What are you doing?" I touched my lips and found them as frozen and numb as the ice in my drink. And they weren't the only thing. A slow paralysis swept through me, concentrating cold down my left arm. Before my sense of smell dulled, I scented my guards nearby. That alone kept me from frying Linen on the spot, before a cast of all-too-human witnesses. Well, that and the fact I couldn't feel my hand. Hard to feed on someone I couldn't touch with deadened mojo.

I wish I had a nifty lure like Shaw's.

"Sparing you." He caught me when I slid off my barstool. "You didn't think Faerie would allow a half-blood upon her throne, did you? As you said, there are rules, and everyone must follow them." He wrapped an arm around my waist, and that nasty string thing bound us together hip to hip, digging in deeper. "Let me take you away from all the politics and protect you from all who wish you harm."

We speed-walked through the pool area and exited the hotel. A black SUV idled by the curb, and when we arrived, a squat humanoid fae shoved open the passenger-side door and leapt onto the curb. He had the look and gestures almost right, nearly human, but his mustache…

Instead of hairs, his 'stache was a cluster of black tentacles. Make that two. Each section rooted above the peak of his top lip, right underneath his nose, and he had combed them—or whatever one did with one's facial tentacles—to frame his plump mouth.

Staring was rude, and his tight frown told me he thought so too, but my eyes were glued to him.

"Thanks for the offer," I said distractedly, "but I don't need protection."

Squid Boy opened the rear passenger-side door, and the breeze caught him just right. Curry and spice. Mystery solved. My money was on this little guy being the one who had followed Mai and me up to our room.

A whimsical image popped into my head of Squid Boy sticking his suction cup mustache to the ceiling of the elevator to avoid being seen when the doors opened. It was probably the drugs talking. Probably.

"Yes, you do." Linen lifted me inside the vehicle and set me on the black leather bench seat like a doll whose limbs he took great care to arrange. "You have made enemies. Luckily, they don't want you harmed."

A cold ball of fear formed in my chest. Following him back to his lair wasn't part of the plan, or if it had been, the guys hadn't clued me into it. But I had scented my guards, and I trusted Shaw to have my back. The filament thing stung, but I could handle it. Tentacle facial hair was freaky, but I could see someone as self-important as Linen employing other monster mashups as his henchmen.

I would have questioned him more, but the pangs in my arm sharpened. Once he finished arranging my hands in my lap, my eyes had fluttered shut.

CHAPTER TWENTY

Bark sliced into the tender undersides of my thighs as I wobbled on a scrawny tree limb. Wood crackled under me when I shifted my weight, and my perch jiggled as I inched my butt closer to the trunk.

"Thierry."

I glanced across from me at the empty tangle of crosshatched limbs where Rook usually sprawled.

"Rook?"

"I didn't know." Regret deadened his tone. "I swear I didn't know."

My stomach clenched. "What are you talking about? Where are you?"

"She didn't tell me." His voice began to fade. "I never meant for this to happen."

"Rook?" A sharp crack rent the air, and my seat dipped. "What's happening?"

"Forgive me."

And then I fell.

"There you are." Linen towered over me with a drink clutched in his hand. "Where did you go just now?"

A long minute passed while I parsed out where I was (*not* safe at my hotel), who he was and why those things should frighten me. I inhaled through a stuffy nose, but the only scent I could identify was the kind of damp smell I associated with the earth.

The dim room loomed tall and narrow behind him. Parquet floors. Knotty oak paneling. Drop ceiling with thick-grain panels stained dark. The decor reminded me of a gentlemen's club straight out of the movies. I half-expected Linen to light up a fat cigar to puff while he swirled port in a squat glass.

My captor leaned closer, and the tickle of alcohol and brine hit my nose. "Did you hear me?"

Shared dreams with Rook were private, almost intimate, and I wasn't about to answer him.

"Where are we?" Lifting my head sent shards of pain knifing through my brain. "What is this place?"

Talking made my jaw throb like I had been punched. Worse was an incessant chattering noise.

My teeth.

When I shoved off the chilly cushions beneath me and sat upright, the whole world sloshed with the motion. I gritted my teeth until equilibrium was restored. The leather couch where I sat had a new-car smell. When I shifted into a new position, gooseflesh raced down my exposed legs. Shorts had been a bad idea.

If I had known I was going to be kidnapped, I would have dressed more appropriately.

"This is my home." Linen, whose real name escaped me, beamed. "You are welcome here."

I stood and swayed on my feet. "I appreciate your hospitality, but I should be going."

He knocked me back with a tap of his index finger. "You've only just arrived." He snapped his fingers, and a door I couldn't quite see from this angle creaked open. A painfully thin woman entered the room holding an oversized tray level with her breasts. A single glass of clear liquid sat positioned in the exact center. Her hair hung in sculpted curls down her back, and the makeup caking her face tricked me into thinking she was human. Until she stepped closer and a sharp whiff of decomposition hit me.

"Don't look at her like that," Linen chided. "She lasted longer than most."

As I stared down my possible future, I had to ask, "Is this what you have in mind for me?"

"No."

He answered a beat too late, and I didn't believe him.

"What did you do to her?" Zombies weren't exactly uncommon. New Orleans, for example, was lousy with them in the summer. But I had never seen one in person, and never one so well-preserved.

Linen approached the woman and brushed the hair from her temple, exposing a small, clean dot the circumference of the eraser on a pencil. He leaned in close and opened his mouth. Another filament, this one a fleshy color, passed from his lips into the hole. The woman—corpse—jolted when he closed his lips and hollowed his cheeks. He drank deep before retracting his strawlike appendage with a soft groan.

I threw up a little in my mouth.

Worse than the floorshow was the knowledge that zombies are unfeeling. They can be controlled by the person who raised them, but they don't act without orders. They're dead. They feel no pain. They don't think, either. They are globs of people-shaped clay for their makers to impress their will upon.

The woman shouldn't have flinched.

Linen enjoyed his production so much, I wouldn't put it past him to give her cues to *act* aware just to unsettle me, but the motions orchestrated by him—her entering the room and carrying the tray—were jerky. Almost like she fought him every step of the way. That one cringe was fluid, responsive. It was real.

The woman, or what was left of her, was still alive.

I tamped down the fury sparking in my palm. I did not want to become more interesting to him.

"You made your point." I balked when the woman extended the tray toward me. Her trembling fingers rattled the ice in the glass, but I took it because I worried what might happen to her if I refused. Certain she wasn't fae, I felt safe saying, "Thank you."

"You're welcome, hon."

Shocked by the warmth in her voice, I lifted my gaze to hers, and recognition slammed into me.

Jenna.

Little remained of the smiling mother of two from the photo Shaw had shown me, but this was no doubt the same woman from the surveillance video.

I wiped every trace of emotion from my face. Showing concern for her might make things worse. For both of us.

"It's not poisoned." Linen's voice dragged my attention back to him. "You should try it."

I sniffed the contents of the glass. Numb-nosed, I had no idea what the concoction was. Not water. It stung my sinuses like alcohol. "I'm good."

"You need to drink," he chastised me. "You don't want to get dehydrated."

"I saw what you did to Mai." Whatever he gave her, she had gone off her rocker. "I'm not interested."

"Mai was a silly girl drinking a fruity drink at a bar. You're a woman who's gone sixteen hours without fluid. You must be thirsty." He tilted his head. "Unless... When was the last time you fed?"

"None of your damn business," I said hotly.

I barely shared that shame with Shaw. No way was I exposing the raw guilt festering in my gut to this psycho. My regret was mine, and I wasn't in an introspective mood.

His expression shifted, and he let the question slide. "Drink."

"Not happening."

"You seem to be under the mistaken impression that you have a choice." The fleshy appendage hissed through his lips, snakelike and threatening. "Perhaps I have been too lenient with you. Perhaps you don't respond as well to the niceties I expected someone of your social status to appreciate. More's the pity."

He snapped his fingers, and Jenna lunged at me. She palmed my scalp and yanked my head back with one hand. Condensation lubricated the glass, and she jerked it out of my hand in one smooth motion.

I had a choice to make. I could hurt her, or I could let her hurt me. No matter who she was to Shaw, it wasn't in me to accept this kind of punishment and not fight back. Time to summon reinforcements.

"Tahlil paque." To me.

My voice rang clear and strong through the room.

And nothing happened.

Linen laughed under his breath, savoring my confusion. "I wondered when we would get to this part."

"What have you done to my guards?" I snarled.

"So protective." He crossed to me and brushed his bony knuckles along my cheekbone. "Would you feel better if I let you see them? If you knew both males were perfectly well and unharmed?"

I nodded as much as I was able. Jenna wasn't letting go. Smart woman. The element of surprise only worked once. No matter. Backup was coming. Between the guards and me, we could take Linen. Jenna too. If we had to.

Linen spoke louder so his voice carried through the doorway. "Odhran, Daire, come in here, please."

Righty and Lefty entered the room wearing somber expressions. Neither looked at me. Probably better that way. They needed to focus on the threat. Any minute now, they would draw their weapons.

Any minute now…

"There." Linen patted Righty on the shoulder. "Is that better?"

"Hi, guys." It was the best greeting I could manage while the not-exactly-a-zombie had my head cranked back, yanking a fistful of my hair out by its roots while she waited for further instructions.

However, it wasn't enough for Linen, who lifted his own glass in a mock salute.

"Thierry, if you could only see your face." He expelled a small, cruel laugh. "You trusted them. You're still waiting for them to spring forward, swords drawn to disembowel me on their way to rescuing you."

I felt the blood rush from my cheeks. "That was eerily similar to the scenario I had in mind, yes."

"We are loyal to Faerie." Righty cut his eyes toward me. "We are faithful to the crown and the one who wears it."

I ran a finger across my forehead. "Last I heard they were sizing it to fit me."

His gaze lowered, and he didn't speak again. Lefty stared at me—hard—but he didn't say a word.

Linen flicked a hand toward the door. "You may go."

They nodded in unison and exited…without as much as a pinky wave at me.

Linen was right. Even now my nerves were strung tight, waiting, expecting the guards to smash the door into splinters, barrel in here and deck Linen before untying me. Then I would feel stupid for the doubt seeping into the back of my mind, making my mouth taste bitter with fear.

But they had left me. *Left* me.

What had Righty meant by saying he and Lefty were faithful to the one who wears the crown? *Duh.* How else would they have gotten this gig? The crown-wearer? That would be *me*. Yet here I knelt, alone and cold, on a hardwood floor with a parasite gloating down at me and a she-zombie cranking back my neck until vertebrae popped.

The more time that lapsed, the more certain I became they weren't coming back.

Linen would expect me to ask, and so I did. "Do they work for you?"

"Not exactly." His eyes rolled toward the ceiling. "They're on loan."

Yeah, to me. Or so I had believed. "They were assigned to me by the consuls in Faerie."

Concern dripped from his words. "Are you sure?"

"Yes, I—" It hit me. "It wasn't the consuls, was it? Rook arranged for them."

Linen patted my cheek. "He did indeed."

Parting words from my last dream came to me in a lucid snap.

She didn't tell me.

"Rook relied on guards from his brother's household." The household he inherited when I killed Raven, a prince, and the rightful Unseelie heir to the throne of Faerie. "Guards who were loyal to Raven."

She didn't tell me.

The Morrigan.

"No, not Raven." It was bigger than him. "The Morrigan."

What hadn't she told him? Which part? That my guards were deep in her pocket? He must have known. So either he accepted the risk on my behalf, or he was complicit. Had he known about Linen? Or had these machinations all been the Morrigan's doing? And if the crown wasn't mine, then whose was it?

Righty and Lefty—they must have been spying on Mai and me since day one. They were plants, obviously, but I figured they reported to Rook. Not this guy. Their betrayal explained how Linen knew where and when to put in an appearance at the hotel, and how he circumvented our *Thierry-as-bait* plan so easily. The guards had been feeding him intel. Easy enough when you can *poof* from one location to another.

"I understand you were unhappy with your marriage." Linen's mouth curled in an approximation of a smile. "That is no longer an issue. The prince regent will soon be a smudge on the annals of Faerie history. That leaves you free to—" he smoothed a hand down his shirt, "—enjoy the pleasures afforded you."

Hot moisture leaked down my cheek, tears I blamed on Jenna's grip scalping me. Stupid, stupid fae. Rook should have known better than to trust his mother.

"No tears." Linen tutted. "The girl who gets her fondest wish can't unwish it."

I hauled my pendant from my shirt and pressed a thumb to its center. "I summon the Morrigan."

He cocked his head, listening, waiting. "She appears to be otherwise occupied." He wrested the medallion from me and studied it. "The conclave should have known better than to expect one such as her to come to heel when called by the half-bloods and exiles of the fae realm. That was their first mistake. The second was allowing your father to set his pathetic threshold with her standing on this side of it." He dropped the necklace and shook his head. "They gave her this world."

The shock of his implications jolted me. Mac was the one who set the threshold?

"You didn't know." He threw back his head and howled with laughter. "Macsen Sullivan loved this world, its people." He pointed to me. "You're living proof of his fascination with mortals. Maybe it was the hound in him. They are called *man*'s best friend, are they not?" Linen paced across the front of the room. "His inane rules not only applied to Faerie, but to the mortal realm as well. It's his law the conclave adopted, and it was his decision to spill his own blood to create the threshold to Faerie, so that he would know who and what crossed into this world through his tethers.

"But Macsen was so flush with power in those days, so young to his new form and so eager to enact large-scale change that he forgot about the small things. He forgot those who were not fae were not his to command. He forgot those who were sworn to other gods were not his to control with his blood-red ink and paper skins."

Linen's tirade lasted until he ran out of breath. Good thing too. My brain was stuffed and couldn't hold any more revelations.

My father had laid the threshold into Faerie.

My father.

The threshold into Faerie.

All this time I figured Mac had slipped out of Faerie on a lark, that he had been bored and came here to play human. But what if his purpose was greater than that? Instead of taking a vacation from his duties in Faerie, what if this had been part of them? Maintenance on this side of the threshold?

No wonder that particular feat wasn't common knowledge. The power it must have cost…unimaginable. And that was the bottomless well from where my power came. No wonder the conclave wanted me kept close.

I swiveled my eyes to track Linen. "What does the Morrigan want with me?"

He kept quiet for so long my back spasmed from Jenna's death grip on my hair. "The Black Dog's blood mends the fence that keeps the monsters where he feels they belong. That's why he ran. He knew the fae were done with their vows of peace and their subservience to humanity. The fastest way to sever those ties was to break the man responsible for them. Only we can't seem to find him."

My father was many things, but he was not a coward. "He's hunting King Moran's killer."

"He witnessed the beheading." Linen slanted a pitying glance my way. "That is a nonissue."

Liar. Mac wasn't a coward. Take Linen's word for it? I think not. "Then why—?"

"He *ran.*" Linen walked two fingers through the air. "Tail tucked between his legs, he vanished. What in all the realms does the Black Dog covet? What does the man who distances himself from those he might be called upon later to end crave? *Connection.* And who in all of his long life did he experience such an event with? A human woman. From all the fae beauties at his disposal, women and men who would have served him until the end of time, he chose a mortal from this backwater realm to be his first and only lover."

Childish hope sparked in my chest. *First and only...* "You can't expect me to be sorry I exist."

"Believe me." He turned sincere. "No one is sorry for that." He grasped my hand and lifted my wrist to his nose. His eyelids fluttered as he inhaled. "Sullivan's blood runs in your veins. Not as rich as the source material, but we can make do when the time comes. It won't take much. A few liters. It probably won't even kill you." He considered me. "Hmm. Do you know whether you're immortal?"

Before I told him where he could stuff his immortality, he inclined his head, and Jenna clocked me in the temple. It felt like a sledgehammer, but it must have been her fist. While I was dazed, she jerked on my scalp harder until my spine bowed impossibly, then busted my lip with the glass's hard edge as she poured the clear liquid down my throat while I coughed and spluttered. Being the helpful soul he was, Linen pinched my nose until I gasped for air. Jenna drained the dregs down my throat and then released me.

Glacial waters swept through my limbs, reminding me of the time I had fallen off a tower during marshal academy. I had ended up in the med ward, hooked to an IV that *drip, drip, dripped* icy relief into my veins.

Paralysis brushed chill fingers down the length of my body, and the eager magic building in my palm snuffed out and left me unable to move my hand, let alone remove my glove or say my Word.

The last thing I remember was the pity welling in Jenna's eyes as she mouthed *Forgive me.*

CHAPTER TWENTY-ONE

I woke inside the mouth of a frost giant who was suffering five-alarm halitosis. That's how it felt anyway. Damp walls enclosed me. I figured that out when I jerked awake and headbutted the stone wall inches from the end of my nose. Whoever I had to thank for my new digs had stuck me inside of an upright box made from natural stone with walls I estimated to be three feet in width if my reach was any indication. I could stretch my arms overhead without touching a ceiling. I was five ten, so if this container had a lid, it was at least ten feet from the ground. There were holes drilled into the wall that let in fresh air and faint light. Normally, I cast my own light, but my magic was on the fritz. The concoction Jenna had force-fed me was wearing off faster now that I was conscious, but I was drained.

Hungry.

The walls were all that kept me on my feet, but I was sagging.

"Thank God—and anyone else listening—I'm not claustrophobic," I mumbled.

"You're new," a tiny voice said from somewhere to my left.

I strained my ears to pinpoint the source. "Did you hear them bring me in?"

"No." A soft feminine laugh echoed. "But only the fresh ones still believe in gods of any kind."

That…was not reassuring. "Where are we?"

"A cavern, but I don't know where." She paused. "I was taken from New Haven Colony."

I whistled long and soft. "How long have you been here?"

It took her a while to answer. "I don't know."

New Haven Colony sounded like it belonged on the page of a history book. It must have been somewhere in the northeast. Connecticut maybe? If that was true, she had been here a hell of a lot longer than Jenna's ten years. Or was a hell of a lot older than her voice sounded. What had Linen said? I had gone without a drink for sixteen hours? That much travel time could have put us outside the state easy, but a Makara required land and sea, and Florida, being a peninsula, made an ideal location. "I was captured in Florida."

Curiosity spiked her voice. "Do you think that's where we still are?"

"It's possible." I shuffled closer to her voice. "Rock formations like these are unusual for the area, but they exist."

"I was transferred from another collection. I'm not sure where, only that I wasn't there long. Faysal, the fae who captured me, traded me to Balamohan." Her voice quivered. "He has...particular tastes...and Faysal owed him a favor."

Trading fae like baseball cards? That explained how Jenna made it here from Port Arkansas. Linen must have scooped her up too, but why? The Valkyrie angle? Did he have a type? What I wouldn't give for a peek inside the other cells for clues.

Imagine an entire network of caverns with fae like him stocking them.

Shudder.

"I remember the walk to my cell," she confided. "This cavern is enormous."

"If we're in a natural cave—" and it sounded like she would know, "—then I think I know where we are. There's only one air-filled cave system in the state—the Florida Caverns State Park." Mai and I had visited it once on our way to Panama City Beach. "It's in the panhandle, near Marianna." I exhaled on a laugh. "Not that knowing where we are helps much."

"Knowledge is power," she contradicted me. "You imparted more than I ever hoped to learn."

With a lifespan like hers, she must be fae. "Can I ask you something?"

"Why not?" She exhaled on a tired laugh. "We have nothing but time."

I thumped my head against the rock wall behind me and focused on not thinking about how long I had been trapped before regaining consciousness. Had a whole day passed since Linen took me out of Daytona? Two days? More? The darkness gave no hints, and my companion's intel was woefully out of date. "Do you have any idea who Linen—um, I mean, Balamohan—has sworn allegiance to?"

More laughter carried to me, and this time it rang sharp with bitterness. "He forsook his goddess, his purpose. What he once was, he is no more. He is a parasite. He sustains himself with his collection." A moment passed during which I worried she had lapsed into hysteria before she cleared her throat and continued as if her near loss of control never happened. "To answer you, his fealty lies with the Morrigan."

Not good. If she was aware of the relationship between Linen and the Morrigan, it was much older than I first assumed.

"You mentioned a collection." I braced myself. "How many of us are there?"

"Hundreds in this cave," she answered in a small voice. "And all of us kin."

I lifted my head. "Kin?"

"We're all death bringers. That's how he feeds. That's what the Morrigan made of him. She was once the only death-touched goddess, you know. Then others arose and diminished her power, and then children of those gods, made with fae and humans, rose to prominence and weakened her further." She sighed as she said, "She yearns for a time which no longer exists, rife with blood and violence. She clutched what tithes she was given to her chest, but once the Black Dog rose, peace reigned in Faerie, and her magic faded as his word became law and his legend took root in the terrified hearts of the fae folk."

If that was true, all of her sustenance was coming from the mortal realm. From the conclave. From *me*.

"She wants him," she said, "wants all that he has."

"She's jealous of Macsen Sullivan?" The question was tinged with awe.

"Jealousy is a good word," she mused. "It conveys her sense of entitlement."

Centuries of careful planning was coming to a head, and all because of me.

I was the weak link in the unbroken chain spanning my father's very, very long life. The resentment bubbling up in me since I realized my own father would have let me die to save his own hide cooled to a simmer.

Now I understood.

During his life as one of the Huntsman's hounds, Mac had run with his pack through the mortal realm, collecting fae souls on All Hallows' Eve. His ties to both realms were solid. Even as a hound, he had held authority here. It made sense his blood could ward this realm from Faerie. Tethers, I had assumed, were natural anchors that conclave outposts sprung up around, but what if I had it backward?

In my father's house, I had walked down a hall filled with doors, and each door opened—not to another room—but to another place. Tethers operated on the same idea, but on a larger scale. What if Mac was responsible for stabilizing those too? It would explain how he could monitor the number of fae traveling to this realm at any given time. Though once they were here, they became the conclave's problem.

One thing I knew for sure. If any fae who wanted to cross into the mortal realm could, humanity would be wiped out in a blink. I had to warn the conclave. Together we could make a stand. I just had to escape my cell in one piece and sidestep the Morrigan's plans to use me as her backup sacrificial lamb first.

"What is your name?"

The timid voice snapped me from my thoughts, and I answered, "Thierry."

"Thierry." She pronounced it *Tee-a-ree* instead of *Tee-air-ree* like I did. "I'm Branwen." Small, shuffling noises announced her movements. "We should rest now, before the feeding begins. Balamohan only ever visits when he's hungry."

A flash of Jenna and that dot on her temple flickered through my mind, and I shuddered.

Sleep wasn't happening.

"Thierry?"

I leaned my head against the rock beside me, placing my ear closest to her voice, the only comfort to be had in this cold, hard place. "Yes?"

"I hate that you're here—" a yawn interrupted her, "—but I'm glad that you are."

"We're going to get out of here." My voice wavered.

"No," she said sadly. "We won't. You'll lose your wits faster if you believe that."

Far be it from me to judge her coping mechanism, but acceptance wasn't my style.

"Rest," I urged. "You sound like you need it. We'll talk later."

A low hum was her answer, leaving me alone to chew over the problem of our escape.

The guards' defection stung my pride. My first line of defense was on the fritz, and my second had gone dark side on me. The three of us hadn't been friends, but we had been friend*ly*. There at the end, I had trusted them.

Shaw was my third and best hope of ever seeing the light of day again. I could summon Diode, but that was risky. If he appeared in my cell, he would crush me. Not to mention he couldn't teleport. Summoning magic didn't work that way. All I would accomplish by calling him would be to trap him in the cell with me.

That put me right back to option number three. Shaw. Magic was, of course, my primary defense, but my palm wasn't sparking. Either the cells were spelled or the drink was spiked, so no help there.

After a while, my thoughts lagged, and closing my eyes seemed like a good way to help me think.

Thanks to the tender spots dappling my thighs, I knew I had been a prisoner for several days. I woke Branwen screaming the first time a frigid needle pierced my skin and pumped me full of stinging fluids. Now I just winced and endured.

The substance Jenna had force fed me in Linen's study? Turned out it was some nutrient cocktail injected into the prisoners daily at chow time.

The combination of boredom, hunger and fear conspired against me. Exhaustion was winning. I hadn't felt any pangs until I began to wonder why I wasn't feeling them. Now that gnawing pain—and my upcoming injection—was all I could think about. Branwen's light snores meant I was alone in my misery.

When a deep throat cleared next to my ear, I shot upright with a shout.

"Marshal Thackeray," a disdainful voice ricocheted off the walls. "You are a difficult woman to pin down."

"Are you serious?" I asked no one in particular. "This faux-British accent is the best my imagination can come up with? If I'm going to hallucinate, can't it be in style? Doesn't Tom Hiddleston do voice work?"

"I am *not* imaginary."

Unimpressed, I fought back using the power of logic. "That's exactly what an imaginary man would say. I'm a big girl. Let me have it. Tell me the truth."

"I am as real as you are."

I flicked my fingers at him. "I'm not up for philosophical debate here. Constructs of my mind would of course *seem* real to me—"

"Gods be praised, the woman has lost her marbles," he mumbled.

"Pretty sure I never had any. Choking hazard, you know."

He remained quiet for several blissful moments until clearing his throat.

"I have a matter to discuss with you."

"No. I'm done talking to myself. I don't want my next-door neighbor to think I'm nuts." I waved at nothing. "Buh-bye."

"But—"

"No," I snarled. "Sanity's all I've got going for me right now, and you're kind of wrecking that for me. Beat it."

"Rudeness is uncalled for." A heavy pause. "Considering the circumstances, you are forgiven."

"Thanks." I would have curtsied if I had room. "For a second there, I was worried."

Worried I was talking to someone who wasn't there.

"Your sarcasm endears you to no one," he said.

I don't know. Shaw seemed to like it. "Why do you sound familiar?"

"We have spoken many times over the phone."

Of course we had. Stress had finally cracked me. "You're the stalker." Of all people, why imagine him? My brain wasn't doing me any favors by visualizing me tying up loose ends. I was not going to die, damn it. "Now that you've found me, what do you want?"

"You arrested my son, Herbert Slosson."

"Herbert, really?" I thumped my forehead on the wall. "That's the best you can come up with?"

"Perhaps this is not the best time— No. It must be done." The voice continued, "I am Nasir, last anointed son of the Warith djinns. You restored my lamp to me, and I owe you recompense. Choose your boon wisely. Once spoken, your wish cannot be retracted nor expanded upon. It is said and will be done." He made an impatient sound. "Fairness urges me to wait, but I cannot. I have little power left, and if I do not use the magic my son poured into the lamp to grant your wish, it will not manifest. We must hurry."

I nodded like everything my imaginary friend had to say made total sense.

Three wishes. I had wanted those once. Even one wish could solve any number of my multitude of problems. I could sever the tie between me and Shaw, ensuring he would survive after I left for...

Crap. Adrenaline drenched me as my mind filled in the blanks the drugs had left empty.

I had been trapped here for days. Shaw got shaky if he held out for more than four days between feedings. He could go a week, maybe more, but once he got ahold of me, he would drain me dry. All this time, I hadn't let the enormity of my incarceration faze me. Shaw was still out there. He wouldn't stop until he found me.

Faced with a ravenous incubus, I might be safer inside the stone prison.

"Marshal?"

I touched my tongue to my chapped lips. "I'm thinking."

One wish. I could go traditional and wish for gold so Mom never had to worry about bills again, but weighed against the life-and-death scenarios playing out around me, I couldn't afford to be that selfish. I touched the wall separating me from Branwen. It was tempting to release her. She deserved it. But after centuries of confinement, even as a fae, I worried her muscles had atrophied. She may not be able to walk, and I wasn't sure if wishing she was free *and* healed counted as two wishes or as a clarification of the first.

The same logic that made me ache to save her damned her in the end.

She endured. She would survive long after I was gone. And where there was life, there was hope.

A final option came to mind, and it felt right.

"Look," I said to the djinn I wasn't convinced wasn't imaginary. "There's a woman. I want you to find her and take her out of here. Her name is Jenna Shaw." I bit my lip. "If you can heal her, do it. If you can't…she would have died here anyway. At least this way her family gets a body to bury."

"As you have said," Nasir intoned, "so shall it be done."

No flash of light. No goodbye. No token to prove the deed was done.

Nasir, the possibly real djinn, was simply gone.

CHAPTER TWENTY-TWO

A hot sting in my gut roused me. I was kneeling, sort of, with my kneecaps braced on the wall in front of me and my feet wedged against the wall behind me. My forehead rested on stone, and the sliver of light my cell was allotted had gone dark. Someone was out there. I balled my fists and hammered against the rock.

"Hey," I yelled. "Who's out there?"

A heartbeat later the same intense prick of agony rippled through my stomach, and I dry heaved until my throat was raw. My arms weighed too much at first, but I strained until I got one raised. My fingers grazed a warm, slick cord. I tugged on it and felt a corresponding pull deep in my abdomen. I took a breath and yanked harder. One last jerk ripped the string free, smashing my hand into the wall and skinning my knuckles. The throbbing in my hand kept me from inhaling as if that would stop the misery. Finally, I had to gulp air or pass out, and that gave me the courage to test my healing wound.

The skin was knitting shut and the blood was drying, but a coin-shaped scab had formed. Clearing my throat, I said Branwen's name.

"You get used to it after a while," she said in a hollowed voice.

Apparently, I had experienced my first feeding. *Please God let it be my last one too.*

"I don't want to get used to it." My arms wrapped protectively around my stomach.

"Balamohan favors the tender parts." Her voice wavered. "The ones that hurt us the most."

I cringed. "He collects personally?"

"He has no choice. Feedings are rare, because he's seldom here for any length of time. I suspect he sips from each of us to keep us alive longer. He devours the accumulation since his last visit, which rejuvenates us." She made a thoughtful sound. "I can hear the screams sometimes. I know there are others nearby, but I have never had a confidante to speak to about such things. The cells beside me remained empty until the day he brought you."

That was curious. "I wonder why he placed us together."

"Would you hate me if I suggested it was a reward for my good behavior?"

I laughed. "None of this is your fault. If I had to be stuck here, at least I have good company."

A bright note entered her voice. "I feel the same."

Though ignorance can be bliss, I had to ask. I wanted to have accurate nightmares I guess.

"You never said…" I turned my head toward her voice. "What is Balamohan taking from us?"

"The accumulation of life." Her voice wobbled. "He consumes that which marks the passage of time until we are held suspended in an eternity of pendulous moments. We do not age while he feeds from us, and his life is extended by the consumption of ours."

I rubbed my forehead. "How is that possible?"

"You are one age today. You will be a day older tomorrow. Balamohan may not visit again for a month or for a year, but when he does, he will drink from you, dissolving the time that passed until you are again the age you are now, the age he prefers." She let me absorb that. "He is particular in his captures. He catalogs us before shelving us, and he means to keep his collection pristine."

I slumped in my cell. "That's why you're still alive."

Not her fae lifespan, as I had assumed, but the inability to age. Ironic that Linen collected death-touched fae not to kill them, but to keep them alive.

"None of us will die. Not until he lets us."

Being immortal was one thing. Being mortal and having the right to die stolen from you was another situation entirely.

But the essence of life as a food source?

The Morrigan's tithes were paid in corpses. Empty husks were all I left her, but then again, I was unique. Besides Shaw, I couldn't name another marshal who fed on souls, let alone consumed them the way I did. Either way I was handing the Morrigan an empty can and asking her to drink. She did, which meant she got something from it, but what? Did she feed off the same thing as Balamohan? Did that mean the essence of life was an element separate from the soul entirely?

I wasn't sure.

When magical beings such as fae died, was a type of retroactive magic triggered to release at the end? Was all the magic inherent in a person distilled and then trapped inside an empty husk until it dissipated or was consumed? Did it exist in the tissues of the deceased? Was that why she consumed the bodies of her tithes?

Instead of snacking on victims with an eye toward maintaining balance like Linen, was she gulping down entire helpings of the stuff? Did she require more to keep her immortality intact?

I wasn't sure of that either.

"You were talking in your sleep earlier." Branwen sounded amused. "Your voice woke me."

Fragments of my talk with Nasir came to mind. "What did I say?"

"You mentioned having a body to bury. That was all I heard." She sounded apologetic. "I didn't mean to eavesdrop."

A shiver rippled through me, and I covered my stomach. "I was having a weird dream."

"I don't dream," she confided. "What was yours about? If it's not too personal to ask."

Personal had flown out the nonexistent window days ago. "I dreamed a djinn offered to grant me one wish."

"What did you ask for?" A dreamy quality filled her next word. "Freedom?"

"Sort of." I thought about Jenna and told Branwen a white lie. "I wished for home."

Thierry. Thierry. Thierry.

My name swirled through my ears. I kept my eyes closed and called out, "Branwen?"

The chanting quieted.

An ear-splitting roar took its place.

The razor edge of fear sent my heart fluttering into overdrive. "Branwen? What's happening?"

"I don't know," she screamed. "The walls. He's tearing them down."

Slowly, I leveraged myself onto my feet and set my palms against the stone. My limbs trembled, and my head bobbled. I took Branwen's word on the walls. Muzzy as my head was, they felt like stacked Jell-O cubes to me.

I strained for a glimpse through one of the cylindrical feeding holes. "Who's out there?"

"I don't know." Her voice cracked. "He keeps screaming your name."

Shaw.

He wasn't yelling now. I slumped against the rock and prayed I was right.

My heart pumped. My breaths labored. My ears rang. All those things I heard, but not a peep from outside.

My knees wobbled, and I collapsed in a heap. "Are you sure? Did he say who he was—?"

The ground trembled beneath me. Bits of rock and dust peppered the top of my head.

A ferocious cry penetrated the stone wall. *"Thierry."*

"Shaw?" I called as loud as I could. My voice broke, so I tried it again. "Shaw? Is that you?"

Rock shuddered, and the holes punched into the front of my cell went dark.

"What is that thing?" Branwen's breaths came harder now.

"That's my..." I couldn't find the right word. "It's Shaw."

A pause. "Is he safe?"

I told her the absolute truth. "I don't know."

More rock crumbled, and she squealed, "Is he some type of enraged troll?"

"Worse." Trolls were stupid. "He's an incubus, and he's starving."

"He's your *mate*?" Her voice shot up several octaves, so high the word *mate* was a screech.

"I— No." I flattened myself against the rear wall. "It's not like that."

Incubi didn't mate. And certainly not to me.

Then again, what did I know? Shaw's brother had been married. What did that make his wife if not his mate?

"Thierry," Branwen said in a voice sterner than any I had heard her use. "There is only one reason why an incubus starves himself."

The thundering in my chest intensified until my heart felt bruised. Hope shouldn't hurt so much.

"Are you all right?" A rising note of panic spiked her tone. "I didn't mean to upset you."

"You didn't," I lied. "I'm fine."

A sniffle from her cell had my hand rising to touch the rock between us.

Lock it down, Thierry. Do your job. Help Shaw. Keep Branwen talking, keep her calm. Hell, maybe talking would keep *me* calm.

I kept my tone light. "How do you know about incubi?"

"When you live as long as I have, you try everything once." Her voice wavered. "I shared a bed with an incubus for six months, and every visit he warned me against his cousin. His cousin lived out in the barn with their livestock, and I was never to go there."

"Okay." Curious despite our situation, I urged her on. "What happened?"

"One night my lover stayed out late, and boredom got the best of me." She cleared her throat. "I sneaked out to the barn and saw him, the cousin. He was a rabid thing. He tried to snap my neck, but I hid in a mare's stall. My scream brought my lover running. He had been at the house looking for me." Her voice gained strength. "He showed me a chain around his cousin's ankle. When I asked what had turned him mad, he said it was love."

Pulled from her story, I frowned. "I don't follow."

"Incubi unions are taboo. They are forbidden within incubi society. If one loses his mate, he will starve himself to death rather than feed from another. Incubi who bond are shunned by their families. When their mates die, most are killed as a mercy." Branwen yelped in surprise when heavier rubble pattered us. "Be careful, Thierry. Please."

No, no, no. Branwen had lost her ever-loving mind.

Shaw was off his rocker because he was starving. Hunger. That was it. My magic had cauterized his mojo. That's why we were stuck together. Not some mystical, fated mumbo jumbo. Wonky magic was at fault. Even if— Not possible. He cheated on me. Soul mates didn't screw around with harpies.

"Thierry." That was Shaw again.

"You're going to frighten her," a muffled voice warned.

He raged at it. "Get out of my way."

"Not until you call your hunger under control."

I covered my mouth to hold back the sobs. *Diode.* He had come too.

"I am in control."

"Calm down, or I will put you down," the prim cat stated.

A full five minutes passed. The wall must have thinned, because now I heard ragged breathing.

"I'm okay," I yelled. "Shaw—*Jackson.* I'm all right."

"Thank the gods," Diode breathed.

Shaw didn't say a word, but the wall separating us quaked. Minutes ticked past. Noises grew sharper. Sounds like fingernails on a chalkboard had me slapping hands over my ears and humming. At some point, I had crushed my eyes shut. A block of rock bounced off my hip at the same time as a burst of glorious light blasted me in the face. *Too bright.* I couldn't open my eyes to see my rescuers.

But then, I didn't have to. I was scooped up and carried into the cavern's fresher air.

Shaw's voice was unrecognizable when he grated out my name.

"Stop sniffing her," another familiar voice snapped. "Get your ass in gear, Shaw."

My eyes still weren't working, but I turned my head toward the sound. "Mai?"

"Everything will be okay, Tee." She touched my face. To Shaw she growled, "Keep those hands where I can see them.

Get moving. Back down the tunnel. Now. Just like we planned. Go, man, *go*."

"No." My arm flailed behind me. "Branwen—"

"We brought reinforcements," Mai soothed. "We're not leaving anyone behind."

Shaw jerked forward with a snarl, and I got the feeling Mai had popped him hard on the ass. His hold on me tightened before he grunted and air whistled past my ears. He absorbed the impact of our landing from a jump that had my stomach hovering over my head, then he hit the ground running.

I bit my lip to keep from crying out as his frantic sprint jostled me.

He stumbled, shoulder bouncing off the cavern wall. I clutched his shirt while he recovered.

"Damn fox," he muttered under his breath.

I was betting Mai had shot between his legs in fox form. It was the only way she could keep up with him. A gentle ripple of magic brushed against my senses. It was familiar enough that I recognized it as Mai shifting to her human form.

"Set her down," Mai ordered. Shaw knelt before settling onto the ground with me on his lap. Mai took my hand, placed it on something warm and slick and held it there. "Feed, Tee."

I recoiled from the word and protectively clutched my belly, twisting on my side to dry heave. I tumbled from Shaw's lap onto the cold parquet floor. I reached out, and warm fur ran through my fingers.

A sandpaper tongue swiped my cheek. "Justice is yours to serve."

"My magic..." I feebly held on to Diode to orient myself. "I can't feel it."

"Killing me...won't save her," a soft voice wheezed.

Sheer panic popped my eyes open, and I winced against the light, but not before I saw him. *Linen.* His trademark linen suit hung in tatters. His torso and head were shredded. The methodology told me his attackers had toyed with him, bleeding him, inflicting small pains, probably working him over before he cracked like an egg and directed them to my cell.

My guys weren't good with restraint. And both of them had left their distinct marks on him. The bone-deep, long swipes of Shaw's claws were particularly evident against Diode's more precise cuts.

Shaw had carried me into the study where Jenna served me for the first and last time.

Mai's fresh scent washed over me as she shoved the cat aside. "You need to do this."

I touched my face and joked. "Do I look that bad?"

No one laughed.

"Leave us," Shaw barked. *"Go."*

"Can you control yourself?" Diode prowled closer to Shaw.

"For a little longer," he gritted out from between his teeth.

"Are you insane?" Mai's fists clenched. "He could kill her when he's like this."

"I don't want you to watch." I turned my face into my shoulder. "Please."

"Okay. It's okay." She touched my arm. "We'll do it your way."

Trembles spread from her hand into me. For her nerves to be this shot, Shaw must have incubused-out.

Without looking, I knew his bronze skin would be snow white. His eyes would swirl opaque and fierce. His claws would be unsheathed. I imagined his blunt fangs, which I had glimpsed only one time, capped the snarl I heard in his voice.

"Hurt her and I'll wall your ass up and leave you here," she growled. "Do you understand me?"

My head snapped up in time to witness a curt nod that appeared to test the limits of his restraint.

A shadow fell across my shoulder. Company was standing in the doorway, awaiting orders.

Diode collected Mai with a hip bump, and they left. I called after them, "Check on Branwen."

"It was…a mistake…" Linen panted, "…placing the crown jewels of my collection…together."

Shaw's punch landed so quickly all I saw was Linen's head snap back on impact.

"Shut. Up," Shaw enunciated crisply.

Unable to get onto my knees, I scooted toward Linen using my hands and the thigh my weight rested on. He was too broken to flee when I palmed his bare shoulder with my right hand, and there was no remorse in his eyes when his gaze drifted up to meet mine.

"By the power vested in me as a marshal of the Southwestern Conclave, I condemn you to death for your crimes." My nails pierced his skin when he tried shrugging me off him. "Your soul will now be extinguished and your remains walled up and left to gather dust inside the prison you created."

A whispered Word released my glove from my left hand. No light rushed to illuminate my runes, and no heat warmed my palm. My magic hovered out of reach.

Linen's laughter at my impotence made things worse. I was hungry. So hungry. The adrenaline dump from being rescued had kicked my body into high gear, but power that usually leapt into my fingertips fizzled out before I could harness its spurting energy.

"I can't," I admitted to Shaw.

He sat on his haunches, leaving inches between us. "You have to."

"I don't feel the magic." And though I used to pray it would vanish, I was desperate for it now.

"You're close." He sounded oddly calm. "Your magic is fuel, and your tank is almost empty."

Close. No further explanation needed. He meant that I— *we*—were dying.

"I could help her…with that." Linen choked on his ragged laughter.

His head snapped back again, and this time his smartass reply didn't materialize.

Shaw had broken his jaw.

What it said about me that violence stirred my appetite I was afraid to know.

The scent of blood, Shaw's nearness and the relentless hunger managed a spark on my palm. A grateful tear spilled down my cheek when I reached for the magic and it leapt into my hand, eager and ready, clawing its way higher up my arm.

The stink of burning flesh made my stomach tighten as new runes joined the old. My magic was growing, runes up to my elbow, consuming more real estate on my body.

The jolt of energy made my fingertips smoke, and then instinct kicked in.

I grasped Linen's bare wrist with my left hand.

Raw, desperate power blasted out of me and electrified him. The dark, rich pocket of energy I sensed in him sickened me, because I knew where it came from and who had given it to him. But my magic only worked one way, and either I consumed it all or it went to waste.

My body quivered as streaming ribbons of green power ripped him apart from the inside out.

It was as if I had flung out a lasso, and the steer I roped was putting up the fight of its life. I knew it was going down. It was running on instinct, but so was I, and mine were honed sharper by deprivation. I yanked on that magical thread until Linen's soul tore free, smashing into me like a cinderblock to the chest. I slumped forward, gasping to fill my empty lungs.

The surge blazed over his skin. It crisped the topmost layers, which sloughed off onto the floor where Shaw ground them to dust under his boot. Only the meat and bones remained in a gnarled, charred heap.

My left hand lifted to my throat from habit, but the days of summoning the Morrigan were over. I fisted the pendant and would have ripped it off my neck, but I had to retrieve my skins from storage first. As much as I hated to, I forced my hand lower. I could stand to wear her mark a bit longer.

"How do you feel?" At some point Shaw had moved a safe distance away. Skin washed out, eyes white, but hanging on to his control.

I took my time answering. "I feel—" My teeth clamped down on my tongue, and my eyes rolled back in my head. Muscles locked up, and my head smashed against the floor when I jerked backward. Tremors kept me writhing and moaning.

My eyes had been bigger than my stomach.

"Too much," I slurred.

"Shh." Shaw's knees dug into my side. "This might hurt."

It didn't.

Once his left hand clasped mine and my runes brushed his skin, I felt nothing at all.

CHAPTER TWENTY-THREE

A familiar sight greeted me when I wiped away the sleep matting my eyes shut. "Hey."

Shaw, who must have been staring at me since our eyes met when mine opened, simply nodded. He occupied a worn pleather recliner positioned at the foot of my hospital bed. His shirt was clean, if rumpled. Hair twisted in clumps all over his head. Several of his reddish-brown curls stood straight.

I continued my assessment, knowing he was conducting a similar examination of me.

His tan skin held a healthy glow. Bright copper eyes, a sign he was in control, hadn't blinked. The tension radiating from him sent my pulse sprinting, and my monitor beeped. Noticing it, Shaw dialed back his intensity, and I found I was able to breathe again. Too bad I smelled bleach instead of him.

Swallowing took effort. My throat was dry, my lips cracked. "Branwen?"

"She's fine." He pushed from his chair and headed to a rolling tray positioned next to my bed. Déjà vu washed over me, bringing with it memories of the first time he had played nurse for me. That seemed like a lifetime ago. And yet, here we were again. "She's a guest of the conclave for the time being."

Guest, huh? "What about the others?"

He poured chilled water over a cup of ice chips and stuck in a bendy straw before holding it out to me. "Two hundred were evacuated. Linen's records show more, but we aren't sure if they're…" His lips pressed shut. "We haven't found them yet, but we will. We rounded up a dozen lesser fae in Linen's employ. Several are directing the rescue crews in exchange for not being executed for their crimes."

The first sip of water was bliss. I took another. "I take it someone else negotiated for their cooperation?"

He lifted his shoulders. "I was removed after killing four of Balamohan's guards at the tunnel entrance."

As the weight of his admission settled around me, I noticed a wide-mouth vase filled with red and yellow tulips sat in the window across the room. I nodded toward them. "Mable?"

Shaw arched an eyebrow. "Who else?"

I screwed up my courage and squinted at him. "How much does Mom know?"

"Not enough." His jaw flexed. "I'm giving you the opportunity to call her yourself. Twenty-four hours. Then I'm picking up the phone if you haven't. She deserves to know her only child is all right."

Guilt pricked at my conscience. He was right. She deserved a phone call. I just needed time to absorb everything that had happened to me before I decided what to tell her.

I scratched my name into the Styrofoam cup with my thumbnail. "Daire and Odhran?"

"I haven't seen them since the night you disappeared." Shaw busied his hands mopping dribbled condensation from the tray. "Can you tell me what happened?"

Reliving their betrayal stung almost as much the second time around.

"Rook borrowed them from the Morrigan. If I had known that…" But I hadn't, and I hadn't even asked where their loyalties lie. I had naively assumed they were with me. "Something changed while we were at the hotel. They got antsy. They tried to stop me from going to Orlando, but they caved in the end. Maybe they were waiting on a signal that hadn't come yet? The fact they transported Diode to Orlando proves they had the ability to jump another person long distances with them. Maybe that's why they figured it didn't matter if I went inland. They had the means to zap me to Balamohan's doorstep at any time."

His expression darkened. "I owed them the benefit of the doubt, but it never sat right with me that they had access to portal magic for casual teleportation. The invisibility gift alone was questionable. I should have pushed harder for restrictions on their powers, but orders handed down from Faerie…"

"No one questioned them." Even with a portal charm hung around my neck, I had trusted them. "We all made the mistake of taking a gift from Faerie at face value."

"It won't happen again." Voice low, I think he meant it as a reminder to himself.

To jerk him out of the blame game, I asked, "How did you find me?"

The intensity of his expression made me think I had yanked a smidge too hard.

"That's the crazy thing." He shook his head. "Jenna, the Jenna no one has seen or heard from in a decade, called me and told me where you were."

"Where is she?" I choked mid-sip. "Is she okay?"

"I haven't seen her, but my brother says she's in rough shape." Shaw stood there, hip even with my pillow, staring down at me. "He found her curled up asleep in their bed. He woke her up, and the first thing she asked for was a phone to call me. She told me what happened to her and demanded I alert the conclave. I asked if she had seen anyone matching your description. She said yes. The rest is history." He bent down to get on eye level with me. "So, this is what I'm wondering. Why Jenna? Why now? How is it she escaped?"

I shrank into my pillows. "You're looking at me like I'm responsible."

"Only three people knew I was looking for her, and you're one of them. My brother and I are the other two." His lips compressed. "You fell off the face of the earth and then she magically resurfaced."

I ran my thumbnail down the scrunched-up neck of the straw. "I thought it was a dream."

"What you went through—" he began.

"No." I cut him off. "I mean, I wished for her freedom."

He blinked. "You what?"

"My stalker? I had this dream where he was Herbert Slosson's father." I laughed. "He offered me one wish to use up the magic his son had stored in the lamp and to square what he perceived as a mystical debt."

Shaw braced his forearms on the safety rail and rested his forehead on top of them. "That would explain a lot." I ruffled his hair with my right hand, and he exhaled. "You could have saved yourself. You had the opportunity to wish yourself home, and you didn't. Why Jenna? Why would you do it?"

"It was the right thing to do. She wouldn't have lasted much longer." I raked my fingers through his curls then brushed his temple on my way to cup his chin and lift his face. "I could afford to make that choice because I knew you would come. I just had to hold on long enough for you to get there."

He turned his face into my hand and kissed my wrist. "I don't deserve that kind of faith."

"Everything that's happened between us..." All the pain and the lies were tempered by the good times. There for a while we had been one hell of a team. "You wouldn't let me down. Not when it mattered."

A hard expression settled onto his face. "I hurt you."

"We've hurt each other." It was the truth. "Maybe that's what it took to get here, to be friends."

He lowered his voice. "I don't want your friendship, Thierry."

"Shaw." My hand lowered to the rail and held on tight. "Don't say something we'll regret."

"The stupid cat was right," he muttered.

"Diode?" I frowned. "What does he have to do with this?"

An odd peace settled over his features. "I never cheated on you."

I snorted. "Um, yes, you did. I caught you. Naked. In bed. With five harpies."

"I was naked with them, but we didn't have sex."

I covered my face with my free hand. "I don't want to do this right now."

He touched my cheek. "Why did we end things?"

"Five harpies," I growled. *"Five."*

"It was over before then, and you know it."

I dropped my hand and glared at him. "We had sex, I fried you and you quit on me."

Maybe later, if I worked up the nerve to be honest with myself, I could admit he was right. He hadn't been all in. Not like me. I had known it was over, that it never really started, but I had a nasty habit of holding on the tightest to dreams I wished would come true the most.

"Something happened that night." He drew in a shaky breath. "It terrified me."

"You could have been killed," I said softly. "It would terrify anyone."

"No." He shook his head. "It was my fault. *I* initiated the circuit. That's why it's one-sided."

"What are you talking about?" I studied him. "Like a simultaneous feeding or something?"

He straightened and anchored his hands on his hips, head tilted back, staring at the ceiling. "You aren't getting it. Maybe you don't want to. Think about that night. Knowing what you do now, think about the harpies. You didn't know about my condition until I came back, but think about it, Thierry."

"Sex with me fried you. You freaked out and went hunting. We broke up and then you left." *Oh crap.* "Except...if I fried you...then you couldn't have fed." Shaw having sex to stay in control, that I could believe. Might even forgive. Shaw having sex for the sake of having sex didn't ring true. He would have known I might work past physical betrayal, but not an emotional affair. I rubbed my forehead. "But I saw you."

"They charge by the hour," he said. "They didn't care what I wanted as long as they got paid."

I flashed the IV piercing my hand at him. "Maybe it's the drugs, but this sounds insane."

He gripped the rail on either side of my hand. "You once accused me of being certain our relationship would fail."

"I remember." *Spectacularly* had been his response. "You also warned me you didn't date."

"You ignored the warnings."

"I wanted you."

"No." His knuckles whitened. "Plenty of women have wanted me for what I am, and none of their faces haunted me like yours." Metal groaned under his fingers. "I saw what my brother had with Jenna, and I knew what it cost him. He gave up his home, his family, everything to be with her. When Jenna disappeared, he lost it. If he hadn't had those kids…"

"I'm sorry." I said it even knowing *sorry* was a drop in a bucket of regret. "How did he…?"

"Feed?" The edge in his voice told me he knew mine wasn't idle curiosity. I was searching for a way to save him, and he was well aware of it. "After our father disowned him, Ian and Jenna relocated to this isolated town populated by incubi and their compeers. After Jenna vanished, the townsfolk initiated the protocols Ian and Jenna had agreed to. They saved him, if you want to call it that."

"Compeer?" That was a new one.

"It's what incubi call their mates," he admitted with a grim twist of his lips. "Groups like the one Ian joined cater to incubi who have mated humans for the most part. Humans are frail, and they only get more fragile with age. Jenna was born null. Too many generations between her and magic for any gift to manifest. She's basically human."

"Those few drops of fae blood might have been the tipping point in keeping her alive during her incarceration." I had my doubts whether a full-blooded human could have survived.

"It makes no sense why Balamohan would have taken her, except that her weak fae blood made her easier for him to control. I think she might have been his touchstone."

That was a new term for me too. "What does that mean?"

"Some fae, especially the older ones, take a human each decade as a kind of tutor. Usually, they release the touchstone after their ten years of servitude have passed. The practice is barbaric and non-consensual. It's also difficult—if not impossible—to prevent. We just don't monitor humans that way." He paused to scrub a hand down his face. "Jenna didn't have a cell like yours. Balamohan kept her like a pet, chained in his office except when he sent her out for supplies, which supports the idea she was his current touchstone. Maybe the Morrigan knew he honored the practice and ordered him to stop abducting humans at the risk of exposing her. His workaround might have been to take a touchstone with a few drops of fae blood, who also fit the Morrigan's profile as a woman with death-touched fae in her family tree."

"It makes sense." I tilted my head. "What about those protocols you mentioned? The ones Jenna and Ian agreed to?"

He shifted his feet, and the pained expression on his face said he had hoped I wouldn't ask. He ought to know better by now.

"The group discovered a means of keeping incubi alive after the inevitable passing of a mate." He dragged his gaze to mine. "From what they explained to me when I went to help with Ian, groups like theirs offer one of two options to their members. You join and sign a waiver of your rights, allowing them to save you against your will, at any cost. Or you sign the equivalent of a DNR, and they step aside and let you end your life however you choose."

I felt like an idiot for blurting, "That's where you went."

"I didn't have a choice." His half smile encouraged me. "Not if I wanted to survive. The treatments worked for several months, but I was sick all the time and couldn't live that way any longer."

I set down my cup before it slid from my hand. "Except you did have another choice."

"I did," he admitted. "But you wouldn't have. You would have been chained to me for life."

"We could have made it work." A sharp edge crept into my voice.

"You would have made it work even if you didn't want it to, because you're stubborn, you don't take no for an answer, and you can't let someone you love hurt when you can help them." He rubbed a finger across his brow like that might help jumpstart his brain. "I fell so hard for you, I couldn't slam on the brakes fast enough to save myself. I couldn't chain you to me when you were so young or when I was…"

"My first love."

"Yes. That." His grizzled tone raised hair on my arms. "You crawled inside my head and scrambled everything my father taught me about why loving one woman is unnatural." Shaw looked up then. "Compeer is an insult. It's a term incubi use for women addicted to the lure. It's the same as a human calling a man's wife his whore."

My teeth clicked together. "It sounds like your brother was smart to get out when he did."

"He was," Shaw agreed without hesitation. "Can you understand why I didn't want that?"

"Losing family is the worst thing I can imagine." Mom was all I had. Losing her would kill me. If being together meant Shaw had to choose me over his family, I wouldn't have picked me either. "I get it. Really. Your family is more important to you."

"Thierry, it had nothing to do with me. Or them. I severed ties with my family after they exiled Ian." Exasperation spiked his voice. "I didn't want that for *you*."

"You're serious." I felt my eyes stretch wider. "You orchestrated our breakup…for me?"

Man logic for the win.

"We aren't fated mates." His thumb stroked the edge of my palm. "We're as *un*fated as it gets."

"Free will is a beautiful thing." No divine hand moving pawns on a chessboard for us. "This doesn't make you the smartest incubus in the realm, but I guess it really does make you mine."

His shocked expression was comical. "You're okay with this."

"Okay is a stretch." A single conversation wouldn't banish my stockpile of bruised feelings and insecurities. Not to mention I had one husband already, and I was *not* interested in starting my own Linen-style collection. What I could do was promise Shaw I would try. "*Okay* is what happens once the IV line stops pumping me full of happy juice, and I can sit on my own couch, inside of my own apartment, and digest all this."

"I'll get Mai." He still looked dazed. "She'll want to know you're awake."

He lifted my hand and brushed his lips across my knuckles before pulling away.

"Hey," I called once he reached the door. "I wouldn't mind if you sat on that couch beside me."

The tender smile he flashed me set my heart somersaulting. "I'll bring the ginger beer."

Two days later Dr. Row unhooked me from the IV pole and signed off on my discharge papers. Mai had offered to drive me from the medical ward to the marshal's office, but I used puppy eyes on the doctor to get her to support my request to walk. Five blocks would work out the kinks in my legs and back, and the fresh air would flush out the antiseptic stinging my nose and the back of my throat.

It would also avoid the whole life-flashing-before-my-eyes thing Mai's driving induced.

Mai passed me a bottle of water. "Tell me this isn't about my driving."

I tossed it in the air and caught it, flipping it end over end. "This isn't about your driving."

Her eyes narrowed. "I'm going to choose to believe you're being sincere and not sarcastic."

I nodded sagely. "You have chosen wisely."

She thumped my ear. "Have you heard from Shaw?"

"Nope." I fumbled the bottle. "Not since the day he dumped the whole *I lied about lying* thing in my lap."

"You believe him." It wasn't a question.

"I do." I huffed out an exhale. "I was so pissed off when he got back, and then Faerie happened. I feel like an idiot for not putting it together sooner. I should have seen the gaping holes in his story."

"Yeah, well, don't beat yourself up over it." She hip bumped me. "I didn't catch on either."

"You were too busy leading the villagers' pitchfork brigade."

"No pitchforks were involved." She spread her hands. "I'm more of a trial-by-flame-thrower kind of girl."

I rolled my eyes and kept walking.

Her voice carried to me. "Shaw knew you had doubts or his plan wouldn't have worked."

My head swung toward her. "Whose side are you on?"

"Yours." She raised both her hands. "He should have told you the truth."

"He hired hookers, Mai." I shook my head. "Who does that?"

With a put-upon sigh, Mai caught up to me and pulled on her serious face. "As much as I hate to be the one waving the *Team Shaw* flag again, I have to say this. I might need to gargle after, but you need to hear it from someone who loves you and has better fashion sense." Her face scrunched like it caused her physical pain to endorse Shaw. "He did you a favor by leaving. You got to learn your job and have a life outside of him, and you're a stronger woman for it. You survived without him. You controlled your powers without him, and you earned a place with the marshals without standing in his shadow, Tee."

"Dial it down, Mai." I flushed beneath her praise. "I put one foot in front of the other, that's it."

"That's it exactly." Her dark eyes searched my face. "I know what he did for you in the caves. It wasn't the first time either, was it? He expected it to happen. I see that now. There I was, urging you to suck Linen dry because I thought you healed faster the more you took. If Shaw hadn't been there..." She bit her lip. "I get it now. I do. He grounds you. Feeding is like tossing back a lightning bolt for you, and he's the surge protector. You guys fit. I got so used to hating him I forgot that part."

Still wearing her *I stepped in cat poop* expression, Mai brushed past me.

I let that sink in before following her. "Is this your convoluted way of giving your blessing?"

"I...guess?" She held out her hand for the water. "All that *nice* tasted bad on the way up."

I let her take a swig to rinse out her mouth before reminding her, "You used to like him."

She spat onto the pavement. "I did."

"Do you think you could like him again?" I kept the question neutral. "Forgive him?"

"Forgiveness is hard," she admitted. "How are you doing in that department?"

I rolled my shoulders. "I might have an answer for you if he hadn't pulled a Houdini on me."

"Our magistrates are partnering with the Southeastern Conclave until this matter is resolved. They loaned out several of our marshals to aid in the rescue. Our office is flooded. I was pulled off my usual job and given a share of the psychological evaluations to process for victims who were assigned to our office." She took another drink. "I haven't seen Shaw either. That could be because he wasn't around to be seen." She polished off the half-empty water. "Chaos." She tossed it in a trash bin. "It reigns."

"Wait." That made no sense. "We're helping the Florida outpost process those cases? What about Georgia or Alabama?"

Ours was the nearest division, yeah, but there were several closer outposts.

"Um, about that." She made a zipping motion across her lips. "I can't say more than I already have."

"With one Texas marshal involved and another one breaking the case…" I cut my eyes her way.

"Puppy eyes only work on the weak. I've built up immunity." Smacking my back hard with her open palm, she shoved me stumbling forward. "Besides, *I* was there too. Remember?"

"That surprised me almost as much as being rescued," I teased.

"Hey, I might have washed out of the marshal academy, but I had perfect attendance. I know the theory. Shaw unleashed his hunger, and there was no way I was letting him come after you without me—" she coughed the words *and a silver dagger*, "—to make sure he didn't slurp you like a juice box."

When the marshal office came into view, I threw on the brakes and tripped over my own feet. A petite woman with silver hair wearing oversized shades, a red skort set and navy flip-flops waved.

"That woman looks a whole lot like my mother." Panic trembled in my voice. "Mai?"

"Shaw gave you twenty-four hours. It's been forty-eight, and you still haven't called her."

I spun around and spluttered, but nothing intelligible came out.

Mai took one look at my face—and my slack-jawed, bug-eyed expression—and sprinted for the relative safety of the office like her life depended on it.

"It had to be done for your own good," she called over her shoulder as she ran.

Mai's brand of love was going to end up killing me if I didn't kill her first.

No one had Mom's contact information except for Mai and Shaw. Shaw might lecture me, but he wouldn't interfere in my relationship with Mom without my say-so.

However, he lacked Mai's "clinical experience", and her habit of confusing *intern* for *licensed medical professional*. She would dial up Mom and spill her guts in a heartbeat if she felt it was best for me.

Too late to turn back, I kept shuffling toward the office, praying this was all some lingering drug-induced hallucination.

"Stop dragging your feet," the woman who sounded suspiciously like my mother yelled.

I kicked it up a gear to a jog tortoises everywhere would envy.

"Oh, for pity's sake." The woman huffed silver hair from her eyes and marched toward me. She reached me before my feet followed my brain's shouted orders to turn tail and run for real. "What in the world were you thinking not calling me? You vanished for two weeks. *Two weeks.* I thought you were on vacation in Daytona." She planted her size seven flip-flops on the pavement. "Was that a lie? Were you afraid to tell the truth?"

Yes. "I did go to Daytona on vacation." My palms went damp. "After I was suspended—"

A terse finger shoved the sunglasses onto her head. *"You were suspended?"*

Her indignation puzzled me. "Yes?"

Even more baffling, her eyes had sprung a leak.

"This is my fault." She gripped my upper arms and shook me. "I made my own child afraid to tell me the truth."

"Momma." I winced while she rattled my brain. "It's fine. I swear."

"That's not what Jackson said when he called this morning. He told me about that man, Balamohan."

Et tu, Shaw? "He did?"

"You are such a brave girl." She brushed hairs from my forehead. "Braver than I ever was."

I shifted on my feet, unsure where to look. I hated seeing her cry, hated making her cry.

"Sorry to interrupt." Mai hooked a thumb over her shoulder. "The magistrates are waiting."

Mom hesitated before taking her first step toward the building. "I'll wait for you in the lobby."

"This might take a while," Mai warned.

Mom was not to be deterred. She set her shoulders back. "We'll play it by ear, then."

Draping an arm around her shoulders, I led her inside the building and straight to Mable, whose eyes widened a fraction before she blinked away her surprise.

I nudged Mom forward. "Do you mind keeping her company?"

Mable, who had been filing papers in a cabinet pushed against the wall, grasped the situational context immediately. Humans with fae relatives were allowed through the door with an escort, but they weren't allowed to leave the waiting area and had to be chaperoned while on conclave grounds.

Throwing Mable and Mom together for the first time and then ditching them was not how I pictured this meeting going down. Actually, I had never imagined the two women who raised me would be in the same room together. Ever.

After patting her hair, Mable thrust out a plump hand. "I'm Mable." She beamed. "It's wonderful to finally meet you, dearie."

"I'm Agnes. Hi." Mom took her hand. "You're sure I'm not taking you away from work?"

"Paperwork will keep." Merry laughter rang out. "This is a special occasion. Come with me."

Mom let herself get ushered toward Mable's private quarters with a last slightly panicked look at me. "Thierry?"

On my way past, I dropped a kiss on each of their cheeks. "Mable will take good care of you."

"Come on, Tee." Mai indicated the stairs. "They're eager to get started."

"Funny thing." I trailed her close enough to breathe on her neck. "Turns out Shaw called my mom."

"Huh." Her steps quickened. "He did that?"

The predator in me was amused. "No sly little foxes put a bug in his ear about it, did they?"

She pointed to herself. "This sly little fox wouldn't touch a bug with a ten-foot pole."

I snapped my teeth near her ear, laughing when she jumped two steps. "That is not an answer."

After bounding up the last flight, she skidded to a stop before the gleaming silver wood doors, braced a hand on the knocker and spun around.

"Here we are," she panted. "Guess we'll have to talk later."

"Yeah." I flashed my teeth. "Let's make that happen."

Shaw might chastise me in private, but going over my head meant crossing a line I had drawn in the sand a long time ago. He wouldn't have done it unless *someone* who knew us both well, *someone* whose judgment he trusted, convinced him that it was time Mom unburied her head out of said sand.

"You may enter," a cultured voice called.

Here we go. I twisted the knob and stood frozen in the open doorway. The entire composition of the room had changed. The creepy mirror effect was gone, replaced by a creepier circle made of spindly silver chairs. Fourteen spots. Three empty chairs. Our magistrates, Evander and Kerwin, filled two, and a petite fae woman I recognized from an old case I had worked with Shaw occupied another. Irene Vause. A magistrate with the Northeastern Conclave. I bet the dour guy bent to her ear was her Unseelie counterpart.

In front of me, three chairs stood empty. On the opposite end of the loop, Shaw watched me.

Subtle inhales carried the scent of rich magic and apprehension, an interesting combination coming from this crowd. Walking into that eerily silent room with zero idea about what had prompted a gathering of this magnitude made my palm crackle from the electric charge in the air. I felt like a matchstick at a powder-keg convention, like if I struck out at the wrong person, the whole room might go *ka-boom*.

Evander seized control of the proceedings by gesturing to the empty seats. "You look well." He affected a sincere demeanor. "I wish we had the luxury of time for you to make a full recovery."

"I appreciate your concern," I said stiffly.

He folded his elegant hands. "You must be curious about what prompted this gathering."

My smile showed plenty of teeth. "I'm sure you'll share when you're ready."

A sharp elbow sank into my side. "Behave," Mai whispered.

"Gentlemen, meet our champion." Kerwin's smirk traveled the circle. "Thierry Thackeray."

Champion sounded ominous. What hoops had they lined up for me to jump through next?

"Let us begin again." Evander drowned out Kerwin. "The situation in Faerie has escalated since you were taken. As you have made no secret of your feelings for your husband, I feel this is a proper setting to announce rumors of the Rook's death are circulating among the fae." He studied me, expecting a reaction. I gave none. "In your absence, with the Rook missing and presumed dead, the Morrigan seized control of the throne. She has named herself as queen."

All heads swiveled toward me. I met each gaze with a serene expression even as Righty's parting shot rang through my head.

We are faithful to the crown and the one who wears it.

Well, this answered my earlier question about their loyalties.

Odhran and Daire belonged to the Morrigan.

"Rook's death doesn't make her queen." I tamped down the dull throb of betrayal. "Faerie's crown is won, not hereditary."

One of the other fae leaned forward. "Are you aware of who shared the prison with you?"

I angled myself in his direction. "I was told they were all death-touched fae."

"Aye, they were." He nodded. "All were gods and goddesses, death portents or their offspring."

Mai's eyes rounded. "She was taking out the competition."

Seething magic sparked in my palm. Linen deserved so much worse than the death I had dealt him.

"With neither the Black Dog nor his pup to intervene," another fae said, "the Morrigan has adopted the old ways. She has seized control by force, and it will require force to wrest the title from her and supplant the true queen upon the Faerie throne."

The moisture wicked from my mouth. "You want me to challenge the Morrigan for the crown?"

"It is yours." The fae stared at me, brow wrinkling. "Do you not wish to challenge her?"

"The Morrigan was gifted the ability to cross realms by your father," a third fae intoned. "She is able to cross his wards and manipulate his tethers, and a skill learned by one such as she is not soon forgotten. She has the advantage. She will enlist Unseelie insurgents and wage a war to win Faerie to her side, and then she will turn her gaze upon this realm. She harbors no love for humans and has no reason to spare them."

Or us was implied.

"I barely survived Faerie the first time." With the direction this conversation was heading, I was mentally preparing for round two. "Without Rook and Diode, I wouldn't have escaped in one piece."

Evander raised a hand for silence. "We would not send you to face an army without provisions."

I leaned back in my seat, wishing I could sink into it and escape this mess.

"You're proposing a suicide mission." Mai's voice carried. "The Morrigan can't be killed."

"She's a *death* goddess," I reminded the room. "Can she be snuffed out permanently?"

"There are two acceptable outcomes," Kerwin announced imperiously. "Either the rightful queen of Faerie will seize her throne or the tethers into and out of Faerie will be severed so that no one can cross realms."

I held very still and reevaluated the fae in this circle. They knew the threshold was Mac's doing, or they wouldn't have expected me to be able to counteract his magic. They knew how he laid those wards. They knew they were asking a blood price from me. Magic like his ran deep, and breaking them might break me in the process.

And not one of them cared as long as their hides were saved.

Burgeoning dread prompted me to ask, "What do these provisions entail?"

"A guide," Evander volunteered. "One who is familiar with Faerie and who will provide for you."

A headache blossomed in my temples. "That's it?"

"Perhaps you ought to ask the guide's identity before you dismiss him," Kerwin advised.

Even knowing I would regret it, I asked the question. "Who is the guide?"

Evander motioned one of the fae toward the door. "Show him in."

Audible gasps had me turning in my chair to examine the newcomer, but all I saw was a familiar neon-yellow cat who had evidently decided to grace the room with his presence. If he was the guide, I might consider the offer. *Consider.* Ha! Like any fae in this circle would give me an honest choice.

I wiggled my fingers at him. "Hey, cat."

With an amused rumble in his chest, the cat replied, "Insolent pup."

Spines stiffened and shoulders straightened in a panicked ripple throughout the room.

Thinking I must be missing something, I stared through the doors into the hall. Empty. Only the cat had been out there. Sure, he was big. Diode was a saber-toothed cat mutation à la Faerie. But that alone wouldn't have caused eyebrows around the room to smack the ceiling when they spotted him.

I was missing something.

Twisting with him, I stroked a hand down his back when he walked past me and went to stand in the center of the circle. I exchanged a puzzled look with Mai then checked Shaw for his reaction. His expression gave nothing away, unless you knew him like I did.

Shaw had anticipated this exhibition.

Kerwin's smile didn't reach his eyes. "I believe you two know each other."

The cat glanced over his shoulder at me, and that one look tightened my stomach. "Yes."

"Enough," Diode's voice boomed. "She is no mouse and I no cat to play such wasteful games."

I tried to find the joke in that, but if there was one, it sailed over my head.

Violent shivers racked his furry shoulders down to his narrow hips, standing his shocking yellow fur on end. A whiff of familiar magic crackled in the air. Before I pinpointed the scent, an explosion of white light knocked me back in my chair.

I scrubbed my hands down my arms and wiped off the prickles of residual energy.

The sounds of chairs scraping in unison across the floor snapped my head up in time to watch as the fae slid from their seats onto their knees. I followed their stares to the center of the circle where a great cat had been a moment ago, where a man now stood, and my arms dropped along with my jaw.

Luminescence writhed at his feet, black and glittering. Magic poured to the ground from jagged, raw runes that looked carved into his left hand by a broken-fingered butcher wielding a butter knife.

Dark emerald eyes gazed back at me, unblinking. Thick black stubble shaded the man's scalp, and his height made staring up at him painful. He wore dark wash blue jeans with a white T-shirt and a crisp button-down that brought out the color of his eyes. But his scuffed brown leather boots kept drawing my eye. Not them so much as the mound of rumpled neon fur draped across their toes and wedged under his heels.

"Hello, Thierry," the man said when it became obvious I was incapable of speech.

I did what any daughter would have done in my shoes.

I got up and left.

CHAPTER TWENTY-FOUR

Jogging down the stairs kept me a beat ahead of the hot tears fuzzing my vision. *I am not crying.* Halfway to the bottom, I slammed into a petite woman and sent her staggering into the opposite wall.

"Sorry," I mumbled on my way past.

"Thierry?" Her timid voice called after me, "Is that you?"

Something familiar about her...

"That's me." After flicking the moisture from under my eyes, I turned around and faced her. "Do I know you?"

Her skin was so pale she appeared bone-white at first glance. Beneath her makeup, her skin held faint grayish tones. Unseelie then. Her eyes were heather gray, and her lips were painted a soft pink shade. A long braid of midnight hair hung over her shoulder, complementing her stark black dress and ballet flats.

A blush swept color into her cheeks. "I'm Branwen."

"Oh. *Oh.* Hi." I initiated a hug that left her smiling. "I didn't recognize you without the rock wall."

Her laughter eased the knot of anger tightening my chest.

"You're in a hurry." She glanced the way I had come. "I was hoping we could talk."

Wood planks groaned overhead, and steady footsteps followed.

I eased down two more steps. "Would you like to come into my office?"

Her eyes sparkled. "Yes, I believe I would."

"It's right this way." I led her down another flight, through a tight doorway, and into a room that smelled like the man I was trying to escape. I pointed to the empty task chair. "Please, have a seat."

A twist of my wrist and a murmured Word activated the spell built into the walls and guaranteed us temporary privacy.

Normally, I would have sat behind the desk, but the oversized leather chair mocked me. Stocked with my father's belongings, the office had always seemed eager for his return. Today it would get its wish.

A low growl climbed up the back of my throat.

Branwen paused with a hand on her chair. "Are you sure now is a good time?"

"I heard surprising news today." I arranged my lips into a smile. "I'm just tense, that's all."

I crossed to her and perched on the edge of the desk so she didn't have to stare so far up at me.

"News, yes, that's why I'm here." She sat and leaned close. "I heard you were going to Faerie."

"Who told you—?" I took a calming breath. "The short answer is I haven't decided yet."

She linked her hands in her lap. "I hope you consider it."

A sense of foreboding swept through me. "What stake do you have in the outcome?"

Branwen blinked up at me. "Surely you've heard."

"I've heard a lot today." None of it good.

"The magistrates summoned me to say my brother is dead." Her chin lifted. "They're wrong."

"Your brother?" I dropped my head into my hands. *No effing way.* "I don't suppose by some small chance your brother is Rook?"

What had Linen said there at the end?

It was a mistake placing the crown jewels of my collection together.

Crown jewels. The Morrigan's daughter and the Morrigan's daughter-in-law.

"Don't mourn him." A small hand covered my knee and squeezed. "Rook isn't dead, Thierry."

Once I smoothed my incredulous expression, I peeked out at her. "How can you be so sure?"

"This." A teardrop-shaped pendant hung from her fingers on a sleek, black chain. The latticework setting clutched a faceted ruby the size of my thumbnail, and the stone pulsed with faint crimson light. "I used to dream of the day I would escape Faerie, escape my mother. I hoped Rook would leave with me, but he thought she would be more willing to let me go if he stayed behind. He thought he could protect me better from Faerie." She handed the necklace to me. "Before I left, he gave me this."

The metal was warm to the touch, and slight vibrations pulsed through the stone. "It's a heartbeat."

"His heartbeat," she confirmed. "He had one made for himself as well."

"This explains a lot." I passed it back, suppressing a shiver. All this time, he had known she was alive. No wonder his belief hadn't wavered. His mistake was in thinking the Morrigan had brought her home to lock her away in the fae realm instead of caging her in this one. "So you left Faerie, and then what? I'm guessing your mother found you."

And then the Morrigan had punished Branwen, because inflicting pain was what the Morrigan did best.

"A year and a day after I fled, Faysal came for me. Mother was so furious." Branwen wore her tears with pride. "After escaping Faerie, I married a fierce chieftain of the gray men, Dónal O'Leary, instead of the Unseelie prince she had chosen for me. She believed the prince, Iasan, was poised to win the hunt, and I cost her influence such a position would have given her, but my heart belonged to Dónal."

They had fallen for each other, defied the Morrigan, and their love had cursed them both.

"Kerwin explained your situation to me." Her finger traced the stone's facets before she clasped its chain behind her neck. "I understand now why what I confided about the incubus distressed you."

That Kerwin. He was one super helpful guy.

I chose my statement with care. "My relationship with Rook was—*is*—complicated."

Figuring Kerwin had already provided her with the official version of events, I decided Branwen should also hear my side of things. As calmly as possible, I outlined how I came to be Mrs. the Rook. I pushed through, adding details I hadn't told anyone else—even Mai—because Branwen appeared so hungry for news of him. Even though my story wasn't flattering, she was a rapt audience until the end.

By the time I finished, Branwen's cheeks were flush and her lips pressed into invisibility.

Certainty flashed in her eyes. "The Morrigan forced him to do it."

The polite thing to do was keep my mouth shut, so I did. Mom would be proud.

Branwen tapped my knee. "Rook wouldn't have forced you if he had known about the incubus."

That was debatable. Rook was charming and handsome, but he was also manipulative and vain. And he had known about Shaw. He just wasn't sure how firm the *ex* was before *boyfriend*.

"What Rook did saved my life, but I won't lie to you." I sat up straighter. "I want out."

"Being used as furtherance for another's ambition is a cruel game." As her story illustrated, she had experienced my quandary firsthand. "I don't hold your animosity toward Rook against you."

"I appreciate that."

A tart smile told me she read my sarcasm just fine. "After our discussion, I realize this is awkward, but I must try. Though this wouldn't benefit you at all—may in fact hinder you—I have to ask."

I cracked an honest grin. "I doubted this was a social call."

"I don't wish to offend you by offering—" she ducked her head, "—but I will pay you any price you name to bring my brother back to me. I don't dare return to Faerie, Mother would kill me, but if the tethers are truly cut, Rook will be lost."

"They're still discussing my fate upstairs." Right now the issues being debated might save or damn humanity. Rook and I were both casualties in the making. "I doubt a rescue mission is on the table."

"I'm not asking you to divert your mission to search for him," she rushed to add. "I only mean if the situation arises…if you see an opportunity to save him and if you think it possible, will you try?"

I resisted the urge to fidget. "I try not to make promises I can't keep."

"I understand." She wrapped her arms around her middle. "I'm leaving today. It's best if no one knows where I go, magistrates included." She produced a small, pink conch shell charm and offered it to me. "Summon me once my brother's fate has been determined. Please."

A spurt of magic expanded the shell to fill my palm, attuning itself to my magical signature, before it shrank again. "However it goes, I'll be in touch."

"You have my gratitude." Her gaze slid to the door then back to me. "I should get going."

Wary of who awaited me on the other side, knowing I had to face him sooner or later, I escorted her to the hall. "Safe travels."

A glimmer of hope lit her smile. "To you as well."

Finding the hall empty, I stood in the doorway and watched her leave. The bright-sharp scent of magic launched me into a sneezing fit. A thick rectangular box like the kind used for gifting sweaters sat on the chair where Branwen had sat. A simple card rested on top of it emblazoned with my name. I flipped it open.

On the day I was freed, I waded into the sea and summoned my Dónal. He told me merry tales of his life and family. We laughed as though we had never been parted. Forever isn't as long as the old songs would have us believe. My Dónal died in my arms, set free on the same day as me.

My eyes prickled through to the end.

We had an understanding, he and I. Despite what the old lore warned, his pelt was his. I never used it to bind him to me. His love was more precious for it was freely given. Now that silky fur is all that remains of the man I spent a lifetime loving and will mourn each day until forever ceases. I will treasure my memories, but I would be grateful if you accepted this endowment. It would only molder with me. I hope very much you wear it again. Through you, my Dónal will live on. Take care, sister.

I lifted the thin paper lid of the box, pushed aside the tissue paper and stroked the soft gray pelt.

"A gift from the gray men?" My father's rich voice rang with power.

"Huh." Taking my time to pack it away, I flexed my fingers to stop their trembling. "The cat doesn't have your tongue after all."

Frustrated magic washed from the man behind me to prickle my skin.

"I admit my deceit." His boots thumped closer. "I spelled the skin to prevent myself from speaking about my plans with you while wearing it. It was a necessary deception to earn your trust. I regret the lengths I was forced to go in the name of protecting you."

I made a noncommittal sound and smoothed the lid back onto the box.

"Selkie pelts have their own magic." He stopped on the edge of my periphery. "You'll have to tame it before you wear it or the first time you get it wet with saltwater, the fur will dive to the bottom of the sea and drown you."

I turned and studied him. "Are you serious?"

His nod was curt. "I learned the hard way."

I anchored my hands on my hips. "Yeah, well, that makes two of us."

He hooked his thumbs through his belt loops. "You're angry."

"I've surpassed angry. I'm beyond pissed. This is me having a freaking nuclear meltdown."

He nodded. "I should not have tricked you."

I snorted. "You think?"

He canted his head in a very catlike manner. "You were attached to the skin."

"I feel like someone ran over my cat." I threw up my hands. "Diode was my friend, and now he's gone."

"I wore the skin," he said quietly. "I am still here."

"You're not my friend," I growled. "That you're my father is a technicality."

A frown knitted his brow. "I cannot place family above duty."

"Above?" I spluttered. "Mom and I didn't rank at all with you. Family is a duty too, you know."

"It is one I take seriously." His lips thinned. "I did as your mother asked. I kept my distance. It was the right thing to do. It protected both of you." He challenged me. "Hour-long visits once each decade... What would that have accomplished?"

"It would have let me know you cared."

I wanted the words back as soon as they left my mouth. They made me sound like an eager little daddy's girl standing in her father's office on career day, trying on shoes so large she drowned in them.

"You are my daughter." Heat touched his voice. "I have watched over you your entire life."

Diode had once said the same thing. Was he speaking as my father then? I wish the cat was still around. Diode had been a safe link to him, a person I could ask questions and who could give me firsthand knowledge of Mac without the emotional acrobatics involved in approaching my mom.

Pushing aside personal questions, I focused on more pressing ones. "Why are you here?"

"Turmoil breeds corrosive magic. The threshold was thinning on my side and required maintenance sooner than anticipated. I decided to inspect your side as well and used a skin to prevent my enemies from tracking my movements." He took his time in adding, "The skin let me interact with you without anger or expectation. You earned my trust, and I hope that I earned yours."

"The trust accumulated while masquerading as someone— some*thing*—else is nontransferable." I spread my hands. "Sorry about that. Lying to someone tends to make them think you're not trustworthy."

A slight grin tugged at his lips. "I can accept that."

How magnanimous of him, considering he had no choice.

"Balamohan claimed you witnessed King Moran's beheading."

The amusement slid off his face, replaced by a stone-cold resolve. "I did."

An unconscious kindling of light in the runes on his left hand warned me away from the topic.

I jerked my chin toward the ceiling where the twelve remaining fae argued the virtues of my impending journey. "Well, Mr. Neutrality, what are your thoughts on the grand scheme being hatched upstairs?"

"I don't consider myself neutral so much as an equal advocate for all sides."

"Of course you would say that." Mac in person was as Zen as a rock garden. For a man with his reputation, it surprised me. "Where do you stand on the issue? Do you think the Morrigan should be stopped?"

His stance relaxed, calling my attention to the fact I hadn't offered him a seat. But it wasn't like I was sitting either. Still, points to him for standing with me and not commandeering his old chair.

"Don't you?" He aimed the pointed question back at me.

"Do I think so? Yes. Do we have the right? I'm not sure. Technically, she didn't break the law." I considered what the Huntsman had told me. "The truce was signed in blood and broken by blood when King Moran was killed. Naming me as princess locked both houses into a holding pattern while they decided internally whether to rebel or to maintain the peace."

"Mutual consent is required in order for a new peace to hold."

I mirrored his pose. "The Morrigan seizing control took that option off the table."

"It seems that way," he mused.

My fingers drummed against my elbow. "You didn't answer my question."

"Tensions must be released in Faerie. That is fact. If this realm is caught in the middle of such a war, it will be destroyed. That is also fact." He sighed. "There is no fair solution to those problems."

As much as I hated to, I agreed with him. "The Huntsman said a war would almost be a relief."

"My father is a wise man."

I gave him an odd look. Seeing Mac standing there as a man, it was easy to forget he hadn't always been one. Once he might have been the Huntsman's favorite hound, but he had been a hound like all the others until fae magics wrapped him in human skin and infused him with power and intellect.

"Then do you think the best thing for this realm is to cut the tethers and fortify the threshold?"

"For this realm?" He nodded. "That is without a doubt the best solution."

As much as I wanted to take that answer and run, it was wrong. "But not for Faerie."

"The houses will divide," he predicted. "Factions will rise, alliances will crumble. There will be bloodshed. Innumerable lives will be lost." Regret threaded his voice. "You can't change the nature of beasts. I might walk like a man and talk like one, but I also run with a pack and howl at the moon. I would go insane if I were confined to one skin, and my laws have confined too many for too long."

"You saved Faerie from the Thousand Years War." He saved her from herself. "It might still be raging without you."

"I was the law for an age." He cast me a meaningful glance. "But that age has passed."

Seeing where this was headed, I reiterated, "I don't want to rule."

"Until that All Hallows' Eve, what I wanted most was to return to my kennel with a full belly."

A knock on the door allowed me to swallow the smartass reply forming in my mind.

Mac didn't turn his head, but his nostrils flared. "I expected you sooner, Shaw."

"Someone *accidentally* charmed the lock on the magistrates' chamber doors." Shaw sidestepped my father and stationed himself against the wall on my left. "Is everything all right in here, Thierry?"

Cold magic radiated from Mac as he faced Shaw. "Do you think I would hurt her?"

Shaw rolled a shoulder. "Twenty-four hours ago, I thought you were a cat."

My glare transferred onto him. "That's twenty-three hours longer than I've known he wasn't."

"He would have told you," Mac admitted. "I forbade it."

"She deserved to know." White flickered in Shaw's eyes. "You let her walk into an ambush."

"I agree." The runes on Mac's hand burned brighter. "That doesn't change the necessity of it."

I angled myself between them. "Where did they break things off up there?"

"They started bickering after you left." He sounded unsurprised. "Nothing will be resolved for days, if not weeks, if the magistrates keep hemming and hawing. Besides, all eleven votes are required for any motion to carry. That means Mr. Sullivan must be present at the polling and his vote tallied."

Mac grimaced in response.

With a nod, I put the same question to Shaw I had to Mac. "What do you think of their plan?"

"The magistrates are looking for a noble excuse. King Moran's death—and now this latest news of the Morrigan—gave it to them." He raked his long fingers through his tousled hair. "Magistrates are powerful by this realm's standards, but it's no secret that affluent families in Faerie place their spare heirs, bastards and screw-ups into those roles to protect them and to keep up appearances. For most magistrates, their position is the most power and influence they can hope to wield in their lifetime. I doubt any of them want to share it with their siblings and rivals if the war spills over into this realm."

"You expect the vote to swing toward severing the tethers and reinforcing the threshold."

"Yes," he said grimly. "I do."

Our gazes held until his eyes warmed to molten copper, and the edges of the room turned hazy.

My father cleared his throat. Loudly. "I should return upstairs."

I didn't disagree with him.

Mac paused on the landing, head lifting and nostrils flaring, scenting the air.

I shot a panicked look at Shaw and mouthed *Mom*.

The seconds Shaw hesitated made intervention unnecessary. Mac turned and climbed the stairs back up to the magistrates' chambers, leaving Mom safe and none-the-wiser downstairs.

After a nod from me, Shaw closed the door behind him and reactivated the privacy spell. A nifty trick since he shouldn't have known the Word keyed to my office.

"That was close," I breathed out on a sigh.

"You can't protect them from each other."

I hated when he was right.

"So—" I rolled my eyes toward the ceiling, "—what's your take on the festivities?"

He rubbed the base of his neck. "All the collective power in this realm is upstairs in that room."

My exhale puffed out my cheeks. "This is really happening."

"Your line of succession has been broken." He sounded relieved.

I wasn't ready to relax yet. "I'm still not free."

"As long as you care, you're never free." He stepped closer. "They can always drag you back in."

"So, we sneak into Faerie, destroy the tethers, reinforce the threshold and go home." I folded my arms. "We separate families, alienate goodwill toward the magistrates and leave a war zone behind."

He stopped an arm's length away and braced his legs apart, making it plain if I wanted closer to him, I had to do the walking. "The only alternative is to wait and see, and if we wait, we won't see the Morrigan coming until it's too late. As cutthroat as the magistrates' strategy is, it's this realm's best hope for survival. Hundreds of thousands or more fae, half-blood and human lives would be saved."

Lives like my mother's.

Mom had no chance against the types of fae who would inevitably jump realms in search of fresh hunting grounds. Old creatures like Linen, who had been kept in check by Mac's laws, would be answerable only to the Morrigan. The prospect of an all-you-can-eat corpse buffet made me doubtful she would step in to prevent the slaughter of innocents.

"This is the right thing to do." I tested the words.

No dice. I still didn't believe them. Not entirely.

"It is." He lent his surety to mine.

"I don't trust him." I didn't need to say who. "He's up to something."

"He's the Black Dog."

"Yes." I exhaled. "He is."

"I won't let him out of my sight in Faerie long enough for him to mark a tree," Shaw promised.

"You're going?" I stepped toward him. "Is that allowed?"

He tucked a lock of hair behind my ear. "I explained our situation to them."

"Oh." Tingles spread through my cheeks.

"Bare bones," he assured me.

The skeletons in both our closets were dancing a jig now. "You told them I was your compeer?"

Pale skin rushed up his throat and into his cheeks. White haunted the rims of his eyes. "No." His voice went hoarse. "I would never do that to you. That is your decision. I wouldn't make it for you."

Right there, that was the difference between Rook and Shaw. Rook got what he wanted through the manipulation of circumstance. Helping me achieve my goals—like staying alive—had benefited his endgame.

Don't get me wrong. Shaw had manipulated me too, and that stung. It still pissed me off that, in the grand and boneheaded tradition of men who thought they knew best for their women, he had made a bad situation *much* worse by lying. He made a life-altering decision for me, just like Rook. But Shaw had almost died to save me from the exact same cage Rook had rushed me into and then barred the door closed behind me.

I knew then I didn't need a couch or ginger beer or a perfect afternoon of contemplation to make the call. Life was not perfect. Making my decision based on an ideal that wasn't realistic was foolish.

I rolled onto my toes and brushed my lips against Shaw's.

White swallowed his irises and his body jerked, electrified. "What was that for?"

"You're a smart guy." I tilted my head back. "Figure it out."

The fingers of his left hand tangled in my hair. "You decided."

My smile broadened. "I did."

He searched my face. "To be with me."

Caught by him, I cut my gaze from left to right. "I don't see anyone else here."

His right hand cradled my cheek, and he lowered his forehead to mine. "This won't be easy."

I turned my face into his palm and nipped it. "Nothing worth having ever is."

AUTHOR'S NOTE

Dear Readers,

When I wrote *Heir of the Dog* as the first book in the Black Dog Trilogy, I planned Thierry's journey to span those three novels and no more. But then I attended the RT Booklovers Convention, and all that changed. *Heir* won the American Idol Contest, and that brought two agents with fresh ideas into the mix. The next thing I knew, the trilogy had expanded to include one more title – *Dog with a Bone.*

Dog with a Bone is a prequel to the series in the sense that the novella cuts a hole into the ceiling of Thierry's past and gives us a glimpse of those first steps that set the events of the trilogy into motion one year later.

With that in mind, I hope you have fun meeting Thierry as a bright-eyed cadet in *Dog with a Bone* and enjoy watching her mature through *Heir of the Dog, Lie Down with Dogs* and *Old Dog, New Tricks* into a woman who knows when laws should be upheld and when they are meant to be broken.

Best,
Hailey Edwards

ABOUT HAILEY EDWARDS

A cupcake enthusiast and funky sock lover possessed of an overactive imagination, Hailey lives in Alabama with her handcuff-carrying hubby, her fluty-tooting daughter and their herd of dachshunds.

Chat with Hailey on Facebook, **https://www.facebook.com/authorhaileyedwards** or Twitter, **https://twitter.com/HaileyEdwards**, or swing by her website **http://haileyedwards.net/**

Sign up for her newsletter to receive updates on new releases, contests and other nifty happenings.

She loves to hear from readers. Drop her a line at **http://haileyedwards.wufoo.com/forms/contact/**

HAILEY'S BACKLIST

Araneae Nation

A Heart of Ice #.5
A Hint of Frost #1
A Feast of Souls #2
A Cast of Shadows #2.5
A Time of Dying #3
A Kiss of Venom #3.5
A Breath of Winter #4
A Veil of Secrets #5

Daughters of Askara

Everlong #1
Evermine #2
Eversworn #3

Black Dog

Dog with a Bone #1
Heir of the Dog #2
Lie Down with Dogs #3
Old Dog, New Tricks #4

Wicked Kin

Soul Weaver #1

Made in the USA
Columbia, SC
18 February 2018